I0673395

THE GRAND
PRIZE

Get the Water Street Crime Starter Library
FOR FREE

Sign up for the no-spam newsletter and get *four* full-length ebooks—the thrillers ***BLOODY PARADISE***, ***FROM ICE TO ASHES***, ***TROPICAL ICE***, and ***SING FOR THE DEAD***—plus two introductory short stories by the author of ***THE GRAND PRIZE*** and lots more exclusive content, all for *free*.

Details can be found at
the end of *THE GRAND PRIZE*,
or go here now:
mailchi.mp/waterstreetpressbooks.com/
waterstreetcrimemailinglist

THE GRAND
PRIZE

DENNIS D. WILSON

Water Street Press
Healdsburg, California

Published by Water Street Press
Healdsburg, California

Water Street Press paperback edition published 2020

Produced in the USA

Print 978-1-62134-425-4
E-Pub 978-1-62134-426-1
Mobi 978-1-62134-427-8

Cover design by **thecovercollection.com**

Typesetting services by **bookow.com**

For my children, who by their example teach me every day how to be a better man. And for Paula, without her encouragement and support, my stories would still be buried deep in my imagination.

"The greatness of America lies not in being more enlightened than any other nation, but rather in her ability to repair her faults."

Alexis de Tocqueville

Chapter 1

Jia Ling, age nine, bounced on the rough-hewn bench of the rickety wooden cart as it swayed back and forth behind the jerry-rigged 150cc motorcycle. Any branding decals had long ago fallen off the scuffed red fuel tank, but the shadow of the Kawasaki logo was still faintly visible, as if the machine was receding bit by bit into time, fading into a memory of the Vietnam era from whence it came. Her smallish round face was framed by close-cropped jet-black hair, and her large onyx eyes were populated with faint white speckles, like galaxies in an alternate ocular universe. But her most defining feature was her gap-toothed grin that burnished every room she entered like a sparkly Photoshop filter.

Today the signature grin was absent, her countenance stone-faced, her forehead wrinkled in concentration, her mouth a tight thin line, and her flawless pale complexion increasingly dotted with a pox of oil that spewed in a mist from the exhaust of the motorcycle's straining engine. She was holding a plastic garbage bag in her lap wrapped in the same nylon cord that served as her seat belt. Without the cord, she would surely be thrown from the cart onto the dirt road that snaked from her farming village in the countryside to the highway leading to the manufacturing metropolis of Shenzhen some fifty kilometers away. With each bump on the deeply rutted road, the cart would lurch, nearly overturning at times, and Jia would be saved by the nylon cord wrapped around her waist. The garbage bag contained all the earthly possessions she was taking with her to her new life in Shenzhen: one change of clothes, a picture of her parents on their wedding day in a hand-carved wooden frame, a book about a young Chinese girl in ancient times, and her only plaything, the Ji'an Li, a hacky-sack-like toy that Jia was very adept at playing for long periods of time in her dirt yard. She could amaze the other children and even the adults with her dexterity, bouncing the Ji'an Li from her foot to her knee to her head, spinning around and then catching it on her other foot, laughing her gap-toothed laugh the entire time.

Although she was leaving her birth home, Jia was happy today. She was looking forward to the reunion with her twin infant brothers. Her grandmother's family had taken in Jia, her mother, and the disabled twin boys after her father died, but the small farm just couldn't support that many mouths, and her brothers had been placed in the crowded, government-subsidized Shenzhen orphanage. And when the torrential storm three weeks later wiped out the crops on the small plot of land, her aunt and uncle had decided to let

Jia join her brothers. Jia's mother, already withdrawn from the loss of her husband and missing her sons, had sobbed and wailed uncontrollably when she left this morning, but Jia hadn't. She hugged her mother and said, "Mommy, I can take care of the boys now." She loved her brothers, and after her father had died, her mother had withdrawn into herself, leaving the boys in Jia's care. Jia's uncle was a stern and gruff man, and when Jia overheard him talking to her aunt at night about the orphanage in Shenzhen, Jia became extra diligent in caring for her brothers, hoping they would be so little trouble to her uncle that he wouldn't send them away.

As she thumped along the unpaved country roads, Jia thought of the little girl in her storybook who, during the Ming Dynasty, had run away by herself and found adventure. Jia pictured herself on just such an adventure, raising her brothers and seeing the wonderful sights of ancient Chinese cities.

At the outskirts of the metropolitan area, the motorcycle and cart turned onto a paved road, and suddenly there were bicycles, motorcycles, cars, and trucks all around her. She had never seen so many vehicles in her life. There had been only a couple of mechanized vehicles in her tiny village, and Jia felt threatened by dozens of metal monsters spitting fumes like giant industrial insects. She felt a knot of nausea in her stomach, and the unmuffled sounds and horns made her ears hurt. She took a deep breath, suppressing the urge to cough, then closed her eyes, wrapped her arms around the plastic garbage bag, and transported herself back to the Ming Dynasty, this time playing with her brothers in a quiet palace garden. In her mind, she replaced the sickening sulfuric exhaust odors with the fragrances of the beautiful flowers in the garden, and the painful sounds of the vehicles with beautiful music from ancient Chinese instruments played by unseen musicians. She kept her eyes closed, playing this comforting scene over and over, and she didn't open them until the cart pulled up to a ramshackle building on a narrow street in Shenzhen. The man driving the motorcycle got off and led Jia and her black plastic garbage bag to the front door. A short stocky man with a bald head greeted her with a wide smile, revealing a mouthful of crooked yellow teeth. "So, this is Jia. Welcome Jia, your brothers have been waiting for you."

Chapter 2

Dean Wister was more curious than concerned as he waited in Conference Room 1 of the FBI Field Office in Chicago. The listing on the directory indicated a conference room, but that was really just a euphemism that fooled no one, especially the unfortunate individuals, most of whom were in some serious shit, who were invited into the oversized closet for a "conference." Dean looked at the three FBI agents from the Washington, DC office who had just taken a seat and thought if he had to write a description, the kind of physical profile that he was often required to prepare as part of his job on the task force that surveilled the complex and wide-ranging crime syndicate in the Midwest, it would be identical for all three—Race: cadaver white; Height and Weight: average; Hair: short but not cut in any way faintly resembling stylish; Facial Features: nondescript; Age: mid- to late-thirties; Sense of Humor: none. In more than twelve years of law enforcement he had yet to hear an FBI agent laugh. Although Dean's agency, the Midwest Organized Crime Task Force, was separate from the bureau, as a sister organization, it answered to the FBI, often interfaced with the Chicago FBI office, and had access to the FBI database and other resources. But Dean had never met any of these men. Within the bureau there is little distinction of rank below the very senior levels, and they were all introduced to him as Special Agents, but the silver flecks in the haircut of the one sitting in the middle—Special Agent Gary Eckles—revealed him as the leader of this team, based more on seniority than merit.

"So, Agent Wister, do you know why we're here?"

"To plan my medal ceremony, right?"

The three men looked confused by Dean's attempt to lighten the mood, so he tried again. "Well, my Supervisor said you wanted to interview me about the Rosati case. But I thought that case was closed."

"Technically, it is. But as you know, we have a new Director. And Director Fanning decided to take another look at the Mario Rosati shooting when he took over for Director Vorhies, just to make sure that all the loose ends are tied up. And since you were the lead investigator on this case, we decided it would be helpful if you could walk us through your involvement step-by-step. You can learn only so much from the files, which we've spent the last week or so reviewing. Oh, and we need to inform you that this interview is being recorded, but of course you already understand that."

Dean nodded, but didn't say anything as he looked up at the video camera hovering above the agent's head that was focused on his face like a robotic metal owl. He knew there was an identical camera behind him that would record the face of the agents interrogating him. The room had no windows, and everything in it was some version of gray: the walls, desk, chairs, even the ceiling. Dean called this color, which was, for some reason that escaped him, now so popular with toney decorators in the gold coast of Chicago, FBI gray. When his wife Sara had wanted to use gray as the color scheme in their Lincoln Park townhome, Dean had joked that there could be *no f'ing gray* in his house. Although the only color seemingly permitted in the bureau was gray, the bureau had acquiesced to their outside decorator's demands and allowed three shades to be prescribed in the written office manual that governed everything from coffee cups to mechanical pencils.

"Agent Wister, I see that you nodded, but could you verbally affirm that you understand this interview is being recorded?"

"Yes, of course, I understand."

"Great, then let's get right to it. We'll just start from the beginning, and you can lead us through how the case came to you in the first place. I understand you became involved when you were in Wyoming? Your jurisdiction is the Midwest Region. What were you doing out there?"

"Well, I was on vacation in Jackson Hole last summer when I was contacted by the Teton County Sheriff. Eddie Torino had been found dead in a car wreck in the Snake River. I knew of Torino from my work with the Task Force in Chicago, and was called in to consult on the case. They thought maybe I could figure out what a mobster was doing out there."

"And you initially thought Torino might be involved in the murder of a local citizen?"

"Yes, Jordy Smith, a real estate office manager, had been murdered late the previous night, and it looked like it could've been a hit. That fit Torino's background, so that made it suspicious to the local Sheriff, and they tracked me down to take a look at it."

"What made you suspect that Torino might be working for Mario Rosati in Chicago?"

"We suspected that Rosati had hired Torino for hits in the past. Rosati was a pretty notorious figure in Chicago, and as I am sure you know, he's been the subject of many investigations by our Task Force and even the bureau over the years. Well, as it turned out, Rosati didn't have anything to do with the murder. We found out later that Torino had been killed for a much different reason. But during the course of the murder investigation, we discovered that Rosati's gang was involved in other crimes in Teton County. Rosati was in the prostitution and human-trafficking business with another Jackson Hole resident, a Russian national, Boris Birkov."

"But that wasn't the only Jackson Hole resident that Rosati was involved with, was it, Agent Wister?"

"No, it turned out that he was also laundering money through a Chicago bank, and their CEO, Charles Kidwell, has a home in Jackson Hole."

"And you arranged for Mr. Kidwell to obtain immunity for his testimony against Mr. Rosati, is that right?"

"Well, I was involved in the negotiations, but the actual decision to grant immunity is above my pay grade, as I am sure you know."

"We want to ask you a few things about your involvement with Mr. Kidwell, because there isn't a lot of information in the files concerning that. Can you tell us what you know about the relationship between Mr. Kidwell and Senator Thomas McGraw?"

Dean frowned, and he could tell that his grimace was noticed by the agents. The inability to maintain a poker face when he was upset was one of his weaknesses; he had about as much control over his facial expressions as an infant tasting spinach for the first time. Kidwell and McGraw? So that was what this was about. Former Director Vorhies had been an old friend of Senator McGraw, who was presently leading the field for the Republican nomination for President. But Vorhies had just left the bureau to take a high-paying job in the private sector, and Assistant Director Fanning, a Democratic Party insider, had taken over. "I don't really have any first-hand knowledge of their relationship."

"Well, didn't the Senator kill Rosati in a shoot-out in the Senator's hotel room in DC?"

"All I really know about it is the report issued by the bureau that ruled the shooting was justified self-defense. As you know from the files, I was unconscious in a hospital in Jackson Hole when that occurred. One of Boris Birkov's men had given me a pretty good blow to the head when I was trying to rescue one of the girls they had kidnapped into prostitution."

"And wasn't Mr. Kidwell present at the DC shoot-out?"

"From the reports I've read, I understand that to be true. But again, I wasn't there. And I don't know why you think I would have any more information about it than you do."

"Agent Wister, do you have any reports or other information about Charles Kidwell or Senator Mc-Graw that you have not included in your official reports?"

Dean stopped breathing for a moment. What could this be about? Where would they get the idea that he might have withheld information about the pair? He could feel the adrenalin start to flow; he was not used to being on this side of the interrogation table, and he took a deep breath. "Ah, no, I do not."

"Have you ever accepted any gifts or other consideration from either Charles Kidwell or Senator McGraw?"

What the fuck? Dean could feel his face getting warm as the blood was diverted to his brain, and he knew it was starting to take on a shiny crimson, the biological facial tell that he was angry. *Gifts? Do they mean gifts as in bribes?* "No, of course not." He instantly regretted letting his irritation show on his face and in his voice.

"Have you ever ridden on the private jet owned by Mr. Kidwell?"

An inner voice came to him now. It was the one that sometimes came to his rescue when he was stressed, when his reptilian brain was trying to take over his body, urging him to fight or flee. He hadn't called on that voice for several months, but he reached out for it now. *Calm yourself. Stay in control. Keep your voice in a monotone. Don't let them see that they're getting to you.* Dean took a deep breath. "I accompanied him on his private jet when he flew from Jackson to Chicago for his immunity conference."

"But that isn't the only time that you flew on the jet, is it?"

"Well, it was a round trip. I returned to Jackson Hole on his jet after the conference."

"Did Mr. Kidwell or any other government officials accompany you on that flight?"

"No, Mr. Kidwell had other business in Chicago, so I came back by myself."

"So, you accepted a flight on Mr. Kidwell's private jet to return to your Jackson Hole vacation?"

"Well, it wasn't like that. I was still working on the Jordy Smith murder case."

"But hadn't your supervisor told you that your work on the case was finished? And didn't he inform you to turn it over to the local officials since it was no longer FBI business?"

"No, I don't believe that's true."

"Agent Wister, our records show otherwise. But let's talk about something else. During the course of this case, did you kill a man when you were in Jackson?"

"As I'm sure you already know, that's how the murder case was solved. I killed the man who ambushed a group that I was with in Jackson."

"Of course, I'm aware of that shooting. I apologize. I should have been clearer. It seems you had quite an eventful summer, Agent Wister. I'm talking about the other man that you killed... the one you killed with your bare hands in a bar fight."

They were really trying to get to him now, and despite his best efforts, they were succeeding. His temper was now completely ignoring his calming inner voice. He should never have been so naïve. This interview wasn't to clear up any loose ends from the case file. It was intended to paint him as some kind of scapegoat. Or maybe it was something else. "It wasn't a bar fight. He attacked me from behind while I was walking to my car, and I broke his arm. He died when a bone fragment went to his lung."

"This other man you killed, which you say was not a bar fight, but it was just outside the bar you both had been drinking in. This deceased man, Fletcher Barns—wasn't he a suspect in the Jordy Smith case when this happened?"

"I wouldn't call him a suspect."

"Agent Wister, we have in your reports that he was on your list as a 'person of interest' and there is a memo in the file summarizing your interrogation of him. Was there ever a formal inquiry into the altercation that led to the death of Fletcher Barns?"

"It was reviewed by the County Attorney in Wyoming."

"But there wasn't a formal inquest, isn't that correct?"

"I'm sure the County Attorney followed the appropriate procedures, and I was cleared of any misconduct."

"Agent Wister, you say you were on vacation in Wyoming when you became involved in this case, but that isn't true is it? Wasn't it really a leave of absence?"

"I think it was called a leave, yes."

"And why were you granted a leave of absence?"

"Well, I'd been working a lot of hours. I had booked a lot of overtime, and vacation time."

Agent Eckles paused. And then he opened a manila file folder from the pile in front of him, studied it for a long moment, and looked Dean straight in the eye. "But you didn't request the leave, isn't that correct? Isn't it true that your supervisor requested it on your behalf, because he was alarmed by your mental state after your wife died?"

Dean glared at Eckles and did not answer the question.

Eckles closed the folder, folded his hands, and then leaned forward and spoke very slowly and deliberately. "Dean, isn't it true that you believe you see your deceased wife, that she actually appears to you in the flesh, and that you still have conversations with her?"

Dean gulped, and tried to speak but couldn't. How could they possibly know anything about these hallucinations of his wife Sara? The only person he'd told about this was his psychologist.

They must have gotten to his therapist in some way. And if they were talking to his therapist, then that must mean that they were trying very hard to target him. All this was bubbling from his unconscious to his conscious mind, threatening to boil over, and as those thoughts came churning to the top of his consciousness, it took every bit of his well-trained emotional suppression techniques to prevent him from acting on one dominant compulsion: to jump across the table, grab Agent Eckles by the throat, squeeze until his tongue stuck straight out from his mouth, watch his blood-red face drain to cadaver pale, and then feel the utmost satisfaction as the life flickered out of his FBI gray eyes. But instead, he stared right into the FBI agent's hound-dog face, and said in the coldest voice that he could muster, "Agent Eckles, kiss my hillbilly ass. This interview is over."

Chapter 3

JIA took the cloth from the bucket of lukewarm water, wrung it out, and gently washed her fourteen-month-old twin brothers. Her first month at the orphanage had been exhausting, and although the facility was rundown and filthy, and the orphanage director, Mao Shu, was a mean and nasty man, in many ways it was a step up from the cramped home in the little farming village. Jia was working sunrise to sunset taking care of her brothers, and also helping out the short-handed staff with the cooking, cleaning and caretaking of the hundred or so other children, many of them disabled, who were housed here, but she didn't mind it so much. She felt a sense of purpose, and she couldn't imagine who had done the work before she'd arrived; probably no one, from the looks of things. She was able to keep an eye on her brothers and make sure they were clean and fed, even if it meant sharing some of her meager rations with them.

The other children in the orphanage weren't so lucky. Nearly a third of them were disabled, some much worse than her brothers. Their cribs, made of plywood and chicken wire, with dirty foam-rubber mattresses, reminded her of the animals' cages she saw on a trip to the Shenzhen zoo. Jia had to avert her eyes when she took care of the other children. She couldn't bear to look at the faces of the wounded little ones who were damaged nearly as much from lack of human bonding as from deprivation and poor medical care.

She looked down at the little boys, *her* little boys. They were small for their age, their growth and development stunted by the dual challenges of poor nutrition and the health complications of their premature births. Still, they were happy babies, and their cheerful demeanor, despite their circumstances, never failed to boost Jia's spirits; she took pride in caring for them. She had finished their baths and was playing a peek-a-boo game with them when the orphanage director looked in. "Jia, come to my office right away."

Jia quickly placed the boys back in their crib and hurried to Mao's office. Mao was sitting with a man with an oddly thin mustache that looked as if it had been drawn on his face with a crayon, and he was dressed more neatly than any man Jia had ever seen before. Mao smiled. "Jia, I have some good news for you. I have found you a job in a furniture factory not far from here. You will be able to earn some money to help defray the cost of your brothers' care. Isn't that great news?"

Jia let his words sink in, her face wrinkled in confusion. "I'm sorry. I don't understand what you mean."

Mao smiled again, more broadly this time, and repeated his words very slowly, as if some of the orphans' mental disabilities may have rubbed off on the little girl. Jia was afraid of Mao, and although he had never beat her, she had seen him strike some of the other children when they committed some trivial infraction, such as making too much noise. But now she swallowed her fear and looked up at him. "I can't leave here. I need to take care of my brothers."

Mao's smile disappeared. "Your brothers will be fine. You need to do this. We have already furnished Li Meng here with several dozen workers, but he needs more. And this is the only way we can obtain the funds to continue to care for the children."

Jia felt a wave of panic at this demand, but the half-formed thought of abandoning her brothers overwhelmed her panic, and she suddenly became very angry, her entire body stiff with rage, as if she could change Mao's mind with her will. "I won't leave my brothers. You need to find somebody else for this."

Mao looked down. "Jia, you embarrass me. You embarrass yourself. Your brothers will be fine. I will make sure they are taken care of."

Suddenly the image of her brothers and the condition she had found them in when she arrived possessed her, and she panicked. She shouted, "No!" and, turning away, walked as fast as she could to the door.

Mao moved quickly, towering over the small girl and grabbing her roughly by the arm. Without thinking, she ran her nails down his forearm and tried to pull away, leaving a streak of raised red welts. Mao squealed in pain, grabbed at his arm, and then, without saying a word, he kicked her feet out from under her. Her face landed with a crack on the concrete floor, the wind forced out of her lungs by his foot on her back. "That was a big mistake, little one," he said.

"Hand me the roll of tape." Mao pointed to his desk, and as Jia wailed and wailed, he and the man with the mustache duct-taped her arms and legs like a little piglet.

Chapter 4

DEAN Wister zipped his Klim storm jacket to the top of his chin, pulled the wrist straps tight on his Gortex gloves, and stole a look at the weather before pulling the ski goggles down over his eyes. He could feel the storm coming now as he flipped the switch on his Ski-Doo Summit X and pulled onto the service road in back of the Mini Mart at Hoback Junction. He forced himself to quash his concern before it turned into full blown panic. It had snowed every single day since he arrived— that was thirty-one consecutive days of snow— and the forecast was for heavy snow for the weekend. The sun was going down and, although he still had visibility, if the wind picked up, making his way up the forest service road for the two-and-a-half-mile trip to his house could be sketchy. The house sat on the ridge overlooking the Snake River and he had already gotten buried more than once on his way there, as he struggled to master the intricacies of the sled.

He smiled at the thought of calling his snowmobile a sled, just as the Ski-Doo dealer in Jackson had laughed at him when he had come into his store to look at "snowmobiles." Over the last month, he'd become more proficient at single-handedly digging himself out of trouble than controlling the machine. All his previous ill-executed maneuvers, and there had been more than he wanted to admit, had occurred in full daylight and clear conditions, but now with daylight running out, his stomach was knotting. There weren't any fluffy snow pillows off the steep ridge on the narrow road—more of a path really—that he had to pilot to get home. He was aware that a plunge off that ridge could be fatal if he ran off an edge into thin air and tumbled down the rocky hillside. The forest service road was the only way home, and it wasn't plowed in the winter.

This remoteness was what made his house both affordable and desirable to Dean. Sara had jokingly called it his "fortress of solitude," or had she said that to him in a dream? Lately he was having trouble with his memories of her, deciphering which occurred when she was alive, which were dreams, and which were the times she had appeared to him after her death, so real that he could smell her unique fragrance on his sheets after she left his bed. When the snowfall had turned into an ice storm last week, the fortress had seemed more like a prison.

He'd been thinking a lot about prison lately. That was what he was doing here, spending some time trying to think of a way to avoid prison. He'd been pretty proud of himself for solving the Jordy Smith murder last summer, but that pride had backfired on him after his interview with the FBI agents last month. His actions had elevated him to near folk-hero status in Jackson Hole, but he knew the risks he took were more a result of his emotional state than good police work.

His good friend, real estate broker Hayden Smith, had been so grateful when Dean had saved his life that he'd found this bargain riverfront property for him. Dean hadn't expected, however, that he would be using the house through the winter. His involvement in the Rosati case had caught him in the crossfire of Washington politics. When he'd terminated the FBI interview, he knew suspension was inevitable, but he also knew he wasn't the real target. The real targets were Republican Presidential Candidate Senator Tom McGraw and his Chicago banker friend, Charles Kidwell, who was the Senator's chief fundraiser and political advisor. Just after Dean's interview in Chicago, the new FBI Director went public with the investigation, accusing his former boss of a whitewashed investigation of the shootout in which the Senator had suspiciously killed Mario Rosati, the Chicago mobster who was also a client of Charles Kidwell's bank and a target of an active FBI investigation at the time of his death. He was calling the whole thing a "rush to non-judgment," and a "politically motivated free pass."

In his heart, Dean knew the accusation that he took inappropriate favors from the subject of a criminal investigation by accepting a cross-country ride on Kidwell's private jet was total bullshit. But he also knew that turning an investigation of "inappropriate favors" into an indictment for bribery was a real possibility, especially when it could be used as a stepping stone to *destroying* the political career of one man—and *making* the political career of another.

Dean twisted the throttle and the sled purred as he traveled up the icy road. Seeing anything was becoming more difficult now as blowing drifts both covered and expanded the route, making the real path, the one with actual earth underneath, hard to distinguish from the false edge that was created as the wind piled ridges of snow like a seductive mirage disguising nothing but thin air below its twelve inches of fluffy powder. He knew that if he put one of sled's skis on the false edge, he would tumble down the steep cliff along with his four-hundred-pound machine, and neither of them wouldn't stop until they reached the river.

He carefully crept up the slope, negotiating the narrow switchbacks until he reached the top of the ridge and, as he turned the corner, he could faintly make out the lights from his house in the distance, though the snow was now heavy enough to cover his goggles. He paused and wiped them clear, held his breath, and slowly began the long steep traverse to his house, which rested at the top of the spine.

Dean had left the house lit up. He didn't have a burglar alarm, not that it would help anyway as there were no land lines and cell phone service was spotty up here, and by the time law enforcement could be notified and respond, any criminals would be long gone. Consequently, Dean figured his best option was just to leave all the lights on when he was away, and any bad guys would figure someone must be home.

The men didn't need to ring the doorbell, but they did anyway, just in case. They'd been watching the Chicago cop for the last month, ever since he had begun occupying the sandstone and log home that sat in the private inholding surrounded by national forest land. They knew he always parked his Ski-Doo in front of the house, and that he left his lights on even when he wasn't at home. They rang the bell several times, just to make sure, then the tall man broke the side light in the front door and reached in and unlatched it.

Cheney, Dean's Border Collie, crouched in the entryway, growling and baring his teeth at the duo when they opened the door. The short man smiled at the dog and pulled from his parka pocket a bag full of fresh sheep organs and bone marrow, waving it back and forth in front of the dog like a canine hypnotist. "Hey boy, look what I've got for you... yum."

The dog caught the scent of the treat and, falling under the trance of fresh sheep blood, let the short man lead him to the laundry room, where the contents were dumped on the floor and the door was closed.

The tall man immediately headed upstairs, as they'd previously agreed, and began sifting through the two bedrooms and loft, methodically searching for items that could be stowed in the medium-sized duffel that he carried. The short man searched the larger lower level, carefully opening each cabinet, pulling open each drawer, looking in the nooks and crannies where only a cop, or a criminal, would think to hide valuables. In three minutes, the tall man had finished his work upstairs and came down to assist the short man. There were more rooms on the first level, and they finished the search as a team. Dean didn't keep any cash or jewelry in the house, and the most valuable items, the furniture and a few large pieces of art work, were too bulky to take out in a duffel strapped to a couple of snow machines. A laptop, an I-Pad, an Xbox, a shotgun, a hunting rifle, and a Nikon DSLR was the extent of their haul. The tall man looked at the short man and nodded. They quickly exited the house and secured their duffels to the sleds that were parked out front.

Had the visibility been better, had the wind noise not been so strong, and had his engine not drowned out the engines of the burglars' sleds, Dean would have spotted them a lot sooner, but they were about twenty yards ahead when he emerged from the blizzard and saw the men leaving his house. He watched one of them throw the duffel on the back of his sled and jump on. Out of habit he yelled, "Stop, police!" although he knew his voice couldn't be heard above the howling wind and engine noise. But when the tall man turned back to strap the duffel down, he caught sight of Dean's headlight. Dean saw him slap his partner's shoulder and point out Dean's approach, and they gunned their machines and pulled away.

Instinctively, Dean pulled his throttle and followed. Dean's Ski-Doo Summit X was one of the fastest stock machines on the market. He should have been able to easily overtake the two men, whose sleds were older and less powerful, but Dean was a novice driver and his skills were no match for them. They quickly disappeared into the darkness. Dean's machine bucked, and he felt himself pushed back on the seat, as all one-hundred-sixty-five horses in the engine he was holding onto galloped after the suspects.

The trail approaching Dean's house was a gradual climb with a few mild switchbacks until the landscape opened to a long slope to the top of the ridge where the house stood. But the trail away from his house was much steeper, the switchbacks much sharper and the trail would alternately enter the forest and then exit to clearings overlooking the river. Dean was not generally considered a particularly reckless man in his world filled with mostly reckless men. He typically evaluated the risk reward of all his actions and, with a few notable exceptions, when a victim or a child was in immediate peril, his judgment had allowed him to escape from quite a few tough situations. But today, the combination of his anger at seeing his home being violated and the trigger of his predator instincts by the fleeing robbers overwhelmed the queasy dread of controlling a machine that he'd climbed on for the first time less than a month ago. With his adrenalin masking the fear in the pit of his stomach, and his anger tunneling his vision, he pulled the throttle wide open and roared after the taillights into the swirling snow and the darkness.

He pulled closer to the sleds on the straight-away, but his inexperience required him to slow for the tight curves and the men pulled farther away. This dance repeated time and again as they followed the road through the woods. Dean could see that the men were pulling farther ahead now, and he knew that he had to take the curves faster or he was going to lose them. He let a little less off the throttle on the next curve and fishtailed through it, feeling the fear rise again in the pit of his stomach. But the sled held the curve, and he opened up the throttle again on the straightaway, narrowing the distance between them. He upped his speed on the next two curves and could see that he was closing the gap.

The men could see that too. The tall man on the sled closest to Dean glanced back on each straightaway, seeing that Dean was gaining on him. If they didn't lose him by the time they reached the next straightaway, they would all emerge from the forest where their truck was parked for their getaway, and that would be bad. Then they might have to kill the cop, and that wasn't what they were here for. As they ap-proached the next curve, the man reached over to a switch that was duct-taped to the dash and pulled it down. Immediately, every light on his sled went off.

Dean had his throttle wide open on the straight-away when the sled in front of him went dark. The snow had become so heavy that his headlamp was giving him only about ten feet of visibility. Until now, he could see the brake lights of the sled in front of him and, as they were activated, had ample warning that a curve was coming and could adjust his speed. But not this time. The sled going dark took him by surprise, as did the sharp curve that emerged from the darkness. He had only a split-second to release the throttle, but that wasn't enough to prevent his sled from jumping through the turn, its ski landing on the false edge of a drift on the outside of the curve. He and his sled sailed into a black abyss.

Thirty feet of thin air was what Dean found himself in, and his instinct to pull up on the handle bars and try to keep the nose of the sled as high as possible probably saved his life. Still, the sled hit hard, six feet of snow cushioning the blow somewhat, but there was hard earth under that six feet. The sled bounced several times before coming to a rest without its rider. On the first bounce, Dean had been propelled up and forward like a greenhorn on his first rodeo bull. When he awoke a minute later, he was neck deep in the ice-cold Snake River, shivering and dazed but alive.

He pulled himself out of the river and limped over to his sled that was miraculously sitting upright. He thought maybe he could ride it back, but his spirits fell when he saw that both front skis were broken off. He wouldn't be riding home. His face was encrusted with ice, and icy water had seeped down the neck of his waterproof suit. His feet started to numb, his expensive waterproof boots not able to protect him from the water that leaked in over the top. That's when the second rush of adrenalin kicked in. He knew that he had to keep moving and get himself back before hypothermia set in. He didn't even know if that was possible, but he had to try. Setting off on foot up the slope, putting one frozen foot in front of the other, he used his mixed martial arts training to suppress his pain, his anger at himself to fuel his stoicism, and his stubbornness to refuse to entertain the possibility of dying alone of hypothermia in the backcountry of Wyoming because of his own stupidity.

When he hobbled into his house two hours later, his front door was standing open, and he couldn't feel his hands, feet or even his face. He passed by the fireplace in the great room and went straight into the kitchen, tapping the buttons on his kitchen stove, knowing his hands were too numb to build a fire. Slumping to the floor, he allowed the heat from the oven and the gas burners to wash over him, exhausted and bone-weary. He awoke an hour later, no longer frozen, actually too warm now, to the sound of Cheney barking. The men had locked Cheney in the laundry room and, thank God, when he let him out, he was relieved to see the dog hadn't been harmed. He picked himself up and checked his extremities. His shoulder was really sore, but amazingly he didn't see any evidence of frostbite. Maybe he had lucked out.

Carrying a mug of hot tea into his sparsely furnished living room, he sat down, now remembering through his mental fog that his house had been robbed. He got up and surveyed the damage. The house hadn't been torn apart; it was almost like they knew what they were looking for. He quickly realized his laptop was missing and, within a few more minutes, he was able to put together an inventory of everything else they had taken. There wasn't much he could do now except wait until morning to contact the sheriff. He fell asleep with his nine-millimeter Glock next to him on the pillow—the one that he almost always carried—hoping they would come back, but he knew that was unlikely.

At 2 AM, he was wide awake and went out to the living room. He'd thought that being in Wyoming would clear his head, give him an idea of how to extricate himself from his suspension, but here it was, a month later, and he still didn't have a clue. It was more than the trumped-up charges that were bothering him; it was how the FBI had found out about his wife Sara. And the irony was that although he had seen her, been with her all last summer, had consulted with her on the Jackson Hole murder case, she'd now disappeared. She hadn't appeared to him since he had returned to Chicago at the end of the case, and that son-of-a-bitch Eckles was using her to imply that he was some kind of bat-shit crazy lunatic. Fuck them.

He looked around the room, and in a loud voice he called, "Sara, where the fuck *are* you? Come back. I can use your help." He slumped to the floor, and whispered. "Please, I really need you right now."

There was a place in his mind that knew she was an illusion, but he ignored that place. Her presence was as real to him as his own flesh. When the therapist who had spilled his secret to the FBI had told him he could be cured with a few more sessions, he'd abruptly stopped therapy. If he was crazy, he couldn't bear to be cured. He sat for a moment, half-expecting her to walk in from the other room, but no one answered his call. Walking gingerly over to the corner of the room, he picked up a bottle of Wild Turkey off the table and drained the last sips from the bottom, dropping the empty bottle to the floor. He reached down and pulled out the last bottle from the case. Could he have already drunk the full case in the last week?

He sat down in his favorite chair in front of the fireplace, next to the stack of James Lee Burke crime novels. He was half-way through the complete set that he'd picked up at the used book store in Jackson. He thought about Dave Robicheaux, the tormented New Orleans cop struggling with his demons and his alcoholism. Was that who he was turning into: an alcoholic cop tortured by regret and vivid dreams of the past? But Robicheaux was more than a drunk. He was so exquisitely evocative in his description of the thunderstorms over the bayou, you wanted to get in your car and drive straight to South Louisiana.

Whenever Dean tried to describe the unspeakable spiritual beauty of the Tetons to an acquaintance and explain why he felt so drawn to this place, he became tongue-tied. He always struggled finding the words to adequately explain why this place spoke to his soul. Maybe the Tetons were just more ephemeral than the bayou, incapable of being described with earthly senses—or, more likely, he was just an inarticulate, illiterate cop. He opened the paperback to his bookmark, took a big gulp from the fresh bottle of Wild Turkey, sat back in his chair and lost himself in Burke's prose, wallowing in guilty satisfaction as Robicheaux went out of control and slaughtered the murderers of his wife.

The book fell from his hand and he slipped into a fitful slumber. In his dream, he was back in Chicago, walking through the home he shared with his wife Sara. She hadn't come home from work, she wasn't answering her phone, and he was panicked. Frantically, he ran through the house, opening every door, calling her name, but she was nowhere to be found. When he awoke, he found himself standing in the middle of the room, thinking he was back in their Lincoln Park townhouse. Then he remembered and fell back into the chair, tipping the bottle so that the burning liquid flowed down his throat, giving him the courage to fall back into his darkness.

Chapter 5

Yao Chen closed his eyes and tried to breathe. He'd just finished a ten-minute coughing fit that left him wheezing, weak, and dizzy. Today his thirty-five-year, two-pack-a-day habit combined with the highest pollution level in the city's history to torture his lungs; the exertion of the short bicycle ride to the Hua Jiaju furniture factory in Shenzhen left him gasping. He stood near the executive entrance to the factory and tried to gather himself. Just back from a three-week, so-called "holiday," he was worried about his job. Holidays were practically non-existent in his world. He hadn't had one in five years, but his mother's illness forced him to take this one. Still, even while he cared for her, he worked—straight through the Chinese New Year, when the factory was shut down—toiling by himself designing a new production layout. When he collapsed by his mother's bedside, from fatigue and anxiety, he was taken to the hospital in downtown Shenzhen and ended up with a stent in his heart. If he'd been conscious, he never would've let them do it. He had scrambled to cover his tracks, exaggerating his mother's illness to get the extra time off to re-cover. He knew his boss would be angry. The factory was re-tooling for a new line of office fur-niture for a new American customer, and, in his absence, Yao's assistant and the factory finance manager had handled the re-tooling. Yao knew this couldn't be good for him—especially if the assistant and the manager had done a good job of it.

When he walked into his office, his assistant, Wei Jinping, was sitting at his desk, studying a stack of reports. "Good morning, Wei. How is the re-tooling coming?"

Wei jumped up from his boss's desk and moved aside so Yao could sit down. "It's so good to see you, boss. How is your mother?"

Yao sat down, leaving Wei standing. Yao didn't like him much. Wei was politically connected and had been forced on Yao. Worse, he was ambitious, and ambition combined with political connections is generally a dangerous combination in a subor-dinate. The truth was that he would already have Yao's job if he were competent. But Wei hadn't an ounce of aptitude for production design, and much of Yao's time over the last eighteen months had been spent teaching and fixing the mistakes of his much younger assistant.

"My mother is still holding on, but she is very ill. I extended my stay so that I wouldn't have to return when she passes. Once production starts, I can't leave the factory. I've said my goodbyes. Thank you for taking over for me while I was out,

Wei. Can you bring me up to speed on the new assembly line?"

"Well, we have it running. Li Meng made the decision to implement those machine modifications that we were discussing before you left, and just as Li said, it should result in significant increases in output." Li Meng was the factory finance manager, and he saw himself as a sort of Renaissance man in the manufacturing business. He was constantly coming up with schemes to increase factory productivity and cut costs.

"Dammit, Wei. Couldn't you fight him on that? You know his machine modifications were basically made to remove all the fail-safe safety controls. It's not like we don't have enough injuries with the controls we have on the machines now. It's going to be a bloodbath on the floor if we allow those modifications to stand."

"You know how Li can be, boss. You can stand up to him, but there is no way he would take any argument from me. Besides, maybe we should give it a try. You know how much pressure we're getting to increase productivity this year."

Yao shook his head. "Let's go take a look at the line."

Hua Jiaju Manufacturing translates into English as Flower Furniture Manufacturing, but there was nothing floral about the thirty-thousand-square-foot facility. Yao knew that most of the world, especially the Americans, thought all the factories in China were clean, streamlined, high-tech facilities with only the minor flaw of exploiting their employees with low pay and overwork. Yao would love to work in one of those factories, the kind that produce the smartphones and laptop computers, but he'd never had the connections or training to get into one of the elite manufacturing programs. His parents had been poor peasants, and he'd had to scrap and fight to get to his present level.

The floor of the old structure smelled of the extremely strong adhesives used in production, so toxic that giant fans in the ceiling ran twenty-four hours a day to remove the corrosive fumes from the building. The line was empty this morning. Normally the machinery, a hodgepodge of refurbished and outdated but still functional equipment would have created a cacophony of sound so loud that Yao and Wei would use ear plugs and need to turn their heads and shout directly into each other's ear to hold a conversation.

"We'll be doing test runs later this morning," Wei said. "Li wants to start full production tomorrow."

Yao walked through the line examining each machine and saw the safety controls had been disabled. He would have to bring this up again with Li. He wasn't surprised that Li had taken the vacuum of his absence to do this. And he couldn't expect Wei to stand up to Li. It would fall on him to fight this fight. "Wei, I want you to stay on the line today and monitor everything. Give me a production report tomorrow. And if there are any accidents, shut the entire line down right away and call me."

"OK, boss."

Yao left his subordinate and sat in a stall in the washroom just off the plant floor trying to catch his breath. Li Meng was the latest in a long line of finance managers Yao had worked with over the years. And he was definitely the most difficult. The others had left Yao alone as long as he met the company's productivity quotas. Li had been at the factory for only about two years, but it had been two years of one battle after another. Li wanted out of the dreary facility, and he knew the best way out was to show marked improvement in the productivity of the plant. Yao gathered himself and walked to Li's office.

Li Meng was a short man with a thin mustache that was intended to make him look older and more authoritative. Instead, Yao thought, the mustache and slicked back hair served only to make him look like an animated cartoon villain— which, Yao also thought, actually did fit his personality. Li looked up. "Yao, so glad to have you back. You look rested. I hope you are ready to get back to work. We have a very aggressive production schedule to fill. And I want the production line up at full capacity next week."

"We'll see how that goes after our trial runs today," said Yao. "But I want to speak with you about the machine modifications. I thought we had decided that those modifications were too risky before I left."

"No, Yao. *You* decided those mods were too risky. While you were on holiday, production decisions had to be made. We couldn't wait for your return. Wei and I agreed on the machine mods and I believe that you left Wei in charge in your absence, no? We decided to give the machine mods a trial, and if we have adverse results, we can always undo them. Doesn't that make sense? You know we are both on the hot seat here. If production doesn't increase, it will not be good for either of us."

"By adverse results, do you mean accidents and severe injuries to our workers?"

"Possibly, but any increases in accidents needs to be considered in the context of increased productivity. It's all about cost benefit analysis, Wei. You know that." Then he continued with his trademark condescending smirk. "Wait, maybe you don't know that. You've had pretty much a free rein here over the years. But with the increase in wages all over China, more and more American companies are moving their business to Vietnam, India, and other countries. If we can't remain competitive, we are both going to be out of jobs, so we have to change things up here." Li paused for a moment, as if he was considering what he should say. "I want to show you something. I know you won't like it, but you need to keep an open mind. We are in survival mode here. Since you've been gone, I've been working really hard on this problem, and I came up with a solution. Come with me."

Li led Yao out of his office and down the stairs to the production line that Yao had just previewed with Wei. Just off the line, there was a door to the warehouse area that had been used to store old equipment for spare parts. Li paused at the door and smiled at Yao. "Yao, meet the solution to our labor-cost problem."

Li opened the door and Yao looked inside. Dozens of little faces looked up at him. For a moment, Yao could not comprehend what he was seeing. Then, his disbelief was replaced by a wave of disgust washing over him. "Li, what the fuck? You can't be serious."

Chapter 6

"DEAN, Dean, are you OK?"

Dean squinted his eyes at the blurry figure standing over him. Why was it so damned bright in here? The sun was shining straight into his face, exacerbating the stabbing pain in the middle of his forehead, and forming a halo effect around the thin figure that stood over him. "Sheriff Cody? What are you doing here?" Dean attempted to stand, but the spinning room made him think better of it and he sat back in the easy chair.

"I've been tryin' to reach you all morning, but you haven't been answerin' your cell. I was in the area, so I thought I'd stop by and see how things are goin'. Jesus, Dean, the sidelight to your front door is broken and here you are passed out with an empty bottle of whisky in your lap. Did you lose your key and have to break in?"

Dean suppressed the bile rising in his throat and replied hoarsely. "Nothing like that. I surprised a couple of guys robbing my house last night and chased them down the ridge on my sled. Took a turn too fast and jumped the sled off the ledge. Broke my skis off so I had to walk home." He tapped the empty bottle on his lap. "Just trying to warm up a bit. It was a long and cold walk home. I landed in the river."

"You sure you're OK? You look like shit and smell worse."

"I'm fine," Dean insisted, but he did feel like crap. He was hungover, and his shoulder was killing him. "Just had a rough night."

"You get a description of the guys?"

"It was pretty dark. One tall guy and one short guy. Not much to go on. They didn't get much —just my camera, a couple of guns and my laptop. I was going to check all the pawnshops this morning."

"Want me to send Rusty down to look around, get some prints?" Rusty Jackson was the lead evidence technician in Teton County and Dean had worked with him the previous summer on the Jordy Smith case.

"I don't think that's necessary. I've got a fingerprint kit here. I'll take the prints and bring them to your office. I'll check outside for boot prints, but it was snowing pretty hard last night, so I doubt we'll get much. I'm guessing it was just a couple of tweakers."

The Sheriff didn't respond immediately. "Maybe. But let me ask you something. The rumor goin' around the state is that the FBI is looking for anything to pin the Rosati thing on Senator Mc-Graw. We both know that your suspension is just another way of tryin' to discredit the original investigation. Is it possible that someone paid these guys to break into your place to grab your computer?"

"My computer?"

"Yeah, your computer. Maybe they wanted to get a look at what you got on there, maybe to get somethin' on you, or maybe just fishin' for something on McGraw. Maybe it wasn't a couple of tweakers, but somebody who wanted to get a hold of your data."

Dean thought about what the Sheriff said. He had given the FBI back his "official" laptop when he was suspended. But when he was working in Jackson last summer he had been on vacation and hadn't had his official issue computer with him. He had been using his personal laptop, the same one stolen by the robbers. He paused for a moment and thought about what could be on that computer that could be used against him, or against Senator McGraw. Could they have been after his data? Dean knew there were notes on his computer that described the relationship between the Senator, Charles, and Charles' alterego Charlotte, and the release of this information could very well torpedo McGraw's candidacy. "I don't think so, Sheriff. I don't think there's anything anyone would be interested in on my laptop."

"Dean, what's this Sheriff crap. After what we went through together last summer, I thought we were at least on a first-name basis."

It was true. After a rough beginning, Dean had become close to the athletic female chief law enforcement officer of Teton County, and she'd actually saved his life last summer. "Sorry, Dani. I've been a little discombobulated since I got back."

"I can see that. If you get any prints, bring them in. If you want, I'll send someone out to the pawn-shops today, so just let me know. Look, the reason I stopped by this morning is that Senator McGraw and Charles Kidwell are going to be in town tomorrow evening for a fundraiser and they want me and you to come. I hate this sort of thing, but I'm running for reelection next year, and it won't hurt to be seen with the Senator and most of the rich folk in the Valley. Want to be my date?"

Dean snorted. "Sure. What should I wear?"

"I don't care what you wear, but you might want to lay off the booze for twenty-four hours. You smell like a Kentucky distillery."

Chapter 7

JIA Ling awoke to a sensation of water dripping on her belly. She sat up quickly and looked across the room, expecting to see her brothers' crib. But she experienced the same disappointment each morning. At first she would think she was in the crowded bedroom of her uncle's farm house; then she'd remember the orphanage and expect to see her brothers in the same room, only to be greeted by rows of metal bunk beds when she sat up and looked for them.

It was the odor that reminded her of her brothers. Most people would consider the amalgamation of odors in the barracks revolting—the damp ancient concrete, the body odor of untold numbers of previous users absorbed into the foam mattress she lay on, and the strong smell of urine from the dozens of pre-pubescent factory workers who found it more convenient to wet their beds than navigate their way to the bathroom in the pitch-black of night. But Jia found it comforting. It reminded her of her brothers back at the orphanage. She never minded cleaning their dirty diapers, and she loved taking them to her bed and nuzzling them for a few minutes each morning before starting her chores. Since she'd arrived, they were the first thoughts on her mind each morning and the last thoughts that launched the fountain of tears that put her to sleep each night.

Jia didn't pray. In her brief life, she hadn't been introduced to the concept that a supernatural figure could grant wishes to humans so long as they weren't in conflict with some grand plan for the universe. The source of her hope wasn't religion. Rather it was born of the purest form of love for her brothers. That and the stubborn will passed down in her DNA that allowed poor ancestral Chinese peasants to survive centuries of subsistence existence. She rolled out of the way of the dripping urine from the bunk above her and considered her options. She was a smart girl, and while she was at the orphanage she had found a way to do her assigned chores and also care for her brothers. She fantasized about running away from the factory and stealing her brothers from the orphanage. But even if she was successful, how would she support them? How would she care for them? Her thoughts were interrupted by the fluorescent lights coming on in the barracks, and the voice on the speaker exhorting the children to arise and get ready for their workday.

It was hot today on the factory floor. Even with the twelve huge industrial fans mounted on the factory roof, the strong chemical smell of the adhesives used in the furniture-making process was nearly overwhelming. Jia had had several bouts of vomiting from the odor until her body adjusted. Today, however, the intense heat somehow made the scent worse, and throughout the day many children would have to leave the assembly line to throw up. The old women who supervised the workers would give the workers only a few minutes to recover, and then would order them back to the line.

The older man was in the factory today and was pointing to some of the controls and arguing with the man with the mustache who had brought Jia to the factory. He seemed very angry about something. Jia had seen the older man several times in the factory but had never seen him angry. There was something about him that reminded her of her grandfather who had died the previous year. On Jia's first day he had brought her a glass of water when she was experiencing one of her bouts of nausea and had patted her on the head. Her focus was brought back by a sharp whack with a wooden stick on the side of her head. The old lady supervisor shouted at her to get busy, and Jia jerked herself back to the assembly line, her head and pride stinging.

Chapter 8

Dean drove to the Teton County Sheriff's Office in Jackson where he met Sheriff Cody, and the two of them rode together to the fundraiser. The event was being held at a house on a butte across from another, lower butte on which Charles Kidwell's home rested. Dean thought about how he'd gotten the property manager to give him a surreptitious tour of Kidwell's house last summer, and how what he'd found there had both shocked him and broken the case open. The information had freaked him out, and he'd been concerned that, by disclosing it to the wrong people, he might be responsible for destroying the Senator's campaign. He'd managed to keep it private, but he also knew that there was some data on his computer that could reveal the secret—if the user knew where to look. His face was frozen in a thousand-yard stare as he thought about all this and, when he looked up, he realized Dani had caught his daydream. "What?"

"Nothing. Just thinking of how these rich folks are trying to one-up each other. I thought Kidwell's house was amazing, but look at that. It's as if this house was located just so he could look down on Kidwell's house."

Dani looked up at the imposing stone home as she drove her county-issued SUV a little too fast around the switchbacks that led up to the top of the butte. "Actually, I think that might be exactly the case. You see, Ron Flag was the most important guy in the Valley for a long time. His daddy owns most of the oil and gas leases in the state. Senator McGraw's daddy-in-law used to own almost as much, but Flag bought him out a few years ago. Then right before the last presidential election, Flag started his PAC, you know, "Americans for an American America." They call it Triple A in the media, but around here they call it God's PAC because it's got more money and has more control over folks than God. But McGraw has never taken any of his money. His whole campaign is based on being this independent cowboy populist, beholden to no one, so, I was kind of surprised to get this fundraiser invitation and see who was hosting it. Maybe he changed his mind when he found out how much it costs to run for president. So anyway, Flag has a thousand-acre ranch east of town, but a few months ago he bought this monstrosity overlooking the home of the chief advisor to Senator McGraw. I don't think it's a coincidence."

"So, you're saying he spent maybe ten million dollars just so he could literally look down on Charles Kidwell?"

"Well, it's not much different than a guy buying a BMW to show up his neighbor's Lexus, is it? Or a guy who has a pit bull instead of a huntin' hound because he thinks it makes him look tougher. You can always spot a guy with who's insecure in his masculinity just by looking at how much he over-compensates."

"Wow, Dani, I never knew you were such a keen observer of the human condition."

"Stick around, Dean. There's a lot about me you don't know yet."

Dean and Dani were ushered into the great room of the house where dozens of people had gathered. The room was a huge rotunda with evenly spaced windows all the way around. The wall space between each window was decorated with Western art scenes, all of them hunting or battle scenes featuring Native Americans: a tribal war dance, a battle showing Sioux warriors slaughtering and scalping American settlers, Custer's massacre at Little Big Horn. Dean looked at the life-sized sculpture displayed at the center of the rotunda. Entitled "White Man's Revenge," it depicted the slaughter of American bison on the Great Plains. Dean thought about the man who had so carefully selected and arranged this display—a display intended to send a message. There were no scenes depicting Native Americans as anything other than savages. The scene Flag presented was one of total domination and humiliation, the ultimate consequences of resistance.

Dean recognized only one man in the room and he immediately greeted Dean. "How's my favorite Chicago cop? I was hoping you would come."

"Senator, it's good to see you too. Are Charles or Charlotte here this evening?"

The Senator grinned at Dean's question. "Charles is around. But I don't think his sister Charlotte will be. She doesn't like being the center of attention, as I'm sure you can understand."

The Senator nodded toward the portly man with a jet-black pompadour holding court at the center of the room. "Have you met Ron Flag? He insisted on holding this little party for me tonight."

"Haven't had the pleasure. I thought he was backing one of the other guys."

"Oh, he is. I think this shows that he's getting scared that I could actually win this thing."

"So, you are going to take his PAC money?"

The Senator laughed. "Shit no. I'm not going to owe him anything. Now if any of his rich friends want to contribute to my campaign, or to Charles' PAC, I'm not going to turn that down. I'm here just to watch him in action as much as anything else.

They were joined by a young Asian woman, resplendent in a red cocktail dress and heels, and she stood so close to the Senator that Dean thought they might have something going on. But since he knew of the Senator's involvement with Charlotte, he doubted that was true. Flag was on a roll with the audience surrounding him, pontificating about how welfare ruined the Native American community by stifling their entrepreneurial spirit. He was going on about espousing the virtues of American self-made men, when McGraw said to the young woman, "The only thing that Flag made himself was his PAC. The billion or so dollars in the PAC is his daddy's money." Then he made a jerking motion with his hand, and she looked over at Dean and shrugged.

Dean never did meet Flag. The rest of the evening he stuffed his face with elk tartar, smoked trout, grouse satay and other local delicacies passed around on trays by uniformed waiters, and spent time examining other rooms containing nothing but Western sculpture along the same thematic lines as the art work in the rotunda.

Toward the end of the evening, Senator McGraw gave a stump speech, during which Dani took him aside. "The Senator wants to meet with you after his speech."

They waited for McGraw to finish, and the Sheriff led him into a large wood-paneled den. A few minutes later, the Senator, Charles Kidwell, and the woman he had seen with McGraw earlier, walked into the room. The Senator gestured for Dean and Dani to remain seated, and the group all took seats at the round wooden table. "Dean, I know this isn't your thing. I asked Sheriff Cody to invite you because I need to talk to you and we're flying back to Washington tonight. I want you to know that I'm aware of your situation. I know your suspension is about me, not about you. And I'm truly sorry that you are involved in this. I promise you that I will make this up to you someday. I owe you for last summer, and I always take care of my friends. They're looking for something in particular, and I think I know what it is. If they had it, they would never have suspended you. But they don't, and it looks like they're not giving up until they find it."

Dean tried to pay attention to what the Senator was saying, but his eyes were drawn to the young woman with McGraw. There was something about her that made it difficult to concentrate on the Senator's words. "Senator, what is it that you think they are looking for?"

"Well, Mario Rosati had a video of me with Charlotte. That's how all this started last year. FBI Director Vorhies assured me that the FBI had found nothing like that in Rosati's property, but I think they started looking for it again after Vorhies left. Dean, if that video becomes public, it's over for me."

"And who exactly is 'they'?"

"I think you can appreciate the politics of this, Dean. The new Director, Fanning, is a Democratic Party flunky. If the Democrats keep the White House, then maybe he gets to be Attorney General. Or maybe he runs for the Senate or Governor. Bringing me down would elevate him instantly to the national stage."

"OK," Dean remarked. And then he waited for McGraw to tell him what he really wanted.

"Right now, there's no one I can trust in law enforcement except you and Sheriff Cody here. Since you obviously have a stake in this too, and you have some time on your hands, I'd like you to find the video before the FBI does." The Senator paused to let this sink in.

Instinctively, Dean knew this was a bad idea. "But you know I have no standing in law enforcement. And I have no resources."

"I've thought of that. Sheriff Cody will deputize you just like last summer. Charles can provide you with whatever financial resources you need, and the Teton County Sheriff has access to national law enforcement records. And I'm sure you probably still have some unofficial relationships in the bureau."

Dean was uncomfortable with the last comment. He knew that FBI informational technologist Mark Jeffrey would help as he had last summer, but it would be risky for Mark, and Dean wasn't sure he should take advantage of him.

"And another thing. You're right—you could use some additional resources." The Senator turned to the woman. "Dean, this is Melinda Johnston. Melinda is an investigator with the Wyoming State Police. She's been assigned to my protective detail, but my wife is giving me a hard time. She's suspicious that something is going on between us. As I'm sure you know, Dean, nothing could be further from the truth, but I decided to kill two birds with one stone. She has great investigative skills, and I am sure you can use another hand to help out with this project."

Dean glanced in her direction, and then quickly turned toward the Senator. "Senator, with all due respect, if I decide to take this on, and that is a *big* if, I'll be working alone. I haven't had a partner for years, and I am not about to start now."

The Senator smiled and turned on the cowboy charm that both men and women found irresistible. "Dean, I'm asking this as a favor to me. You would be doing me a huge solid. Give her a shot. Let her work with you for a week. Then, if it's not working out, I'm sure I can find something more suitable. Please, it would mean a lot to me."

Dean looked at Melinda, and she met his gaze. He couldn't read anything at all into her expression, but she didn't avert her eyes, rather looked directly into his as if she was looking right through him. The directness of her look unsettled him, and he turned back to the Senator. "OK, we can give it a try. One week."

The Senator rose and, as they started to leave the room, Melinda whispered to him, "Dean, could we speak for a couple of minutes?"

The woman wasted no time, Dean thought, but he remained at the table as the others left. When they were alone, he let her speak first.

"From the looks you've been giving me... I think I have only this week to prove my worth. Why don't we meet tomorrow and develop a plan? I'm staying at Charles's house while I'm here. Want to meet there in the morning?"

Dean looked around the room, avoiding her eyes. "I'm skiing in the morning. We could get together after that I suppose."

"You mind if I come along? I'm a boarder but never skied here before and I've been trying to find some time to get on the slopes."

"Suit yourself. I'll pick you up at 7 AM sharp. Be ready."

Chapter 9

Ron Flag was unwinding after the party was over. It had accomplished exactly what he had planned. After spending a quarter of a billion on the last election, he had won both houses of Congress but had failed to win the grand prize. He was determined that would not happen again. With both houses, the best he could do was create a stalemate. If he could win the presidency this time, he could advance his agenda—one that would control the direction of the country for decades. His personal assistant, Luis, brought him a drink in a crystal cocktail glass on a gold tray. Luis had been his valet since Flag was a twelve-year-old boy. Flag's father had been concerned with the bullying that his son had been suffering at his exclusive prep school, so he'd replaced Ron's nanny with Luis, a former Mexican boxer with a fighter's nose and facial scars that belied the perfect English he had garnered through hours of practice with the language tutor hired by Flag's father. Ron's new "manny" had toughened him up—at least that was how Flag chose to remember it. But it was the presence of this intimidating figure at his side as much as his pugilistic instruction that scared off the upper-class bullies. Luis would walk Flag into the school each morning and would stand next to the car that picked him up from school each day. His fighter's stare and knowing nod to each of the preppie bullies was enough to scare them off.

"Luis, let me know when my guests arrive. I really need to unwind tonight."

"Will do, boss."

Flag thought about his mistakes in the last election. He hadn't accounted for the charisma of the president, but now the president's inability to grow the economy had made him extremely unpopular. It seemed it would be much easier to elect a Republican this time around, but he needed it to be a Republican he could control. He had embarked on an "anyone but McGraw strategy" and it had failed miserably. He was shaken by the way the Republican base had responded to McGraw and, thus far, McGraw had seemed bulletproof to negative campaigning. He snorted at his own metaphor. Bulletproof. Ever since McGraw had killed the Chicago mob boss in the Washington hotel, the voters could not get enough of the cowboy Senator. Consequently, he decided he would try to woo McGraw with a combination of carrot and stick.

Tonight was the carrot. About ninety-five percent of the wealth of Wyoming was at the fundraiser tonight. He couldn't wait until McGraw found out what a failure it had been. Flag let it be known behind the scenes to each of the attendees that the whole thing was for show. He'd opened the door to the vault and let McGraw peer in, but Flag wasn't unlocking it. Not yet. Not until McGraw agreed to play ball. He didn't need to totally abandon his crazy populist, anti-capitalist rhetoric. He just needed to realize that most of his wild ideas were anathema to the money people. Oh, he'd let McGraw continue to give his folksy speeches, and maybe pick a couple of insignificant gestures to keep the little folks happy—stuff that wouldn't cost him any money. But McGraw was going to have to give up his bigger, more revolutionary schemes—the scaling back of oil and gas leases on public lands, outlawing fracking for natural gas, and a Federal carbon tax.

He still couldn't believe McGraw was member of his party. The media was now calling him a modern-day Teddy Roosevelt. His followers on social media were calling themselves The Rough Riders.

"Rough Riders, my ass." Flag actually said this out loud, but unlike most of his proclamations, there was no one else in the room to smile and agree with him.

He knew that McGraw was almost out of money, so he had shown McGraw a tantalizing blank check tonight. But blank checks always came with conditions. There was absolutely no way that McGraw could raise enough money from the Republican money sources without Flag's support.

Flag's silent soliloquy was interrupted as Luis ushered a man into the room who hadn't been at the party. When he recognized his best friend, his face erupted into a grin.

"Sorry, I couldn't make it, Ron, my flight was delayed because of weather. Tell me about the fundraiser. How did it go?"

Flag spoke the thoughts to his friend that he'd just been turning over to himself. Colonel Ned Wood disliked McGraw as much as Ron did. Maybe more. Flag's dislike was mostly based on self-interest, but Wood's was ideological, and that kind of dislike ran much, much deeper.

Flag had few true friends—most people were only friendly to him because they either wanted something from him or were afraid of him. Ned Wood was a true friend, asking for nothing more than friendship, and Flag felt a strange brotherhood with him. *We're both professional soldiers*, Flag thought. True, Wood was a former full-bird colonel from Marine special ops who'd retired from the military and morphed into a CIA contractor and Black Ops specialist. He was a different sort of warrior than the political soldier Flag considered himself to be. In some ways, fighting political wars could be even more dangerous and more patriotic than the military battles. And the fact that this symbol of American macho had befriended Flag when he'd retired to Jackson Hole after Iraq, well, wasn't that a kind of affirmation of Flag's manhood? Flag had been curious how a career military guy could afford to live in Teton County, immerse himself in Wyoming politics, and be a major donor to conservative causes. He'd done some checking and suspected that some of the tens of millions that his friend had been in charge of distributing to Sunni tribal leaders to buy their loyalty had found its way to Jackson Hole. And Flag didn't have a problem with that. The Iraq war had been a complete failure in its political objectives, but it had been an extremely profitable adventure for a number of capitalists. Just as Flag was finishing the debrief, Luis appeared at the door. "The girls are here."

Flag jumped to his feet and turned to his friend. "You ready for a party?"

Chapter 10

DEAN was at Charles's house at 6:45 AM the next morning. "I'll wait outside until exactly 7:01," he thought, "then I'm out of here."

At 6:47 a young woman decked out in a purple ski jacket and form-fitting black ski pants, carrying a matching purple backpack and snowboard, bounded out the front door. She jumped in the front seat with a big grin. "It's beautiful this morning, isn't it?"

Dean looked around. It was indeed a beautiful morning. About four inches of snow had fallen during the night and the sun was out, illuminating the snow crystals in a painfully dazzling light. He realized he was in such a sour mood that he hadn't even appreciated how gorgeous the morning was. Jackson Hole gets a tremendous amount of snow in the winter, and the price for that is, on most winter days, the sun is obscured by snow-filled clouds, unlike the endless blue-sky days of summer in the mountains.

"I guess." He mumbled, then took a long drink of coffee from his travel cup and nodded to the thermos. "There's a cup in the side pocket if you want some."

"Thanks." She poured herself a cup. "Guess you're not much of a morning person."

"That's not true. I am one of the most morning people I know."

"So, this is really your normal personality? I guess the Senator was just bullshitting about your charm..."

Dean laughed. "You are something else, aren't you?"

"Look, I don't need to come along if you want to be alone. I thought this would be a way for us to get to know each other a bit. But I guess I did invite myself, didn't I?"

Dean looked at her for the first time this morning. She was looking at him the same way she had yesterday. Her eyes penetrated him so deeply that it made him uncomfortable, presenting a striking figure with her dark eyes and jet black hair, but looking nothing like the stereotypical fragile Asian princess. She was strong and athletic, even muscular in the way that reminded him of an Olympic gymnast. Damn, she was pretty. He didn't know why, but it pissed him off. "Look, Melinda, it's fine. I'm sorry I'm such a grouch this morning. It's been a tough few months for me, and Tom blindsided me yesterday. I'm not sure taking this assignment is such a good idea."

"Well, that makes two of us. Tom told me quite a bit about you and your situation. And although our investigation could make it worse, it could also make it better. Do you have a better plan?"

That was just the problem. He not only didn't have a better plan; he had no plan at all. Recently, his plan had been to drink himself into oblivion every night waiting for Sara to show up and rescue him. Even if this assignment turned out to be a disaster, at least he had the ability to fuck with them instead of only being on the receiving end.

Dean rolled down his window, took a deep breath and felt a jolt as the fresh, cold mountain air filled his lungs. Looking out the frosty window of his Jeep at the snow-covered Teton Range, he felt embarrassed. This was one of the most beautiful winter days he'd ever seen in Jackson. Above the pine trees, the sun melting the overnight snow had created icicles that looked as if they were carefully placed on the drooping pine boughs. Wispy clouds swirled over the range like Christmas garland, and sunrays reflecting off the granite face of the Grand Teton sprayed silver glitter with each gust of wind.

"I'm sorry, Melinda, I've been in a funk and it's not your fault. I've been fucked with a lot over the last few months. And I've been sitting on my ass letting it happen. Let's shred this mountain and then figure out how to turn the tables on these assholes."

They both were boarding, but Dean had just switched from skis to snowboarding this season, and the conversion was not going well. Melinda was an expert, and Dean's pride would not permit him to ride anything but the blacks. At noon, after tumbling down the blacks and several near-misses with boulders and trees, they adjourned to the Four Seasons bar for lunch and drinks.

"So, Dean. What's with the accent? I thought you're from Chicago."

"Grew up in West Virginia. Never really lost it. It confuses people. And it makes me seem dumber than I really am, which can be an advantage in certain situations."

"It also makes you seem more charming than you actually are, which can also be an advantage in certain situations, I imagine."

Dean ignored the remark, not willing to think about whether it was flirtatious or insulting. "Somehow I get the impression that you know a lot more about me than I know about you. What else did Tom and Charles tell you about me?"

"Pretty much the whole story of last summer. How you killed a couple of guys in Jackson, saved a playboy and his girlfriend, and almost died saving some little girl from a Russian gang." She gave him that dazzling smile and penetrating look again. "Oh, and how you protected the secret of the Senator and Charlotte."

"So, you know about that then?"

"Yep. I haven't met her yet though. I think Mc-Graw and Charles keep her pretty well hidden."

"Obviously his wife doesn't know, if she's jealous of you."

"Ahh, Lydia McGraw. I can't see how she doesn't know. She's very sharp. Maybe she does know, and she just doesn't like me."

"Does she like anybody? From what I've seen, she's a pretty tough nut," said Dean.

"Actually, I have a great deal of respect for her. She knows what she wants, and she doesn't take shit from anybody. I can see that the Senator cares a great deal about her. He's very respectful of her opinions. That's one of the things I really like about him."

"Well, she's always been a bit of a mystery to me," said Dean.

She stared at him again. "You are the enigma, Dean Wister."

"That's a big word for a cop." Dean looked into her eyes. She had opened her jacket, revealing a good deal of cleavage in her tight-fitting tank top. He had written off the extra cleavage yesterday as cocktail attire, but maybe this was her everyday style of dress. "But I'd say *you* are the enigma. How did you get assigned to the Senator's campaign, and why does his wife hate you?"

"I got assigned by the luck of the draw. Wyoming has a budget shortage, and I was coming off an assignment at just the right time—I was the only one available. As for his wife... well, let's say she's suspicious of any woman under fifty that spends time with him."

Back at the house Melinda asked Dean to walk her through the case from the beginning. "I've heard the story from Charles and Senator McGraw, but I'd like to hear it from you. Somehow I get the feeling that they were leaving a few things out."

"OK. But this may take a while. How about a drink?"

"Sure. What's your pleasure?"

"Bourbon?"

"Sounds good to me. I'm a bourbon drinker myself." She went to the bar, filled an ice bucket and brought a couple of glasses and an unopened bottle that she put on the table between them. "Will this do?"

Dean looked at the bottle. "Whoa. Pappy Van Winkle 23. Do you always start off a new investigation like this?"

"I think we're worth it. Don't you?"

Dean laughed and held up his glass. "Thank you, Charles."

Melinda clinked his glass. "Actually, I think it may belong to Charlotte. I understand she's a bigger drinker than her brother."

Dean took a big sip and felt guilty as the warm, comforting liquid flowed down his throat. Just one drink, to take the edge off, he thought, and settled back in the distressed buffalo-hide easy chair. "OK. From the beginning. I came out here last summer. I hadn't had a day off in over a year and needed the R&R."

Dean paused. He left out the part about the death of Sara and the sentimental reason he chose Jackson Hole for his vacation. This was the place they had met, and where their romance had blossomed, and he wasn't about to reveal her nocturnal appearances after her death.

"While I was here, a Chicago hitman named Torino was found dead in a car accident in the

Snake River. When Sheriff Cody found out about his mob connections, my boss told him I was in the area, and he called me in to consult on the case. Torino's involvement led us to Rosati, a Chicago mob boss. But we uncovered two different crime trails. The first led us to discover that Rosati was working with a Russian national living in Jackson by the name of Boris Birkov, importing Russian girls for prostitution. That's how I happened to rescue Tatiana when she escaped from a brothel down in Rock Springs. The second trail led us to discover that Rosati was laundering money through Charles Kidwell's bank. I suspected, but was never able to prove, that Rosati was blackmailing the Senator and that's why Charles was looking the other way. In any event, FBI Director Vorhies was a close friend of the Senator, and we were able to arrange a sweetheart deal that allowed Charles to cooperate in gathering evidence against Rosati in exchange for no charges against him."

Melinda frowned. "OK, so how did Rosati end up with a bullet through his brain in Senator Mc-Graw's hotel room?"

"Well, I'm sure you read the report. McGraw says Rosati pulled a gun on him and it was self-defense."

"Doesn't that seem like bullshit to you, under the circumstances?"

"Well, remember, as far as I know, the former FBI Director did not know about Charlotte and the Senator and the possibility of blackmail being involved. At least as far as I know. But yes, it seems pretty suspicious on its face. And that's the justification that Director Fanning is using to reopen the investigation."

"OK, so how did you end up suspended?"

"Well, they called me in and accused me of accepting illegal favors, a free plane ride back to Jackson on Charles's private jet after a meeting in Chicago. But they were hinting if maybe I located any information that I somehow 'forgot' to include in my official report, then my problem might go away."

"And did you give them anything?"

"I told them to kiss my hillbilly ass."

Melinda laughed out loud, swallowed the rest of her bourbon and reached over to refill both of their glasses.

"My house was burglarized this week. They got away with my camera, my computer and a few guns. The Sheriff thinks they were after the data on my computer."

"What do you think?"

Dean picked up the glass and took a long swig. "I don't know what to think."

"So, Dean, what happened to this girl, Tatiana?"

"Well, she was living with some friends of mine down in Alpine after she escaped from the brothel, but the Russians followed me and kidnapped her. I got myself into a little bit of trouble trying to rescue her, got my brain rattled, but luckily Sheriff Cody's boys came on the scene just in time."

"And what about that shootout on the Snake River I heard something about?"

"Well, this is where it really gets strange. I was taking a group down the Snake River—I used to be a river guide—when this guy started shooting at us. He wasn't that great a shot, so I was able to chase him down and take him out."

Melinda didn't say anything for a minute. Finally, she looked at him and said. "Shit, Dean, that's some awesome summer vacation."

Dean turned his thoughts back to their assignment. "We need to try to get a lead on how far along the Bureau is on locating the video. I'll check with my sources inside and see what I can find out." The real truth was that he didn't have any actual *sources* within the FBI. His sole source close to anyone in the Bureau was data specialist Mark Jeffrey. And he worked for the same organization that Dean was suspended from—the Midwest Organized Crime Task Force, a federal agency that was a sister agency of the FBI. But Mark had access to the FBI database, and he had a good working relationship with many people in the bureau.

Melinda's voice jarred Dean from his thoughts about how Mark might be able to help them. "I'm getting a pretty good buzz. You want something to eat?"

"You go ahead and eat if you want…" Dean held his glass aloft a little off kilter, "I prefer liquefied corn, wheat and barley."

"You're drunk, cowboy."

"Maybe." And for the first time since he arrived in Jackson, Dean smiled.

Dean awoke to a spear of sunlight piercing his pupils, realizing after a moment that he must be in the guest room at the Kidwell residence but struggling to remember much about the evening. He had no recollection of events after he told Melinda he would stick with liquefied food. His mouth felt as if it was filled with barf-flavored cotton, but— his head foggy, his stomach churning—he got out of bed and realized he was naked. He looked for his clothes, found them in a curvy line beginning in the bathroom and ending in the hallway just outside his door. Why were some of his clothes outside of the bedroom? Had he and Melinda...?

He walked downstairs to the kitchen. There was no sign of Melinda. He put the thought out of his mind, found Charles's French press and a bottle of aspirin in the cupboard, took two of the pain pills with a slug of water, and made some coffee. His head began to clear, but there was still no recollection of the night before. His stomach still churning, he knew he needed food and started to make breakfast. He was deep in thought, chopping onions, when he felt her behind him, her breasts pressing against his back as she stood on her toes and looked over his shoulder. "What're you making?"

That simple sensory stimulation put his nervous system into overload. It took him back to the previous summer when he would awake to find Sara in bed with him, her naked breasts rubbing against his spine so he could feel her nipples. He was instantly aroused.

"Good morning. Making my world-famous Western omelets. Have a seat and I'll get you some coffee."

She sat, and he brought coffee to her. She was wearing a silk pajama top coming only down to the middle of her bare thighs, and it was obvious she wasn't wearing a bra. Maybe the nipples he felt on his back were not just his imagination. Her hair was deliciously askew, and she obviously hadn't showered so her intriguing perfume wasn't from her body wash or shampoo, it was her natural fragrance. These thoughts added to Dean's discomfort. And she noticed.

She looked right at his crotch and grinned. "Geez, Dean."

"I'm sorry. It sometimes happens the morning after I drink. And how you're dressed isn't helping matters."

"Oh, do you want me to go up and change?"

"No, it's fine. It's just that it's been a while since I've had breakfast with a woman dressed the way you are. Just stay right where you are and let me distract myself and get you something to eat."

He served their omelets, and she took a big bite. "Damn, Dean, this is spicy."

"Whoops. Sorry, I should have warned you."

"No, I love it. I'm really into spicy food. It just surprised me. A lot of things last night...surprised me."

Dean took a long swig of coffee and thought about the evening. "I'm kind of foggy about the end of the night last night. Did... anything happen?"

She frowned at him. "Are you telling me that you don't remember you screwed my brains out last night? I can't believe that you don't remember. This is why I don't fuck cops."

Dean stammered. "I'm sorry. I just, I just had a lot to drink. I do remember that we had a great time."

She looked at him. "I'm fucking with you, Dean. Absolutely nothing happened. You were a perfect gentleman. You did give me a very sweet good night kiss, but that was it. Your honor is intact."

Dean cracked a grin, offering her a refill on her coffee. "I'm glad to hear that. I mean, I'm not glad that nothing happened. Oh, shit."

Melinda laughed, waving the coffee pot away. "If you don't mind, I'm going to get showered and dressed. And you were going to talk to some of your contacts with the FBI, if you recall. And I have to make a few calls myself. What do you say we touch base later today about our next steps?"

Chapter 11

Driving home Dean couldn't shake the feeling that he'd somehow cheated on Sara. His wife had been dead for nearly two years, but she was still the first thing he thought about when he woke up each morning. Last summer, when he was hospitalized, he'd said goodbye to her, and he'd thought he was OK with that, but then his job suspension shoved him into a downward spiral. He kept expecting—no, *hoping*—that she would show up again. Did nothing really happen with Melinda last night? If not, then why did he feel so guilty?

He dialed Sheriff Cody, who picked up on the first ring. "Hi Dean, recovered yet from the fundraiser? I've never seen so many assholes in one place in my life."

"You must have lived a sheltered life, Dani. I was wondering if you could do me a favor. Are you close to anyone in the Wyoming State Police?"

"A couple of people, why?"

"My new partner, Melinda Johnston, that Mc-Graw is insisting I work with... You think you could make some inquiries and find out what her story is? Like how she ended up on loan from the state police and on McGraw's crew."

" Yeah, I'll make some calls and see what I can dig up."

"Thanks. Just trying to see what I might be in for." His cell phone beeped, and Dean could see another call coming in. "Got to go, Dani. Get back to me when you have something."

He missed the call, but in a moment saw there was a text message from an unfamiliar number. "Hey, redneck, call me. Important."

He dialed the number of the only person who would dare to use that moniker, and a familiar voice picked up immediately. "Dean, are you alone?"

"Yeah, Mark. What's up?"

"A bunch of stuff. First, why have you been avoiding my emails? You disappeared when you left town and I've been worried about you."

"Sorry about that. I kind of figured that fraternizing with me would be a very bad career move for you. And since you just called me from what I assume is a burner number, I bet I'm right."

"Fuck that. You can't just ignore your friends. Are you OK?"

"I'm fine. Just been hanging out in Jackson, perfecting my skiing and snowboarding. I even bought a snowmobile, but that part isn't going so well." Dean thought about his near miss a couple of days ago.

"Good to hear. Maybe you could invite me out there some weekend? This place has really gone to shit since you left."

"Dude, you have an open invitation. Get your ass out here. I can't wait to see your puny butt tumbling down the mountain."

"Let me check my calendar. Maybe I could get out for the football playoffs. There's another reason I'm calling this morning, though. Eckles knows about your shadow investigation for Senator McGraw and he's really pissed. He called your former boss a little bit ago and said if you interfere with their investigation, he's going to arrest you."

"Who'd you get this from?"

"Your former boss Alvarez told me. I'm sure it was intended to get back to you."

"Fuck, why wouldn't Alvarez call me himself? But it figures, I guess—he's always been an ass-kisser. Mark, the Senator just put me on this about thirty-six hours ago. And very few people, just the McGraw inner circle, know about this. There's no way Eckles could have found out. He knows I'm tight with McGraw and he knows I'm out here. He's probably just warning me to stay out of it."

"Well, watch your step. You don't want to make things any worse than they are."

"Thanks for the heads-up. By the way, what do you know about the FBI investigation of the Senator? He thinks they have a lead on some dirt they're trying to dig up on him."

"That's exactly right. They've made some kind of deal with Mario, Jr. and he's trying to locate a video file his dad had on the Senator. After Mario, Sr. was killed, the search of his property turned up pretty much nothing useful, other than a little info about the Russian girls that incriminated Boris Birkov. They're somehow convinced that Mario, Jr. can locate it, and they're working with him. I've got a pretty good source at the bureau on this."

"That girl you were seeing last year?"

"Maybe, maybe not. You know I don't kiss and tell. Look, Dean, this Eckles... he's a real bastard. Let me help you out. I can feed you any info I'm getting, then maybe you can stay out of the way and also stay out of jail."

"I don't know if that's a good idea. This seems pretty dangerous for you. I'm already fucked. I don't want you screwing yourself too."

"I'm pretty good at covering my tracks. Let's just say that if they try to trace any of our communications, it won't point at me. Put this burner number in your contacts with an alias. You'll be getting emails from a new email address in the future. If you need anything, call or text this number."

Dean thought for a moment. He could use Mark's help, but he knew it was risky, and he'd have a problem living with himself if Mark's career was derailed by helping out. He made a mental note to call Mark only when absolutely necessary. "Thanks, Mark. I really appreciate this."

Dean hung up and wondered if Eckles was bluffing. There were only four people in the meeting at Flag's... What were the chances the room had been bugged?

Chapter 12

JIA was concentrating on the face of Juan Fu, who was focused on the chess board between them on their bunk. Juan Fu, roughly translated to English as curly blessing, wasn't her real name, but it was the name that everyone called her because of her locks, which were unusual and fascinating to the other children in the makeshift dormitory. Juan Fu was the physical and emotional opposite of Jia. Even after an exhausting day on the assembly line, she always had a smile on her face. After work and their meal, there wasn't much to do other than watch the same incessant boring videos that were provided to entertain the children in their off hours. Jia's grandfather had taught her to play chess, so she had fashioned a chessboard and pieces out of random parts from the factory floor. Juan Fu was a bright girl, and she caught on to the game quickly. She had been looking at the board for several minutes, her lips pursed in concentration.

"Juan Fu, this isn't the chess championship. We have to go to sleep soon."

The girl looked up at Jia and then down at the board, touching her queen and then moving her small chubby fingers over to her knight. She picked up the piece, paused with it in mid-air, and then slammed it down hard on the board, shouting "checkmate," scattering the pieces all over the bed, jumping up and dancing around the room, spinning around like the toy top that the children played with at the orphanage. Jia took her chess as seriously as everything else in her life, but the sight of the curly-headed little girl, leaping like a deranged Chinese Shirley Temple, made her laugh. She couldn't help herself, and soon they both were rolling around on Jia's bunk laughing and squealing.

Eventually their giggling fit petered out and they lay looking at the ceiling. Juan had been at the orphanage with Jia, but they had hardly acknowledged each other there. Jia's single-minded obsession with her brothers' care left little time for socializing, but since coming to the factory, Jia had befriended Juan and they'd become inseparable. "Juan, how did you end up at the orphanage?"

For the first time since she had known her, the smile left Juan's face, and she looked away before she spoke. "My mother, she made these beautiful Chinese dolls, old fashioned ones made from beads. They were beautiful Chinese princesses from the five ancient dynasties, and they all had the most wonderful gowns. She would sell them at the tourist market. My father said this would be the way that we could earn the money, so I could go to school. One day I was sick and did not go with them to the market. They didn't come home that evening and an older man from our village came and told me that there had been a traffic accident. My parents and sister were killed. Then they brought me to the orphanage." Juan began to cry quietly. "I brought one of the dolls with me here, but now I can't find it. I think one of the other children stole it."

Jia put her arm around her. "I will keep my eye out for it, Juan. I will try to get it back for you."

Chapter 13

Toby Landers, the McGraw campaign manager, dropped into a chair at the Senator's breakfast table, nearly spilling the bowl of oatmeal Tom McGraw was staring warily into.

"Watch it, TL," said McGraw. "It you spill my oatmeal, I swear I'm going to place an order of biscuits and gravy, and that will really upset my nutritionist." Tom called him TL, which Toby interpreted as a reference to his initials, but it really referenced the secret nickname Tough Love that Charles had given him, based on his all-business, all-the-time demeanor. "Before I forget, update me on the progress on your adoption. It's been awhile since I've heard anything."

TL shook his head. "It's a slog. We've decided to go the international adoption route, and Melinda has been really helpful, I don't know if you're aware, but her parents adopted her from China, and she's still involved with several Chinese adoption agencies. China used to be the main resource for international adoption, but that's pretty much dried up. Now the only Chinese children available are disabled. Chinese orphanages are full of disabled children. We're willing to take a disabled child, but depending on the severity, the cost of care can be astronomical. There are many Americans willing to accept disabled children, but the financial commitment can make it impossible."

"So what you are saying is that China has spent decades taking our jobs, and now they're sending us the children they don't want to take care of," McGraw said.

"That's pretty much it."

McGraw thought for a moment. "You know, this could be a winning campaign issue for us. Maybe assistance for American families who have children with disabilities. Put together a briefing paper for me on this, would you? What else you got for me?"

TL looked down at his spreadsheet, "Well, as of the end of the week, your campaign is officially out of money."

"What do you mean we're out of money?" Tom McGraw dropped a glob of oatmeal on his shirt and glared. "How can that be? What about Charles's PAC, and what about the fundraiser in Jackson?"

"The PAC Fund is getting low. Most of the contributions have been from Charles's personal funds, and we've had little luck with the normal Republican sources. We netted only about twenty-five grand at the Jackson fundraiser. Most of the folks there are waiting to see what Flag does. We aren't in critical mode yet, but we need to get proactive on this. We're going to be broke in the next few weeks."

Charles Kidwell came into the room as TL was delivering the bad news, picked up a napkin and dabbed at McGraw's shirt. "I'm going to make a substantial contribution later this week."

"What are my other options?" the Senator asked.

TL handed Tom a spreadsheet. "We're going to need big money to see us to the finish line, and the only place to get that is with PAC money. There are two columns on the sheet that list all major national PAC contributors, and the column on the left shows our best bets. The column on the right is 'no fucking way'—those are either supporting Democrats or actively committed to your opponents."

Tom frowned as he perused the list, looked up and sighed. "Look at these names: mostly banks, energy companies, and Flag's cronies. I'm breaking up the banks, I've come out for strong environmental protection, and I'll be damned if Flag will own me. Come on, TL, you know I won't be beholden to any of these groups. That's what my campaign is all about."

TL couldn't help but smirk. "I know that's what you've been saying in all of your speeches, but getting to the White House takes money. You're going to need north of a billion dollars. Most of it from this point forward. You're not going to get that with hundred-dollar contributions. You need major PAC money, and if you aren't willing to court the PACs then you might as well throw in the towel. I think you've been a bit naïve, thinking that your wife's money, Charles's money, and a few rich friends could fund your campaign. I hate to tell you this, but that won't even get you to the end of primary season." TL paused to let his words sink in. "Take a look at the list again. Aren't there at least a few on the list you could take money from?"

Tom put his reading glasses back on and, using his black sharpie, he went through the list again, crossing out the PACs one by one. "The NRA is going to make me sign a pledge that I won't ban assault weapons, and that it's OK for a guy to buy a gun fresh out of the looney bin. Not going to do that. The retirees are going to make me promise not to change Social Security. But you and I both know that we're going to need to reform it when I get in office. Not going to bring it up in the campaign, but it's going to happen. Oil, gas and coal— they're going to make me slack off on the environmental regs and that's not going to happen either. The big bankers all hate me, except for Charles here." When he handed the spreadsheet back to TL, it was a mass of black lines.

TL was speechless and just stared at the Senator. "So, are you withdrawing?"

Tom laughed loudly. "Fuck, no. This is what we're going to do. What is my number-one issue in this campaign so far, TL?"

"Jobs?"

"TL, you're saying that like it's a question. Of course its jobs. Not minimum wage, fast food and retail jobs. Real middle-class wage-payin' jobs. Manufacturing jobs. Like the ones that could provide a working man with a middle-class lifestyle before they were all shipped off to China. Is there a PAC on this list dedicated to that—and don't say the labor unions; they don't have the resources these days like they used to."

"The banks?"

"You have to be fucking kidding me. Do you know what tellers make? And most of the middle class aren't going to become investment bankers or bond traders, and the investment banks are all about Silicon Valley startups that will send even more manufacturing jobs overseas."

TL shook his head. "You tell me."

"No, there isn't a PAC dedicated to job creation, is there? Just a bunch of businesses that want their industry to receive preferential legislative treatment. So, here's what we're going to do. We are going to create our own PAC. Let's call it the 'Coalition of Job Creators.' That has a nice ring to it, doesn't it? And just by coincidence, that PAC is going to want me to pledge the things I already want to do to create jobs. Incentives for private job training, expansion of our community college system, infrastructure investment, manufacturing tax zones, disincentives for foreign manufacturing, and on and on. Compile a list of the top 100 US companies that employ US workers already at middle-class-wage jobs. Let's start with them. I think they might like to have a president beholden to helping them extend the agenda they're already pursuing. And I wouldn't mind saying in my speeches that the number one supporter of my campaign is the 'Coalition of Job Creators.' What do you think?"

TL looked at the Senator. "I think it's a great idea. But why do I think somehow that you've been thinking of this for a while and just didn't come up with it on the spur of the moment?

"Maybe it's because you never asked me. Don't just sit there. You just told me we don't have much time to get this together before we run out of money," McGraw said, dismissing TL. "Charles, please stick around."

When TL left the room, McGraw put his hand on Charles arm. "I don't want you to contribute any more personal funds to the campaign—"

Charles interrupted, "I don't mind, really. I want to do it."

"Stop. I wouldn't even be where I am now if it weren't for you. You're the chief architect of this whole campaign. I owe you more than I can ever repay, and I won't have you spending any more on the campaign. I won't have money coming between our friendship. Even if you say it won't, if I lose, you'll have spent your fortune on me. And I just can't have that. We have to find a way for the campaign to stand on its own."

"So, what do we do? Do you really think this job-creators thing can work?"

"It will if you take charge of it. Can you find a surrogate who can spearhead this whole movement? Some business owner who can be the face of this whole issue?"

Charles thought for a moment. "There's a customer at my bank, a pair of brothers actually. They'd be perfect. Let me get to work on them."

Chapter 14

DEAN stood in front of a dirty trailer just outside of Jackson, rust leaking from its seams like bloody tears. He'd observed this little part of town last summer. It was where the weird man was staying who had been abusing the Border Collie Dean had rescued and named Cheney. The investigation into the break-in at Dean's home was at a dead end. There were no fingerprints or other clues left at the scene, no videos or witnesses to the men other than those Dean had turned up, and a survey of the pawn shops in the area had not produced any of his stolen belongings. But then Dean's Internet search of online ads led him to this trailer park in the section of Jackson reserved for a surprisingly diverse hodgepodge of mostly transient residents: minimum-wage workers who served the wealthy vacationers, or cleaned and maintained the homes of the even more wealthy citizens who made Jackson their second—or their third—home, ski bums and climbers who hot-bunked the only semi-affordable housing in Jackson with like-minded adventurers who wanted to experience the thrill of some of the most dangerous terrain in the lower forty-eight before they settled down to a mundane middle-class existence. Then, of course, there were the unlucky few who'd never given up on the dream and now found themselves struggling with a disability resulting from decades of doing battling with nature, who never remained gainfully employed long enough to fund the kind of medical care that aging athletes require.

He knocked on the door a third time and was nearly ready to leave when he heard some rustling and a thin, stooped man with a weathered face opened the door. "Yes?"

"I called earlier about your ad? You have a Nikon camera for sale?"

The old man nodded. "Yeah, come on in."

The trailer looked barely habitable. It had the kind of faux, pressed-wood paneling that Dean remembered from some of the homes in his childhood in West Virginia, and piles of collected clutter were stacked floor to ceiling over most of the space, radiating an earthy odor of wet paper and mildew. Buckets placed strategically caught drips of snow filtered through dirty insulation bulging from the ceiling tiles. The old man nodded to a chair, hobbled over and removed a stack of newspapers. "Sit down and I'll get the camera."

He came back a minute later with a shoebox containing the same Nikon model as the one that had been stolen.

"I'm sorry. I've been rude. My name is Dean Wister."

"Good to meet you, Dean. My name's Will Munson."

"Will Munson? *The* Will Munson? The first guy to ski down each of the Teton peaks?"

"One and the same."

"Well, I'm honored to meet you Mr. Munson. I've got the poster showing each of your runs in my house."

"That is a nice poster; too bad I never made a cent from it."

"Really? That sucks. But it did make you immortal."

The old man smiled ruefully at the compliment. "Ah, yes... immortality. Doesn't pay the bills."

Dean looked through the camera lens. "So, why do you want to sell your camera?"

"Well, I saw it on an online ad, same as you. I don't get along too well now. This is the first year I haven't been able to ski. My hips got to the point that it won't let me. Hope to get a new one, maybe next year. Anyway, I always like takin' pictures and thought maybe I could take a few. Something to get me out of the house." The old man paused. "But the truth is I was little drunk, it was a crazy idea, and I couldn't really afford it. When I sobered up, I realized I didn't have enough left to get through the month. Pictures are pretty, but they don't put food on the table."

"I understand. Where did you get it?"

"Just some guy from the ad. Don't know his name. Met him down at the Mini Mart on Broadway."

"Can you describe him?"

The old man looked at Dean skeptically. "OK, I ain't stupid. What's this about?"

"Mr. Munson, I'm a deputy with the Teton County Sheriff's Office. A camera of this model was stolen in a home robbery a few days ago. I've been looking at pawn shops and online ads to see if one came for sale. I'm surprised I didn't see the ad for the camera that you answered."

"Well, the ad I answered wasn't for the camera. It was for something else. Just so happened the guy also had a camera for sale. As I said, I'd been drinkin', so I wasn't exactly clear-headed."

Dean grinned. "Well, some other things were also stolen. What else were you trying to buy?"

The old man hesitated. "Well, see, my hip gives me a lot of pain. And I can't afford the medication. So, the guy had somethin' for that too."

Dean looked at the old man and wondered if all those decades of adventure were worth the price. Munson was a legend not only in Jackson, but in the North American skiing community, and now couldn't even afford his pain meds. "Don't worry about that. I'm just looking to recover the stolen merchandise. What can you tell me about the person you bought this from?"

The old man didn't answer his question at first. He seemed to be thinking of something else. "How do you know this is the camera that was stolen?"

"I don't right now. But digital cameras generate EXIF data, a unique serial number that's on each digital picture file. If the EXIF data from this camera matches the pictures that the owner has, then we know it's the stolen camera."

"So, assumin' it is the stolen camera, does that mean I'm out of luck here. I'm out the five hundred I paid for it?"

Dean grimaced. "You paid only five hundred for this? And you're asking a thousand? You got a good deal my friend." Dean took a wad of cash out of his pocket and peeled off ten one hundred-dollar bills. Here you go. I want to make sure you can get your meds this month. So, now, what can you tell me about the guy who sold it to you?"

Will Munson pocketed the money before he answered. "Not much, I'm afraid. Really tall, skinny guy. Driving a dark-colored Subaru Outback. And, oh, he had a Russian accent."

Dean called Dani as soon as he left the trailer. "What the fuck is it with these guys," he said. "Why can't I get away from the fucking Russians?"

"Have you been drinkin'? You didn't get into another bar fight did ya?"

Dean ignored the jab about his little altercation the previous summer. "I think I found my camera —the one that was stolen. Don't know for sure but will as soon as I match it with the EXIF data from my picture files. But I'll bet you a thousand it is. I bought it from an online ad, and that guy said he bought it from a tall Russian."

"Shit, Dean.... I'm afraid I have some more bad news. Boris Birkov is back in town and at home under house arrest. They let him out on bail."

Chapter 15

MELINDA was waiting outside the house when Dean arrived. "Sorry. I stopped by the sheriff's office. Cody got an artist to draw a description of the guy who sold my camera to Munson. I picked it up, and we can show it to Boris. Also, they looked at the EXIF data and it's definitely my camera."

"Not a problem." Melinda was looking more rested than when he left her the day before. "Do you really think Boris will tell you even if he knows who it was who was fencing the camera?"

"Probably not. But if he doesn't, and we can prove the thief worked for Boris, then maybe we can bring Boris in on the robbery. Or at the very least show that he's being uncooperative, which may eventually add to his sentence when he's convicted."

"Don't you mean *if* he is convicted?"

"They caught him in the act of kidnapping and beating the girl. It's about as airtight a case as I have seen."

"I was talking to Charles before you got here. He's worried that somehow someone got to the judge to let Boris out on bail. The prosecutors were pushing hard to keep him as a flight risk. And if someone can get to the judge, who knows what will happen at trial. I'm sure you've seen stranger things in your career."

Dean thought about what she said. The Chicago judicial system had a reputation of world-class corruption. He'd had to worry about judicial malfeasance in every major case he was involved in. Of course, she was right, but the truth put him in a bad mood, and he became quiet.

They drove for a few minutes in silence, and then Melinda asked, "Look, you aren't getting all weird on me about the other night, are you? I thought we had a good time."

Dean looked over at her and forced a grin. "No, Melinda it's all good. I was just thinking about that asshole, Boris. You know he would have killed Tatiana if he hadn't been arrested. I was hoping he'd be put away for a long time." What he didn't say was that he knew Boris would also have killed him if back-up hadn't shown up in time.

They drove in silence the rest of the way and pulled into the gated community where Boris resided. Dean showed his badge and they drove through. Melinda was looking out the window at the houses as they drove through the winding streets of the development. "So, I understand you're good buddies with Dick Cheney."

Dean started to respond, but when he looked over, he saw a mischievous look in her eye, the look that his wife used to give him when she was pulling his leg. "So how did you hear about that?"

"Senator McGraw was at a dinner with Cheney a few weeks back and Cheney told him the story. It's a damned funny story, Dean—you actually knocked on his door and thought it was Boris's? And he invited you in?"

"Yep. I thought we had a nice conversation. I didn't realize he would be making fun of me with all his political buddies."

She giggled. "You sure do have thin skin. As I understand it, the story was told affectionately. I got the impression that the Vice President actually likes you. I can't imagine why, though."

They pulled into the driveway and walked up to the door. "If you don't mind, I'll handle this," Dean said.

"No problem, officer. He's all yours."

Boris answered the door himself. A hulk of a man, he wore a Nike track suit and had a conspicuous ankle monitor just above his flip flops.

"Dean Wister, it's been awhile. What can I do for you?"

"We're working on a case and thought you might be able to give us some help. Can we come in?"

"Of course, I'm always available to help Wyoming law enforcement." He opened the door for the two to enter but remained standing in the entryway and did not offer them a seat. "I thought you went back to Chicago, Dean."

"I did. But when I found out that you made bail, Sheriff Cody asked me to come back to keep an eye on you."

"I see. And you really think you're up to the task? As I remember, some pretty rough things happened to you the last time you were following me around."

That stung, but Dean ignored it. "Boris, a tall Russian man has been linked to a robbery in the area. Since you know just about everyone in the Russian community, we thought we would talk to you. The Sheriff's Office has prepared a sketch." Dean pulled out the sheet of paper and handed it to Boris. "Recognize this man?"

Boris took the picture and held it up to the light, looking at it for perhaps thirty seconds and then nodded. "Yes, I know this man. I know him very well. In fact, I saw him right before you got here."

Dean, now on alert said, "He was here?" And then, realizing the man might still be here, he put his hand on his weapon. "Where is he?"

Boris put his hand up. "Relax. I said I saw him *before* you got here. I didn't say he was actually here." He smiled broadly and poked his fat finger at the image on the paper. "Dean, look at this picture. Right before you arrived, I was watching an old movie. I love your American cinema, especially comedies." He paused and scratched his chin. "Now as I look closely at this picture, I realize your artist has drawn a very realistic picture of the comedic actor Jim Carrey. It's most definitely him. Have you seen *Bruce Almighty*? It's very funny, Dean."

Dean didn't say a word but turned to Melinda. "Let's go."

In the car, Dean stared straight ahead while Melinda laughed hysterically. "You know, Dean, he's right. That picture looks exactly like Jim Carrey."

"That motherfucker should have stayed in jail." Dean turned to Melinda. "I'm sure the guy who robbed my house is working for Boris. If we can make that link, his ass will belong to someone named Bubba in a federal max-security pen."

Chapter 16

Mario Rosati, Jr., didn't look like a gangster. Sure, his dark wavy hair and brooding good looks were consistent with movie star gangsters, but he had a pretty, nearly effeminate look about him. Maybe it was that he was a little too coiffed. He wouldn't leave his house until the curl that graced his forehead was placed just so. Or maybe it was that his chiseled features were just a little too perfect. He was the kind of man that women would turn and look at when he entered a room, and he knew it. But Mario had two different personas. The charming solicitous Mario was almost universally irresistible to women. After they had succumbed to this persona, his alter ego would be revealed. The narcissistic Mario would inevitably surface, and then would come the obsessive controlling, demanding, belittling—and the violence. It was impossible for any girlfriend to acknowledge him sufficiently, and so his relationships with women resulted in an endless chain of victims.

This morning, he stared at the wall of colorful wrestlers' masks as he sat in his office located in Luche Libre, his girlfriend's restaurant in the trendy Wicker Park neighborhood of Chicago. Well, it wasn't really his office. His real office was a small contemporary chrome-and-glass room he rented on the second floor of the building, but he liked to spend time at the bar, sipping the sweet /spicy piloncillo-and-cayenne flavored coffee that was a specialty of the restaurant. As the flavors titillated his tongue, he would imagine himself the owner of this restaurant, the Don of one of the most desired neighborhoods of the city, giving thumbs up or down to the favors requested by an endless queue of millennials who often congregated on the sidewalk in front of one of the hottest restaurants in the city. The harsh reality of his situation was that the restaurant and building were bought with his girlfriend's family money. He had met her when he rented the office on the second floor, and she, like the dozens of women before her, had surrendered to his spell.

Mario was a Don only in his fantasies. He was the son of an actual dead Don, and, except for his looks that he shared with his late father, he was the exact opposite of Mario Rosati, Sr. Junior wasn't a Don, or even a Don in the making. Junior was a snitch. An informant. The FBI's little bitch. That's what he thought of himself when he awoke in the middle of the night in a cold sweat, and this realization interrupted his fantasy world multiple times each day, triggering a self-loathing that he found nearly unbearable. He hated his FBI handler, the skinny little red-haired twit, but he hadn't had much choice after his father was killed. It was either cooperate with the FBI or go to prison.

And so he had given them the location of the brothels his father had used to work the young girls Boris would bring in from Russia, and other miscellaneous information he had about his father's operation. There wasn't much really. He wasn't in his father's inner circle and didn't know that much. Instead, he had given them info on the criminals who laundered money through his chain of currency exchanges. Although over ninety-nine percent of his customers were hard working but undocumented immigrants, or other members of the underclass without the where-withal to use traditional banks, a small percentage used his business as their laundry. He gave the FBI some of those, the ones he deemed least dangerous to himself. In return, the FBI hadn't charged him. Not yet anyway. They were using the possibility of dropping all but the most benign of charges as the carrot to squeeze every bit of information they could from him. They had insisted he give up the business, the business that his father had let him take over. He'd turned it over to his father's lawyer, Joe Hoffman, and although Joe was sending Mario a royalty off the top every month, he knew damned well that it was only a fraction of what Joe was really making from his business. Without the ability to oversee daily operations, he had little choice but to take the money and contemplate his next big move.

At first, the FBI had been satisfied with the intel he had given them, but now they wanted him to help them get the video that his father had used to blackmail Senator McGraw. He hadn't actually seen the video. His father had bragged about it a few times when he'd had too much to drink, but Mario didn't doubt that it existed. Otherwise how would the Senator have gotten to know his father in the first place? And why would the Senator have shot his father in that Washington DC hotel room? In truth, he'd been thinking about the video before the FBI asked him about it, and if he'd had any idea how to get it, he'd already have it. *There are plenty of ways to monetize that asset*, Mario thought. Maybe he'd sell it to the Senator's political enemies—he had plenty in both parties —or maybe to a tabloid. Or maybe he'd use it to blackmail the Senator like his father had. But of course, his father had ended up on that hotel floor with two bullets in his head. His father was tough as nails and ballsy, but Mario, Jr. had no doubt that he was smarter and more cunning than his dead dad. Maybe he could find a way to turn the tables on the Senator, but he couldn't tell the FBI that. No, he should do everything he could to find the video and then give it to the FBI. Give it to them right after he had monetized it.

This morning, as he sipped his coffee, he asked himself the same question over and over. *Where would the old man have stashed it?*

Chapter 17

THEY had just finished with the morning production meeting when Li Meng paused, took off his glasses and looked straight at Yao Chen. "Yao, you need to get rid of that little girl Jia Ling today."

"What do you mean," said Yao. "I've observed her, she is a very hard worker, and also she is very fast."

"Yes, but she is also a pain in the ass. She is always complaining, and she has infected the other girls. They are now complaining also. I want to show you something." He walked over to his desk and motioned for Yao to follow him. Yao watched while he clicked on a folder on his desktop and up came a log with video files by date. He clicked on the one labeled the previous day and brought up a video showing the entire production floor. He could see Jia talking animatedly to the older female supervisor. Li Meng used his mouse and zoomed in so that Yao could see that Jia was shouting something at her supervisor. "You see how disrespectful she is. We can't have this. I insist. You must get rid of her today."

"Let me talk to her and tell her we are giving her one more chance. If her behavior does not improve immediately, then we will terminate her."

Yao left the meeting and walked to the production floor, glancing up at the cameras that Li Meng used to monitor all the activity from his office. He thought he was probably being watched right now by Li.

Jia was busy setting up her machine, and he went directly to her. She looked up when she saw him and beamed.

"Jia, I need to speak with you about a very serious matter. Li Meng tells me you are always complaining, and that you are talking back to the supervisors, and that you have gotten the other girls to start complaining also. You cannot be doing this. If you have a problem, you need to see me. If this does not change immediately, Li Meng is going to insist that I fire you."

Jia looked up at the old man with a serious expression on her face. "Well, the supervisors are mean to us. And things are very bad for us here. Girls are getting hurt all the time. And I don't mind if you send me back to the orphanage. Then I will be able to see my brothers again."

"Jia, you don't understand. If we terminate you and send you back, it will be very bad for you and your brothers. The director of the orphanage will not accept you back. He will send you to another orphanage or put you out on the street. Then you will never see your brothers again."

The little girl seemed to consider that for a minute. Her face crumbled, and she began to sob. "Please... no, my brothers are my life. They are my responsibility. Please, don't do this to me."

The old man put his hand on her shoulder. "I'll tell you what. If you will change your behavior, do your job, keep your mouth shut, and stop stirring up the other girls, I will take you to see your brothers on your next day off."

"Really, you would do that?" Her tears stopped as abruptly as they had started.

"Yes, I will. But you have to do as I say. If you go back to your old ways, it will be very bad for you and your brothers. Do you understand?"

"Oh, yes. I promise you. If you take me to see my brothers, you will not have any more trouble from me."

Yao Chen turned to go, and she grabbed him by the sleeve. He turned, and she put her arms around the old man and planted a kiss on his cheek. "Thank you, thank you, thank you!"

Yao glanced up at the camera. He hoped Li Meng wasn't watching.

Chapter 18

DEAN didn't speak for a long time after they left the Birkov residence. Melinda let him brood as they drove on Highway 89 south of town. Finally, because she couldn't tell where they were headed, she broke the silence. "Where are we going?"

"I think I may know someone else who can identify the Russian. I have a friend who runs a social marketing company, and he has a lot of Russian members. I thought we could stop by and see if the drawing resembles anyone he knows."

Melinda wrinkled her forehead. "What's a social marketing company?"

"You might have heard of it under a different name. It used to be called direct marketing, and before that network marketing, and before that multi-level marketing or MLM. The industry changes its name every couple of years to stay up with the current jargon, and make the industry seem cutting edge. The first company to make it big with the business model was Amway. Some people call them Ponzi or pyramid schemes, and some of them are. But this one is on the up and up. By the way, don't ever say pyramid scheme in front of my friend Daryl. He's very sensitive about it."

"Got it. Your friend Darryl? Is that the same Darryl that was on the boat with you during the sniper attack last summer?"

Dean glanced over at Melinda. "Have you been doing research on me, Melinda?'"

Melinda grinned. "Damn right. I go to work for some gunslinging Wyoming senator, and then he tries to pawn me off on a crazy Chicago cop who also killed a couple of people on the same case—you better believe I'm going to do a little homework on it."

"Then you may know that Daryl's actually a pretty good guy. He was living down in Alpine, but he and his girlfriend Amber just bought a new place, and I haven't had a chance to see it yet."

Dean turned off on a narrow road and drove awhile, getting quiet again. He kept glancing off to the side of the road as if he was looking for something.

"What's wrong, Dean?"

"Nothing."

"Are you looking for the place where you had that run-in with Boris?"

"I think right over there." Dean pointed to a warehouse behind some weeds, about a hundred yards off the road.

"Does it bother you to be here? I know that was a really close call for you." Melinda spoke softly.

"Not really. What bothers me is that I can't remember a lot of what happened. All I know is what the sheriff, Mark, and Tatiana told me." This was only partially true. It did bother Dean that he had very little memory of what happened after he turned off onto Fall Creek Road while tailing Boris, but what bothered him even more, what really haunted him, was that one of the last times he spoke with Sara was when he was in a coma while he was recovering from his head injury. She had been with him all summer, but after his stay in the hospital, she'd pretty much disappeared. He wasn't certain he would ever see her again.

About a mile past the warehouse they came upon a big wooden gate with a huge sign proclaiming: "EV Enterprises, Daryl Fay, Regional Vice President." There were a couple of cars pulling in ahead of Dean, and when he pulled up to a man who was directing the cars to park, Dean rolled his window down. "Is Daryl Fay around?"

"If you're here for the EV meeting, there's parking behind the auditorium." The man gestured to a large red barn, which Dean surmised was what he was calling the auditorium.

"I'm actually here from the Teton County Sheriff's Office. I need to speak with Daryl."

"I saw him a little bit ago in the auditorium. He's getting everything ready for the presentation."

"Thanks," Dean said, and drove to the back of the barn and parked the car.

When Melinda and Dean walked into the barn, Dean was shocked. The barn had been transformed into an actual auditorium. The dirt floor had been planked with pine boards, dozens of chairs faced a stage that was constructed at the front of the barn, and a colorful banner welcomed

"Western Region Distributors".   On the stage, Daryl was directing the setup of the podium, and he looked up as Dean and Melinda approached the stage.

Jumping down from the platform, he embraced Dean in a full body hug. "Dean Wister! I heard you were back in town. I'm so glad you came. I know when you see our presentation today, you're going to want to sign up. I don't have a distributor in the law enforcement community and you could be the first."

Dean grinned. "I appreciate the opportunity, Daryl, but I'm too busy right now to devote the time I know this opportunity deserves. Melinda and I are working on a case and thought maybe you might be able to help us."

"Sure. But I don't have much time. We're expecting about two hundred distributors today for our new product rollout. All our products are now vegan, gluten-free, GMO-free, and hypo-aller-genic. This is going to open a whole new segment of the market to us."

"This will only take a minute, Daryl." Dean took out the picture and showed it to Daryl. "This is a drawing of a guy who robbed my home last week. We believe he's Russian. I thought you might rec-ognize him because I know you have a lot of the Russian community here involved in your busi-ness."

Daryl looked at the picture for a long time. "It looks a little like Ivan Chersky. Do you know if this guy is very tall?"

"He sure is."

"Could be him. He actually took over a lot of Boris's business when Boris went to jail. He should be here today. Why don't you wait around, and Amber can point him out to you?" Daryl called out to a plump blonde woman who walked toward them.

When Amber saw it was Dean, she screamed and planted a red-lipstick kiss on his cheek. She glanced at Melinda. "Are you going to introduce me to your girlfriend?"

"She's not my girlfriend. This is Melinda, she's a criminal investigator working on a case with me."

Melinda offered her hand to Amber, and Amber gave her a look as if she didn't believe what Dean had just said. Then she turned back to him and pushed him on the chest. "Dean, I am so mad at you. Why didn't you call us when you got back in town? And you haven't been returning our calls. Why are you avoiding us?"

"I'm really sorry, Amber. Maybe we can get together soon."

Amber smiled. "We would really like that. We miss you. What do you think of our new place? Isn't it fabulous?"

"It sure is. But, Amber, I didn't know you were expecting. Congratulations."

Amber rubbed her belly. "I know, I'm huge. Twins."

Dean put his hand over Amber's and grinned. "It looks like you two are doing really well. I promise I'll call and we'll get together soon, but today I'm afraid we're here on official business. Daryl said maybe you can point out this Ivan Chersky to us when he comes in? We need to speak with him about a police matter."

Amber didn't act surprised at the mention of a "police matter". "Sure. Just go to the back of the auditorium. Tatiana is working with the video guy and she can point him out to you."

As they walked to the back, Melinda said, "Is this the same Tatiana that you rescued down the road?"

"One and the same."

The petite, dark-haired girl at the back of the auditorium greeted Dean with a hug that lasted so long Melinda thought she would never let go. Dean introduced Melinda to Tatiana, explained who they were looking for, and they waited at the back of the auditorium as the Western Region Distributors filed in. But no Ivan. The lights went down as Daryl introduced a company-made video highlighting the potential of the new EV product line. When the lights came back on, Daryl returned to the stage to work the crowd into buying into the new line. Dean had been to a Tony Robbins seminar once in Chicago with Sara, and he had to admit that Daryl had something of the Robbins gift for exciting his listeners. The kid he'd met the year before in Alpine had come a long way.

When Daryl finished his presentation, another man took the stage to explain more details of EV's marketing and distribution plan for the new products, and Dean whispered to Tatiana, "Do you know how to get in touch with Ivan?"

"I'm sure Daryl will be calling to find out why he wasn't here. I'll have him call you when he knows something."

"Good. Just make sure Daryl doesn't mention we're looking for him."

They started to leave, but Amber came running after them before they could make their exit. "Wait a sec." She grabbed a blue and a red gift bag from the stack near the door and handed them to Dean and Melinda. "You guys need to try these. They're fantastic."

On the way back to town, Melinda studied Dean as he drove. "You're smiling," she said. "What is there about those three that changed your mood?"

"I don't know what it is. Maybe something about their naïveté. They're just so relentlessly positive. And they've come so far from where they were when I met them—especially Tatiana. She's been through a lot."

"I know. I read the report. It is pretty amazing."

Melinda started going through the items in her gift bag. "This is some pretty good stuff, Dean." She held up a large bottle and read the label: "'Rejuvenating Massage Lotion.' What do you think?"

Chapter 19

Dean spent a quiet evening at home, setting up the new computer he'd picked up in town, cooking and thinking about the case. Cheney sat next to him in the kitchen and waited patiently for Dean to toss him scraps as be prepared his flank steak stir fry. His mind wandered to Melinda—he was tempted to take her up on it when she held up the massage lotion, but part of his problem was that he didn't know if she was serious or just teasing. Half of him thought she was just fucking with him. He felt as if he'd been out of the flirting scene too long and was lost without some liquid confidence, but he realized he had a problem with that too—his drinking had gotten out of hand. He realized that right now he needed to show some discipline. He couldn't be hungover on the job. He took his last bottle of Wild Turkey, still three quarters full, and thought about Melinda as he poured it down the drain. His attraction to her made him uncomfortable. Thankfully, his cell phone interrupted this train of thought. He picked up, "Wister."

"Hey, Dean. It's Daryl. Sorry I didn't get back

to you earlier, but things were really crazy around here this afternoon. I hope you'll give some thought to being an EV rep. As I said, I think there's a big opportunity in law enforcement and you're my guy. I don't want to ask anyone else until you've had a chance to think about it."

"I appreciate you thinking of me, Daryl, but I honestly think you should find someone else. I'm just too busy right now to take it on. What I'd really like is for you to tell me where can I find Ivan."

"Well, that's the thing. He told one the guys in his downline that he was leaving town for a bit."

"Where did he say he was going?"

"He didn't… and didn't say when he was coming back either. And I'm kind of pissed because this puts us in a bind covering his business."

"Can you give me his cell number, and maybe his home address?"

"I'll text them to you when I hang up. But I tried his cell as soon as I found out and I got a recording that it's been disconnected. You think he knows you're after him and took off?"

"Probably. Text me that info right now. And if you hear from him, let me know. And you know not to say I'm looking for him, right?"

"Sure, Dean. And, Dean? I thought this guy was straight. I asked him about Boris and he said he didn't have anything to do with him."

"Don't worry about it, Daryl. Just keep your ears open, OK?"

"You got it, buddy."

Dean hung up and dialed the Sheriff. When Dani picked up, Dean was right to the point. "I've been able to ID the guy who sold my camera. Daryl Fay knows him, and I just found out he skipped town. His name is Ivan Chersky. I'll text you his information. Do you think we can get a search warrant for his house, or to put a trace on his phone? Although he's probably tossed the phone by now…"

"OK, but you have your camera back, and we now have an ID on him. What is it exactly that we are searching his house for?"

"Dani, don't you remember? You're the one that said they wanted my data. My laptop's still missing, right?"

"Yeah, right. I'll get on it and let you know when the warrant is ready. I think you should lead the search since you know what you're looking for. You good with that?"

"I wouldn't have it any other way."

"Also, I have some info for you on Melinda Johnston. She's got mixed reviews down in Cheyenne. She's a smart one and received several commendations for her investigative work, but some of the guys are suspicious about how she uses her sex appeal. It seems she filed a sexual harassment complaint against her supervisor. He got slapped on the wrist, and the next thing you know, *she's* working for the Senator."

"So, what's your conclusion about all this?"

"Well, you have to understand it's tough being a female in law enforcement in Wyoming. We're about fifty years behind the times in gender relations. Accusing a woman of sleeping her way to the top is par for the course in this country, but if that was her plan, filing a harassment complaint was a dumb way to go about it."

An hour later, Dani called with the warrant and Dean met her at Ivan's place, a one-bedroom apartment in east Jackson. It was small, around six hundred square feet, and even though it was packed floor to ceiling with EV products, the search didn't take long. The warrant listed the property stolen from Dean's house—the guns and his laptop—but also listed "data contained on the laptop or camera of the victim." Not surprisingly, he didn't find the guns or the laptop, but expanding the search to include data allowed them to scour meticulously for a memory card or a flash drive. They found absolutely nothing of interest, but left with Ivan's laptop. Dean would hook it up at the Sheriff's office and Mark Jeffrey could search it remotely for any evidence of files downloaded from Dean's computer.

On his way home, Dean dialed Melinda to update her on the search. She answered with a sleepy rasp. "Did I wake you," Dean asked.

"I just drifted off. What's up?"

Dean filled her in on the search and there was a pause on the other side. "What's wrong?

"I'm surprised you didn't call me. I thought we were partners and you execute a search warrant without me?"

"I didn't think it was a big deal."

"Did you shut your partners out like this back in Chicago?"

Dean thought for a moment. "You're right. I'm sorry. I don't know why I didn't call you. Maybe I got too used to working alone for the last year or so."

"Call me in the morning," she said, pointedly not letting him off the hook.

When Dean hung up the phone, he thought about why he hadn't called her to execute the warrant. He was avoiding her, and he knew the reasons would lead him to a place he wasn't ready to go.

Chapter 20

Ronald Flag threw the front section of the *Wall Street Journal* at the bespectacled little man standing in front of him. "What am I paying you for? Your only job is to monitor all the moves of Senator Roy Rogers and I have to read about this on the front page of the Journal? What the fuck is the 'Coalition of Job Creators'?"

The man stuttered. "I just found out about it yesterday and I wanted to get all the facts before I brought it to you. Apparently, McGraw is starting his own PAC. It's comprised of several hundred small and medium-sized businesses. His strategy is to focus on American businesses that have been hurt the most by overseas manufacturing. He's appealing to their self-interest, and he's promising to bring those jobs back to America. He's calls it 'Re-Patriotizing American Industry'. He's setting up a convention in Las Vegas. I think he's going to use it to make a major speech and try to shake them down for money."

"Can you get me a list of those companies?"

"I can try. What do you have in mind?"

"I'm not exactly sure yet. But we need to find a way to crash this little party. From now on, I want someone on the ground following his campaign. Got it?"

Flag sat at his favorite table overlooking the Teton Pines Golf Course in his usual weekend casual attire—navy blazer, white shirt, camel-colored slacks, and Italian oxblood tasseled loafers. He was sipping his very, very dry Stoli Elit vodka martini, crunching on a bleu cheese-stuffed olive, and contemplating what he was going to say to Ned Wood. So far, they'd only been friends who shared political views. Well, that is, friends who shared political views as well as the addiction to the aphrodisiac of power and the vices that come when humans believe they can exist outside the normal boundaries of society and the law. Flag's power came from his money and its ability to buy and control people and policy. Wood's came from the hubris of a warrior who had operated his whole career skirting the boundaries of international law and the established rules of war, in places where the ends are justified by the most effective means available—where a man had almost no limits on his behavior as long as he was prepared to accept the consequences. True, they shared a common political philosophy, albeit Flag was a major influencer on the national stage, while, as far as Flag knew, Wood limited his operations to the State of Wyoming. Wood was eccentric—no doubt about that; maybe even a little too crazy in his views for Flag's taste—but

Flag needed him now. *If I limit the information I feed him,* Flag thought, *I should be able to control him.*

A tall, wiry man grabbed the chair across from him. Retired Colonel Ned Wood was also decked out in his favorite casual attire—olive Henley, camo pants, tactical field boots, and a big black GPS watch that could track him anywhere in the world; the kind of attire that suggested he'd just parachuted into an anti-terrorism mission in the Tetons, if he'd been only twenty years younger. "Sorry, the Sierra Club committee meeting ran late. I'm sure you'll forgive me for that." Wood chuckled at his own joke, knowing that his friend absolutely hated the Sierra Club.

"How coincidental. I was just on a teleconference call earlier today to see if we can get a bill introduced to permit hunting in the National Parks. I think we may have the votes to get that passed." He chortled at this repost even louder than his friend.

"What's so important that you needed to see me before I leave town?" Wood waved at the server and ordered a protein shake.

"I'm sure you can guess. I think we have a mutual interest in stopping Senator McGraw."

"I've been telling you that project needs extreme measures, and you kept telling me you had it all under control."

"A lot of Democrats are crossing over to vote in our primaries, and there are so many candidates we're splintering our core voters. I still don't think he can reach the convention with a majority. I've succeeded pretty well in drying up his fundraising, and I thought that would squeeze him out."

"That hasn't worked, has it? I've been following his new PAC and it looks like he's getting quite a bit of money, and great PR for his Vegas convention." Wood lowered his voice. "Maybe it's time for a Stauffenberg solution."

Flag was not a history buff, and Wood was always showing off by making obscure references to old military battles, to which he would generally either nod as if he got the reference, or change the subject. Today he did both. "Maybe, but I was thinking there might be a way we could disrupt his little party in Vegas."

"What did you have in mind?"

"Didn't you tell me that the Las Vegas police chief was in the Seals with you? From my experience with these sorts of gatherings, I'd suspect there might be some illegal partying going on at the convention by some of the McGraw supporters. Even if there isn't, maybe we can find a way to present them with some irresistible if not wholly legal temptations. If you could solicit the help of the chief, we could provide him with some intel and point him in the right direction to make arrests. The headlines could take out the senator, and they might help the chief's next re-election campaign as well."

Wood paused when the server brought the smoothie, making sure he was out of earshot, and took a long gulp. Flag thought he looked ridiculous in his commando outfit, and the green protein smoothie mustache made him look as if he'd just given a blow job to a bullfrog.

"You know what?" Wood asked. "Most of the time your schemes are pretty asinine, but I guess even a stopped clock is right twice a day. And I do have personal knowledge of your skill at setting up extreme parties. I'll talk to the chief, you set up the sting and let me know the coordinates for the party. Maybe we can arrange for it to be crashed."

Chapter 21

MELINDA looked at the number on her mobile and picked it up on the first ring. "Hey, Dean."

"Are you up for a road trip?"

"Sure, where are we going?"

"There's a nonstop flight to Chicago this morning. I thought we would do a little snooping around."

"I'll be ready in a half hour. Just let me throw a bag together."

The wind nearly blew them over as they exited the cab in Wicker Park and entered the Mexican restaurant where Mark Jeffrey had agreed to meet them. The cold took their breath away, and they both had faces chafed red from the wind as they followed the server to a table in the corner.

Mark laughed when he saw them. "I thought it was cold in Wyoming. A little old Chicago winter shouldn't cause you that much trouble. You guys look like you're returning from a camping trip in Siberia."

"Nice to see you too, Mark. It was about the same temperature when we left Wyoming, but there wasn't a fifty-mile-an-hour wind. Melinda here hasn't experienced a Chicago winter before. Melinda, this is Mark Jeffrey."

Melinda gathered herself and leaned forward, nearly touching Mark's face. "It's so good to finally meet you, Mark. Dean has told me everything about you." She grabbed Mark's hand and placed it between hers. "Your hands are so warm. I hope you don't mind warming mine up a bit."

"Oh, not at all." Mark blushed.

Dean rolled his eyes, taking off his coat and waving at the server. "What can you tell us about where the FBI is looking for dirt on the Senator."

Over habanero-infused margaritas and a variety of spicy Mexican tapas dishes, the trio had a leisurely dinner at Luche Libre and discussed the case. "The FBI is using Mario Rosati, Jr. as their primary informant and lead on the case but, to tell you the truth, I think he's just jerking them around. Either he doesn't know anything, or he's not telling. For my money, the most interesting lead would be Mario, Sr.'s former attorney, Joe Hoffman. He handled all of Mario's affairs," Mark said.

Dean took a long drink of his margarita. "So why doesn't the FBI have Hoffman under surveillance?"

"Oh, they did for a while, after Mario was killed and his crew was arrested. But Hoffman filed a harassment lawsuit against the Bureau. He was representing several of Mario's crew, still is actually, and the court made the Bureau back off."

"So, our best bet is to investigate Hoffman," Melinda said. "And maybe our tactics should be a little more unofficial than the Bureau has tried."

"She thinks like you, Dean. And that could be dangerous."

"So where do you think we should start with this? What do you know about Hoffman?" asked Dean.

"Well, he's a classic mob lawyer and accountant. He's very good at helping his clients hide their money. Actually, he's now also running the currency exchange business that Mario, Jr. was in charge of. He thinks of himself as a lady's man. Besides his mob clients, he represents women in divorce cases and has been known to use some of his mob contacts as extra motivation for the husbands to give their wives a favorable settlement. Dean, you're the king of the unofficial investigation techniques. How would the king go about this?"

"Somehow, I don't think that's a compliment," said Dean. "But I'd have to give it some thought."

Melinda cleared her throat. "It seems pretty obvious."

"What do you have in mind?" Mark asked.

"You two guys ever hear of the 'honey pot'?"

"Of course, I've heard of it," said Dean. "But only when there's enough law enforcement support to make sure the 'honey' is safe. It's just going to be you and me, Melinda. I'm not sure that's a good idea."

"What, you don't think I can handle a middle-aged accountant? You wouldn't hesitate to be alone with him. I can take care of myself, so spare me the paternalistic bullshit."

Mark looked at Dean. "I think she might have a point, my man. I bet she can take care of herself."

Dean had rented out his Gold Coast condo temporarily when he was suspended and while he was living in Wyoming, so Charles had made a reservation for him and Melinda at the Four Seasons. After they checked in, they agreed to meet for breakfast the next morning to hash out the details of Melinda's plan. Dean was half-expecting the knock on the door between their adjoining rooms that came an hour later, while he was watching ESPN, but he wasn't sure if he welcomed it. Half of him was aroused by the possibility, the other half not sure if he was ready for this.

When he opened the door, he expected to see Melinda wearing some slinky lingerie, but she was dressed in jeans and a baggy tee shirt, holding a bottle of wine, and she wasn't smiling. "Can we talk?"

Dean shrugged and invited her in. He sat on the bed and Melinda in the chair beside it. She opened the bottle and Dean declined a glass. "I'm taking an alcohol sabbatical for a while."

Melinda nodded, but wasted no time thinking about why Dean didn't want a glass of the merlot in hand. She got right to the point. "You're acting really strange toward me. You got weird after that night at Charles's house, and then you didn't take me with you for the search for your laptop, and then today, when I suggested the honey pot thing, you protested way too much. I'm sure you've run honey pots many times in Chicago with drug and prostitution busts, and trying to put the kibosh on mine was a bit overprotective, to say the least, but that doesn't stop you from looking down my shirt whenever there's a half inch of cleavage showing. What's the deal? You've never had a female partner before?"

Dean paused, taking in what she was saying. "I've never had a female partner, but I've been on the job with many women... Just not any like you."

"What the fuck does that mean?"

"Well, it's how you dress, you know—provocatively. And you're always making suggestive comments."

"Oh, my god." She shook her head. "You're just a fucking guy, aren't you? By provocative do you mean showing a little cleavage, liking my clothing to fit tight?"

Dean nodded.

"Stand up."

"What?"

"I said stand up!" she ordered, and Dean obeyed.

"You know what I see? You have on a shirt so tight that I can actually see your nipples poking though. You've got your sleeves rolled up over your biceps. Your pants are so tight that when you were sitting down, I could estimate the size of your dick by the log resting on the inside of your pant leg. Very nice, by the way. Now turn around."

"I'm not going to turn—"

"I said *turn around.* You accused me of dressing provocatively, now I'm pointing out you do the same thing."

"I get the message." Dean sat back down.

"I don't think you do, officer. If you would have turned around, I would have pointed out that those form-fitting pants do a great job of highlighting your tight ass. And you know what? It's not just you. Every male cop under forty with a nice body is a fucking peacock, strutting their stuff around the station house. But you have the fucking audacity to hold it against me, because I'm not ashamed of my body either? Dean, your misogyny is showing."

Dean didn't say anything, and she continued. "If you had a male partner who dressed like you do, and made wisecracks filled with sexual innuendo throughout the day, would you have a problem with that?"

"I might. If I was attracted to him."

"That's what this is about?"

Again, Dean paused. "I honestly don't know. I don't know whether you're flirting with me, or if that's how you talk all the time. And maybe my misogyny *is* showing. I've never had a female partner before, and I've never thought about the way guy-cops dress. I'm sorry."

Melinda took a sip of her wine, studying Dean from over the rim of her glass. "Look... I'm attracted to you too." Then she looked away and he could see that tears were welling in her eyes. "I've been told before that I'm too flirty and dress too provocatively, but I decided I'm not giving in to that double standard. I decided a long time ago that I'm not going to let men define who I am. It's not like dressing like a librarian inoculates a woman against sexual harassment. It's something women face no matter how they dress." She shrugged. "I'm an outrageous flirt, but I'll admit I've been flirting with you a bit more than normal. Do you want me to stop?"

"No, please don't."

Melinda nodded again and smiled. And then she left, taking her wine with her. Dean went to bed but couldn't sleep.

Dean was already drinking his first cup of coffee when Melinda showed up at the hotel restaurant and sat down at his table. "About last night—"

"Let me talk," Dean held up his hand. "I thought a lot about what you said, and you're right. I was being chauvinistic, misogynistic, and everything else you called me. I'd like to start over. Could we do that? I want you to feel free to be completely who you are around me. I have a feeling I might like that very much. So... can we start over?"

"Yes, we can." Melinda smiled her dazzling smile. "Thank you. Now, take a look at what I'm wearing. I want to make sure it's seductive enough for a mob lawyer." She stood and turned around, so Dean could get a good look, before sitting back down. She was wearing a low-cut top and skin-tight yoga pants.

"Well, it would be for most normal, red-blooded American men."

"Well, how about for you? Aren't you a normal, red-blooded American male?"

"It's not me you're trying to seduce. These mob guys, they have a different image in their minds of the ideal female. And your outfit doesn't go quite far enough. You're beautiful and sexy, but the mob guys don't even know what sexy is. Do you have anything really slutty with you?"

"Dean, you're taking away my self-confidence. This is the sexiest thing I brought. If I'd known about the honey pot thing before we left Wyoming, I might have packed a little differently."

"Well, I guess we're going to have to go shopping. Did you say you have Charles's credit card?"

"I sure do."

"So, let's go on a reverse *Pretty Woman* shopping trip."

Dean remembered that Sara always had to stop and watch that movie whenever they passed it while channel surfing, and he could never understand why. Wasn't it the antithesis of a feminist movie? Sara had informed him it was merely a modern Cinderella fairy tale, and even contemporary women fantasized being Cinderella.

"Remember the scene in the movie where Richard Gere takes Julia Roberts shopping? She has nothing but hooker clothes, and he needs to buy her something respectable for a high-class party?"

Dean nodded.

"Well, we'll be doing the reverse. We'll go shopping in my semi-respectable clothes, and I'll try on hooker clothes, and you can decide which are sexy enough to seduce a mobster. I trust what you're saying, but it's hard to believe this outfit is not nearly sexy enough for a mobster." And she leaned forward so her bosom was nearly popping out over Dean's plate of scrambled eggs. "This should be a lot of fun." She laughed and tousled his hair.

Dean thought she was probably right. *This could be a lot of fun.*

They spent the rest of the morning and most of the rest of the afternoon at the shops on North Michigan Avenue. Melinda would try on outfits while Dean sat in a chair, and she would come out and model them. They stopped for lunch and each had a few cocktails, and Dean was able to loosen up. After lunch, the outfits became sluttier and sluttier and they ended up in the lingerie department at Victoria's Secret. She came out in a translucent teddy with nothing on underneath, and Dean nearly fainted.

Chapter 22

DEAN sat in the car outside the small office park where Melinda went to meet with Joe Hoffman. She had been gone for over an hour and Dean was starting to worry. What if, somehow, he didn't believe her cover? Dean knew that Hoffman was not a tough guy, as far as the mob guys go, but who knew what he might do to a woman he suspected was trying to scam him? Dean was typing a text to her to see if she was all right when the car door opened, and she jumped in. "Let's roll," she said.

Dean pulled onto the main thruway. "You were in there a long time. I was beginning to worry that maybe he didn't buy your cover."

"Oh, he bought it all right. He alternated between trying to look up my skirt and trying to look down my shirt. I'm not even sure that he was paying much attention to my cover story."

"What did you tell him?'

"Just as we planned. I'm thinking of divorcing my husband and remembered his name from conversations with Mario, Sr. He wasn't too impressed with my occupational choice."

"Well, we picked bartender because it's not a stretch that you might have met Mario, Sr. in a bar. Also, because my bar owner friend will vouch for you."

"Joe said that with a body like mine I could make a lot more money in a gentleman's club. I said I'd thought about it, but I thought maybe I was too old."

"And what did he say to that."

"He said that from where he sat that seemed like nonsense. But he would have to see a lot more to give a legal opinion."

Dean laughed and looked over at her. "So, the honey pot got the honey bee buzzing."

"I'd say so. I'm meeting him for drinks this evening at his steak house hangout that Mark told us about. But let's go back to the hotel. I'm going to need some time to get ready."

"Oh, I think you look pretty fine to me."

"Well, thank you, Dean. But as you told me yesterday, your sluttiness standard is a little lower than a mob lawyer's. I think I need to crank it up a notch for cocktails."

"Melinda, if you crank it up much more you might give him a heart attack. But who am I to argue?"

Jake's Chop House was an old-school supper club with velvet-lined half-moon booths and waiters in waistcoats and bow ties. Jake's was known as much for the five mafia hits that occurred in its parking lot in the seventies and eighties as for its prime beef and made-at-your-table Caesar salad.

Located just barely within Chicago city limits, Jake's North Side location was in an area that, in the heyday of the Chicago mob, contained more organized criminals per capital than any neighborhood in the United States. In the 1970s, the ward's alderman was notorious as a made-man in the Chicago outfit, with powerful connections in City Hall as well as in Springfield. Since the 1980s, the traditional clientele of Jake's had gradually dried up, thanks to the FBI's successes in breaking up the Chicago mob and the takeover of much of the drug business by Chicago street gangs. Consequently, Jake's had morphed from a mob watering hole to a tourist attraction, and, oddly enough, a museum of sorts for food historians. While *The Sopranos* had spiked an interest in mob nostalgia, and foodies had rediscovered traditional southern Italian cuisine, Jake's authentic ambiance of the Sinatra-era supper club brought hundreds of five-star reviews on social media. The large half-moon bar was where Joe Hoffman held court and networked. He was at the restaurant nearly every day for lunch, and back again most evenings at six for cocktails. This evening, he was excited about the date he was bringing to dinner.

He almost couldn't believe his good fortune. Sure, Mario Rosati, Sr. had been a good client in many respects, as good as a mob client could be. He paid in cash and on time, and he had a fair amount of legal work, most of it involving some government investigation or another. He also provided a fair amount of legitimate, business legal work—it had been Joe who had designed the nearly incomprehensible labyrinth of domestic and foreign corporations that was designed to hide Mario's wealth from the government. Mario had always had a gorgeous girlfriend or two on the side, but the girl who had walked into Joe's office today would have put any of them to shame. A couple of times he imagined she was going to let her tits fall onto his desk. He knew her come-on was probably designed to get a deal on his legal fees, and he was OK with that. Most of the women he got lucky with lately were middle-aged widows with a few pounds of excess fat deposited at some random point on their bodies, like some practical joke that God plays on all of us when we reach a certain age. Except for an occasional stripper, which he didn't count, he hadn't had a shot at pussy at this level for a long, long time. The regulars at the bar would be impressed, which wouldn't be a bad thing for his reputation, or his law practice. He was awakened from his reverie by a pair of soft pillows on his back, followed by a warm whisper in his ear. "I hope you haven't been waiting long."

He turned, and his eyes had trouble deciding where to focus, darting between the creamy, exposed cleavage and the clearly outlined curves of the hips, all encased enticingly in red silk. He stuttered first, and then recovered. "I think I've been waiting all my life for this moment. Melinda, you're gorgeous."

"Why, thank you, sir." She grinned, flashing her blindingly white teeth.

Joe couldn't wait to get her alone, into one of those semi-circular booths, but he also wanted to show her off to some of the regulars at the bar—make sure they saw what he had landed. "Let's have a drink before we get a table."

The bartender's response was quick and solicitous. "What can I get you, miss?"

"Dirty martini… very dirty." She grinned at Joe, stroking his hand with her manicured one.

A singer who almost certainly hadn't yet been born during the heyday of the Rat Pack was doing a passable imitation of Sinatra, crooning "the girl that I marry…her nails will be polished….and she'll purr like a kitten."

"You have beautiful hands, Melinda."

Melinda let herself giggle and wiggled her red-tipped fingers. "The color's called Little Red Roadster. But my girlfriends have another name for it."

"What's that?"

She looked around, as if to make sure no one was listening. "Hand Job Red."

Joe looked up, not quite sure what to make of her.

Melinda took a sip of her drink and said, "Why don't we move to one of the booths, so we can have some more privacy. Would you like that, Joe?"

Dean waited in the car in the parking lot outside the restaurant. He'd had misgivings about the honey pot in the lawyer's office, but now he was getting more and more nervous as the minutes passed. He had used female detectives before as decoys, mainly in vice investigations, but in those

cases, the circumstances were much more controlled, and there was always backup involved.
Melinda could handle herself, he was sure, but
in Chicago, the wise guys often ran in packs, and
sometimes passed a girl around, especially if she
came off as a real slut, which he had no doubt
Melinda was doing at just that moment. And in
that dress… As his anxiety increased, a text came
through: "In the ladies'. He's pretty drunk and
raring to go. Heading back to his place. I'll text
you later."

Dean watched as they exited the restaurant and
got into Hoffman's car—Hoffman with his hands
all over Melinda, Melinda responding as if his
school-boy groping was arousing. Hoffman pulled
the short, red dress up over her round bottom
and, from this distance, Dean couldn't see her
thong; her bottom looked completely bare and
Dean found himself wondering if this over-the-
top-display was really necessary.

He followed them to Joe's house, keeping a safe
distance, and then parked on the opposite side
of the street and a couple of doors down. When
he saw the garage door at Joe's go down, he took
out his field glasses and waited. He waited a really long time. The longer he waited, the longer he
worried about whether or not the honey pot was a
really, really bad idea.

An hour later he received Melinda's second text:
"All clear. Come to the front door."

Melinda opened the door wearing only her red
Victoria's Secret bustier and the matching thong

panties, her hair askew, her lipstick smeared and her mascara smudged.

"I'm fine," she hissed in a whisper, cutting off any inquiry from Dean about her disheveled condition. "I had to put a double dose in his drink. He just wouldn't go down... so to speak." She led Dean back to the bedroom. Hoffman was lying face down on the bed, naked, snoring loudly. His pale white ass had bright red marks on each cheek.

"Melinda," Dean gasped, "did you have sex with him?"

"Of course not," she spat back. "But I had to tease him a bit. I told you, he was really frisky and just wasn't getting drowsy. Turns out he's a bit kinky as well." She picked up a ping pong paddle with holes in it. "After I used this on him for a while, he passed out."

Dean closed his eyes, trying not to envision the scene. "Where are his pants?"

They fished his keys out of his pants pocket, and Dean texted a number on his phone. "Shouldn't you get dressed so we can get out of here?"

When the mobile locksmith's van pulled up a few minutes later, Dean took Joe's key to them and, when he returned to replace the original set of keys in Joe's pants, he was relieved to see that Melinda was fully dressed and already downloading the hard drive on Joe's computer to the flash drive Mark had given them. While the files transferred, he and Melinda searched the rest of the house and were disappointed to find nothing they determined to be significant to the case they were trying to make.

Taking full advantage of Joe's incapacitation, they drove to the strip center that contained his law office. Dean parked in the back of the office and got out of the car. "Text me if anyone comes by," he said. "If there's an alarm in his office, we're screwed," he added as he jogged the few feet to the back entrance to Hoffman's office and inserted the key in the door. When it swung open easily, and silently, he allowed himself a breath of relief.

Dean and Melinda dropped off the flash drive—which now contained the downloaded files from both Hoffman's home and office computer—with Mark before returning to the hotel. "What do you say we hit the minibar and unwind?" Melinda suggested as Dean parked in the hotel's garage.

Dean turned to her to tell her that, his alcohol sabbatical be damned, that was a great suggestion, but he got a good look at her for the first time since she'd let him into Hoffman's house.

"What?" Melinda asked when he started laughing.

Dean reached over and pulled down the sun visor so that Melinda could look in the makeup mirror. A streak of bright red lipstick smeared under her nose. "Holy shit. I look like a twenty-dollar street walker," she said, and started laughing herself.

Maybe it was the two long years of sensual deprivation. Or maybe it was the fantasy pinup vision of Melinda in her perfectly chosen Victoria's Secret attire hidden underneath the silk kimono. Or maybe it was her strawberry nipples peeking out of the bra that was fitted just a little too small. Or maybe it was the feeling that jolted him to the core when her soft lips met his, her tongue darting softly into his mouth and her body melting into his. But whatever it was, desire flowed through him with a force he hadn't felt in a long, long time.

The first, second and third times they coupled that night couldn't be called lovemaking. It was raw lust, plain and simple. Later, in the early hours of the morning, he entered her gently as she spread herself wide for him, pulling out and teasing her as she grabbed his butt and tried to pull him deep into her. Then, he supported himself on his arms and looked down at her face as he moved slowly and rhythmically, their eyes welded and searching, as if they were trying to merge their souls as well as their bodies. As he released himself inside of her, he pressed his lips against her face and said softly, "Where did you come from?" And then they both collapsed into a sweaty, satisfied, sleep.

As Dean emerged from his sex-and-champagne fog, he wasn't sure where he was until he opened his eyes and saw Melinda in a hotel robe walking toward him with Mark Jeffrey in tow. Mark looked down at Dean, smirking, and Dean self-consciously pulled the sheet up over his body.

"You have got to be fucking kidding me. I'm spending the entire night going through these flash drives, and you two are in some kind of weird cop orgy? Anyway, if you're not finished, tell me and I can come back later. Otherwise, I'll get some room service coffee going. We've got a lot of work to do."

Chapter 23

Mario, Jr. sat in the visitation room of the Metropolitan Correctional Center in Chicago. The maximum-security, federal high-rise prison, located smack dab in the downtown city center, housed federal prisoners awaiting trial and sentencing. Across from him sat the widest man he'd ever known, a man who seemingly had no neck and four visible chins, the deep creases in his neck suggesting there could be several more buried deep within. Pete "Double P" Pisano was even bigger than the last time Mario had seen him. His nickname stood not only for his initials but his ability to consume prodigious amounts of his favorite food, pizza pies. As Mario, Sr.'s long-time bodyguard, driver, gofer and confidante, Double P knew him better than anyone, including his son. Double P had been housed in the facility for several months, awaiting sentencing, and had little to do other than consume copious amounts of calories from the carb-rich prison cafeteria, and friends in Mario, Sr.'s old crew made sure that the guards were rewarded for smuggling his favorite foods to his cell. As a career violent offender, sentencing guidelines mandated an effective life sentence for his offenses, which Double P tried not to think about. Mario, Jr. knew that if anyone could shed any light on where the video might be stashed, it would be Double P.

Double P picked up the phone and nodded, "How ya doin', Junior? I heard you got out. How'd you beat it?" Double P was breathing heavily and paused. "People are sayin' you turned snitch. But I don't believe it. No way would the old man's son snitch."

"You got that right, Double P. Nobody needs to worry about that. They won't get nothin' from me they can use."

The truth was Mario, Jr. had given the feds the info to bust the prostitution operation, and he would have absolutely no problem ratting on anyone to cut a deal, but he had nothing more to trade.

"How're you doing? Are they treating you OK in here?"

"It's not so bad, kid. The gangs, they don't mess with me. There's a few of us dagos in here, and there's a few guards we've taken care of over the years."

Mario paused and looked straight into Double P's eyes, which were mere slits due to the accumulation of fat on both his upper and lower eyelids. "You tell any asshole that says anything about me that I ain't no snitch. You know that. Mario Rosati's son is a stand-up guy."

Double P nodded. "I know, I know."

"So, here's the deal. The FBI is going after Senator McGraw. The new FBI Director, this guy Fanning, is a Democrat, wants to get him bad. Fanning knows my dad was gunned down in cold blood in that hotel room 'cause Dad owned McGraw. The reason Dad owned McGraw, according to Fanning, is that he had some kind of video of McGraw screwing a whore or some important guy's wife or something, and they want me to help find it 'cause they searched everywhere, and they can't. Do you know anything about the video?"

Double P was sweating now, and Mario remembered how much he used to sweat. He remembered how the leather in the front seat of his father's car would always be slimy with Double P's perspiration. "I don't know about helping the FBI, kid. They asked me about it, and I told them to go fuck themselves."

"I know, I know. But here's the thing. If we don't help the FBI find the video, that cocksucker McGraw may end up being president. I know what Dad meant to you. Do you think we could stomach that—to do whatever it takes to destroy McGraw, even if it means working with the fucking FBI? This isn't about helping the FBI. It's about fucking McGraw. And get this, if you can help me find it, there may be a way to cut a deal to reduce your sentence. I know you're looking at a tough road."

Double P wiped the sweat away from the counter in front of him with his sleeve and thought for a moment. "You know, if I could get out of here, I'd kill McGraw myself, with my bare hands."

"I know you would. But you'd never get close now, he's got Secret Service all over him. This might be the only way we can stop him. This tape can destroy him. And then, when he's a private citizen in a year or two, with no more Secret Service, then we can get to him. But not now. What do you say? Can you help me, Double P?"

Double P coughed and drops of sweat sprayed the Plexiglas between them. "I heard your dad mention the video a couple times. He said something about it being in a real safe place, but I don't know where. I've been thinking that it might be with Doris. I heard she disappeared after the shooting and everyone got arrested."

"You have any idea where Doris could be?"

"Maybe...I got an idea. You know about the Key West and Vegas places?"

"No. I never heard about any Key West and Vegas places."

"I thought you probably didn't. I don't think anybody did except me, your father and Doris. He wanted a couple safe houses that he could hide out in if he had to. So, your dad bought a couple of places for him and Doris. I would go with them sometimes. A little house in Key West and a condo in Vegas."

"You got the addresses?"

"I don't recall the exact addresses, the street in Key West was some flower name or something, the one in Vegas named after some singer, but not the rat pack or anything, I'd remember that. But I think I could find them. They weren't in her name —your dad used some fake names or something.

When I was with them once, I heard your old man say he was going to put the property in the name of Doris Day, but I'm pretty sure he was just joking around."

"What's funny about Doris Day?"

"It was just a thing they had. He called her Doris Day, and she called him Rock."

"You mean like Daryl Johnson?"

"No, not fucking Daryl Johnson, Rock... like Rock Hudson, the first Rock."

"Rock Hudson and Doris Day?"

Double P laughed. "Kid, you don't know who Doris Day was? She was a fucking hot blonde from the sixties, and your dad's girlfriend, Doris Bertucci, looked just like her."

"OK, so listen, Double P, I got an idea. If I can get you out of here on bail, we can go looking for Doris. And if we find the video, we can squeeze the FBI on your sentence."

"That sounds good, kid. But you got that kind of money? My attorney got them to set bail while I'm waiting for my sentence, but its two hundred fifty grand. Cash."

"I don't have that kind of money, but I know somebody can maybe help with that. Let me make a call to a friend of mine who's got as big a hard-on as the FBI for McGraw. Are you up for doing whatever it takes to find this tape? I might need you to use your persuasive powers."

Double P sniggered. "Kid, have you ever known me to shy away from usin' my persuasive powers? As long as we can butt-fuck McGraw, and as long as I don't have to snitch on nobody, if we get to anybody who knows anything, I'll get it out of them. Don't you worry about that."

Chapter 24

Dᴇᴀɴ, Melinda and Mark looked at a file containing information about Mario Rosati, Sr.'s empire on the screen on Mark's laptop. Mark pressed the screen and enlarged a section of the diagram. "I got this off Hoffman's flash drive. All these companies are what Hoffman put together, and I bet Mario had to pay a pretty penny in legal fees for all this intricate corporate structure." Mark pointed to one of the boxes. "There's this LLC with an address in Wyoming, but that address is just an office that warehouses corporations so they can have a Wyoming headquarters on paper." The diagram had several other boxes linked to the Wyoming company. "He also had sister companies in Illinois, Nevada, Florida, and Texas, and companies headquartered in the Cayman Islands and Belize. But why so many companies to run a chain of currency exchanges?"

"Tax avoidance and money laundering," said Melinda. "Other than Illinois, these other states don't have any state income tax. And Belize and the Caymans not only have no income tax, they also have strong banking secrecy laws, and the banks themselves go out of their way to protect the anonymity of their customers."

"And how do you know all this?" asked Dean.

"Maybe because I'm a CPA. Do you know what a CPA is?" said Melinda.

"Of course, but why didn't I know you're a CPA?"

"If you'd bothered to ask about my investigative background, you'd have known. I thought it would help me get into the FBI. And they did make me an offer, but after seeing how that organization operates, I knew I'd never fit in."

"Kids, stop bickering," said Mark.

"I'm just busting his balls, Mark," said Melinda. "The Caribbean, huh. I'm going to need some new bikinis."

"You may not need to go to the Caribbean, at least not right now," Mark said.

"Doesn't the FBI have this information already?" asked Dean.

"The bureau located the Illinois, Cayman, and Belize bank accounts from currency exchange records shortly after the bust of the Russian ring. But Mario kept only a small amount of working capital in the Illinois account, and the foreign accounts were drained of around five million in assets before the bureau got there. We been monitoring those accounts since, and there's been no activity."

Dean thought for a moment. "You mean he didn't pay any US income tax on the five million? "Of course not, that's the point," said Melinda. "But that's small potatoes. There's hundreds of legitimate US companies doing the same thing.

There are trillions of dollars overseas, some hidden, some not. The biggest, most profitable US companies are engaging in this kind of tax avoidance, most of it completely legal. I'm not sure if Mario's scheme was legal—Hoffman's no genius. But you can be sure the major corporations have high-powered attorneys and accountants working to make their schemes pass the sniff test."

"The FBI already knows about these companies?" asked Dean, waving his finger at the computer screen.

"Only some of them," said Mark. "The FBI doesn't know about the Florida, Nevada, and Texas corporations. Their ownership records don't show Mario's name because the registered owners are a D. Day and R. Hudson, but the company mailing addresses are a P.O. box address in Chicago that's owned by Hoffman. I searched the property records in those states for Mario, Sr., Hoffman and the corporate names, and I got a couple of hits. A residence in Key West and one in Las Vegas are owned by those corporations."

"So, he had real estate in Florida and Las Vegas that the FBI doesn't know about?" Dean said.

"Either homes or maybe investment property," said Mark. "But the FBI's been trying to find his mistress, Doris Bertucci, who disappeared right after Mario was killed. She may know something about the missing money and maybe even about the video file. It's possible Doris could be holed up in one of those places. At least it gives you a place to start."

Dean and Melinda stepped off the turboprop plane into the brilliant sunshine of Key West International Airport and took a taxi to the address in Old Town that Mark had given them. The driver, a talkative Cuban man, gave them a tour of Duval Street on the way, the mile-long main drag in Key West lined with bars, restaurants, clubs and several dozen tourist gift shops. Mario, Sr.'s house was a modest-looking canary yellow cottage with white shutters located only a couple of blocks off Duval. Dean and Melinda rang the buzzer on the gate of the wrought iron fence several times, with no answer.

"So, what do we do now?" asked Dean.

Melinda looked up and down the vacant street. "Put your hands together and give me a boost." She stepped on his joined hands. "On the count of three push me up and over."

Dean crouched, pushed up hard and launched Melinda over the top of the gate; she opened the latch to let Dean inside. They knocked loudly on the front door. When there was no answer, they peered into the windows. The interior was dark, no sign of anyone home.

"Now what?" Melinda said.

Dean scanned the front porch, and then lifted up several potted plants, one after the other. He stood up after the third plant with a key in his hand.

"We're really going to do this?" Melinda asked.

"Well, I don't know about you, but I didn't come all the way down here just to get a sunburn."

"And if the police show up?"

"It's a welfare check for my Aunt Doris."

They opened the front door and Melinda called, "Hello, anyone home?" The house was much more luxurious inside than the modest exterior would imply, with an open airy floor plan featuring tile floors, tropical ceiling fans, and a breakfast bar, with stools, dividing the kitchen from the living room. The furniture looked high end, and either Doris had a gift for decorating or a professional had been hired. Off the kitchen was a screened-in porch and a private, lushly landscaped yard surrounding a small swimming pool. "Pretty nice love nest, huh?" said Melinda.

"Let's look at the bedrooms," said Dean.

There were two bedrooms, one with a large *en suite* bath featuring a huge shower with two rainfall shower heads, multiple body sprays and the kind of bench you might see in a spa. They looked through the walk-in closet where there was both men's and women's clothing, and the same in the dresser. Over the bed was an oil portrait of a voluptuous blonde woman lying in bed with a sheet partially covering her in a pose reminiscent of a famous photograph of Marilyn Monroe. "Stop staring, Dean," said Melinda. "She's not that hot."

"Oh, I think that may be a matter of opinion."

On the dresser were several pictures of Doris and Mario together. Dean reached over and picked one of them up. "What the heck is this?" asked Dean. The picture appeared to be taken at some kind of festival. Mario was wearing a Zorro costume, standing next to him was an extremely large man dressed as a gladiator, and between them was the same blonde woman in the portrait wearing nothing but tropical body paint, a colorful parrot donning each breast.

Melinda took the picture from Dean. "Ever hear of Fantasy Fest? It's the week-long Halloween party here. It's Key West's version of Mardi Gras, but more laid back and a hell of a lot warmer."

"And, apparently, nuder," Dean said.

"Oh, much, much nuder. There are thousands of women roaming the streets wearing body paint like Doris here, some not even wearing that much paint."

"And you know this how?"

"I plead the Fifth." She smiled and walked into the bathroom while Dean searched the rest of the drawers.

"I got nothing," said Dean. "Not even a receipt or an unpaid bill."

"I don't think she's been here for a while," Melinda said. "All her cosmetics are missing. From the pictures on her dresser, she didn't go anywhere without her makeup."

"OK." Dean sighed with frustration. "Let's go get something to eat. I'm starving."

They walked the few blocks to Duval Street and looked up and down at all the cafes, restaurants and bars. "Where should we eat?" Dean asked.

"Right across the street, the Bull and Whistle. There's a bar on the rooftop with a tremendous view of downtown Key West."

Up three flights of stairs, the open-air café was lined with tables and tropical plants. A man in the corner wearing a Bob Marley tee was playing the guitar. They each took an empty barstool, and then the bartender, a young woman wearing shorts but no top, each breast painted like a large blinking eye, handed them menus. Dean grinned at her and asked for the daily specials. After they ordered, and the waitress had gone to get their drinks, Melinda said, "Keep your eyes in your head, cowboy."

"What? I was looking directly into her eyes." Dean laughed. "If this is casual Friday attire at all the bars in town, maybe we should stay a little longer."

"It's kind of a special place—The Garden of Eden Bar. As far as I know it's the only one like it in town."

They ate their fish tacos and conch fritters and talked about the empty house. "So, you think she hasn't been there in a while. How long?" Dean asked.

"Well, the house is very clean, no dust on any of the furniture. Either they have a regular cleaning service, or it hasn't been that long. Maybe she's just out of town. Let's go back and talk to some of the neighbors. You tell them you're in town and just checking in on your Aunt Doris."

"Why me?"

"You have that Southern boy sincerity, and that irresistible accent. Plus, you're hot as hell. Who wouldn't talk to you?"

"What if their neighbor is a guy? Under that theory, shouldn't you do the talking?"

"Are you kidding? Look at me, Dean, do I look like I'm related to Doris? And this is Key West.

Most every boy in town would want to jump your bones."

A plump middle-aged couple, both wearing Key West baseball caps but nothing else, and carrying plastic cups that read "Eve's Appletini," walked over. "Mind if we join you two?" the woman asked and placed her chubby hand on Dean's shoulder, her heavy breasts leaning into him.

"Of course," Dean stammered. "But we were just leaving. We have a plane to catch."

"That's too bad," the man replied.

"Yes, it is," Dean said as he waved to the bartender. "Can we get our check?"

Melinda looked up at Dean and smiled. "We have a little time, don't we, honey? Can't we stay just a little longer?" She looked at the naked woman who was still leaning against Dean. "I think my husband is way overdressed, don't you?"

"Oh, yes," said the woman. "Way overdressed. Let me and Vern buy you two a drink."

"Really, honey, it's a lot later than I thought," Dean stammered. "We have to run that errand, and then we have to get to the airport. We can't chance missing our flight. It was really nice meeting you two—" Dean extended his hand, trying not to look at the woman below her eyes.

"Well, if you say so, dear," Melinda said. She slid off her stool. "Sorry, we have to go. He's always in a hurry, if you know what I mean." Melinda winked at the woman.

"Oh, I sure do. These men are always in too much of a hurry for me."

Melinda and Dean walked down the stairs and out onto Duval. "What was that about?" Dean said.

"Just having some fun. Did anyone ever tell you that you're a little uptight?" She reached up and kissed him on the cheek.

Doris's neighbor on the east side wasn't home. The neighbor on the other side was a friendly, bald man about Dean's age, with sleeve tattoos on both arms, and he smiled when Dean, with furrowed brow, explained their surprise visit to his aunt. "Doris has been gone a couple of weeks," the man said. "She goes to Vegas every couple of months. She didn't say when she was coming back. I'll tell her you stopped by."

"No, that's all right. We didn't say we were coming. We just decided to detour from Miami at the last minute. I have a cell phone number for her, but she must have changed it, it's not working. Do you have her cell phone number?"

"Give me yours and I'll message it to you."

Out of the corner of his eye, he could see Melinda smirk at the request. Dean thought it a little strange he didn't just give him Aunt Doris's number to write down, but this was a way of getting the neighbor's cell without having to ask for it.

While he was texting the number to Dean he asked, "You guys going to be in town long?"

"Actually, we're leaving today."

"That's too bad. Well, if you ever get back in town, look me up. I'd love to show you around."

"What did I tell you?" Melinda asked on their way back to the airport.

"About what?"

"That guy was totally hitting on you."

"Really?"

"Why do you think he got your number? You are equally desirable to men and women of all ages." She snuggled against him in the back of the taxi.

Chapter 25

THE first annual Coalition of Job Creators chose the Flamingo Hotel in Las Vegas for their convention—or, rather, the Flamingo Hotel chose them. The convention center at the Flamingo was the only hotel in Vegas with enough space to host the convention on such late notice. Thus the hotel, founded by the notorious Bugsy Siegel and the namesake of the mobster's girlfriend, Virginia "Flamingo" Hill, came to host several thousand of the most successful small business owners in America, all who hoped to be able to wield the same level of influence over the next president that their richer and more influential counterparts among the Fortune 500 took for granted.

Charles Kidwell was the driving force behind the small business PAC that was founded by his surrogates, Chavez Designs, a major customer of his Chicago bank. Twin brothers Hector and Rigo Chavez had taken an abandoned steel factory on the south side of Chicago and turned it into one of the leading manufacturers of office furniture in the United States. Moreover, they had become a model for the public/private partnership espoused by Senator McGraw. Most of their employees had been moved from welfare and unemployment rolls into well-paying, non-union jobs.

Charles had gotten to know the brothers five years earlier when he was trolling for business at the North American Commercial Design show in Chicago, where the pair won the Innovation Award, the first of many that would propel them to the top of the industry. Hector's revolutionary designs had wreaked havoc in the staid office-furniture industry with motifs that were at once striking and simple, futuristic and classical, clean and intricate—the best part of US, European, and Japanese design articulated in a line of highly profitable furniture. Each piece in the office suite integrated seamlessly with the other components, and the overall effect was genius of such simplicity that it made every designer think he or she could have created it. The designs had become so popular that Hector had begun doing custom residential work for some of the world's richest individuals.

But even after these awards, and a blue-chip customer list, the company was now hemorrhaging cash because of competition from cheap knockoff manufacturers in Asia, all of which were subsidiaries of US companies. The brothers had assumed that their patents, filed with the help of an expensive Chicago patent attorney, would protect them. But now they found that there were several Chinese companies that specialize in reverse engineered patents. These companies took a popular consumer product, made a few changes to it, and then filed design and utility patents on that product. Just enough changes were made from the original designs to sustain a patent challenge, but not enough changes so that customers noticed the quality or the design were different in any observable way from the original. The knockoffs were then manufactured with inferior materials and cheap labor in Asian factories.

The Chavez brothers felt trapped. Their options to regain competitive advantage in the market were to move their operations overseas, reduce the quality of their product, or both. Charles wasn't sure he could help them with their business problem, but he saw the political angle for Senator McGraw right away. The Chavez brothers were the human face of the jobs problem that the Senator hoped to make into a national referendum on shoring. A couple of anchor babies, children of illegal immigrants, obtained their citizenship by right of birth, embraced the American dream, played by the rules, created thousands of good-paying American jobs, only to see their designs stolen by American companies and shipped overseas, along with thousands of jobs of their countrymen. And then the same American companies avoided paying taxes on these ill-gotten gains through the use of foreign tax havens and complex tax-code loopholes. American voters might not have understood the complexities of these issues, Charles thought, but they would understand the Chavez's story. Charles convinced Rigo, the twin in charge of operations and finances, to found the Coalition of Job Creators, and arranged for a local filmmaker to create a documentary chronicling the Chavez brothers' struggles. This would be shown at the convention prior to the keynote speech by Senator McGraw.

Charles Kidwell entered the makeshift green room of the Grand Ballroom at the conference center and could see right away that something was wrong. Hector was standing over Rigo, who was sitting in a chair looking as if he was about to pass out. His face was pale, and he was dripping with sweat. "I... I just don't think I can do it, Hector."

"Bro, you have to. I can't do it by myself. Our whole presentation is based on the two of us. And for once, you're the straight man, so all you have to do is deliver your lines deadpan, and I'll take care of the punch lines. It should be simple."

Rigo began hyperventilating and put his head his hands. "I know, I know, but I just don't think I can do it."

"Hey, guys." Charles walked over to the two men and gave Hector a big hug. He tried to do the same to Rigo, but Rigo turned away. "What seems to be the problem?"

"Rigo has a bad case of stage fright and he doesn't think he can go on."

"Oh, shit," Charles said.

"I know. I told him he doesn't have any choice, but he insists—"

"I'm sorry..." Rigo was now speaking barely above a whisper. "But I think I'll throw up right on the stage if I try to do this."

Charles sighed, pulled out his phone and dialed a number. He explained the problem and handed the phone to Rigo. "Someone wants to talk to you."

Rigo said hello and listened for several minutes without saying a word, frowning at first, but gradually the frown turned into a small smile, and finally a chuckle and then a full-on laugh. At the end of the conversation he said, "Yes, Senator, I feel better now. I'll give it a try. I appreciate your confidence in me."

"What did he say?" Hector asked, stunned at his brother's turnaround.

"He said he had the same problem when he got into politics. He actually vomited in the lap of a lady in the basement of a church the first time he ever spoke."

"That sounds encouraging," Charles said.

"He told me he stumbled on two things that made all the difference in the world," Rigo continued. "He takes two shots of whiskey before every speech, and then he picks out the best-looking people in the audience and imagines them naked."

And that's exactly how it went down. While the large hall was enraptured with the documentary depicting the amazing journey and struggles of the twin Mexican entrepreneurs, Rigo sipped his liquid courage backstage. The audience gave them two standing ovations, the first when they were introduced after the film, and the second after straight man Rigo, his inhibitions lowered by three shots of tequila and some licentious imagery, delivered his lines with even more extraordinary humor and humanity than his more outgoing brother.

Chapter 26

Since eight that morning, Dean and Melinda had been sitting in front of a condo building a few blocks off the strip, at the address Mark Jeffrey had given them, waiting for someone resembling Doris Bertucci to emerge. They had called the landline of her unit, provided by Mark along with a snarky commentary about baby boomers holding onto their landlines as some kind of security blanket, but there had been no answer. It was now 11 PM and Dean was tired and cranky. He hated stakeouts. They were incredibly boring, and one of his weaknesses was impatience.

Melinda yawned. "I know you're in a bad mood. Your face doesn't hide anything. Did you know that? Look, I'm bored too. You know we don't really know that much about each other. I mean, other than we're both great in bed. Tell me about growing up in West Virginia."

"Not much to tell. My dad worked at whatever he could get. He was handy. He drank too much. My mom cleaned houses. The town I grew up in was a backward little place."

"So how did you get out of there?"

"Football. I got a scholarship to play at the University of Illinois. If not for that, I'd probably be doing six-to-six in a coal mine or something."

"Somehow I doubt that."

"How about you?"

"I grew up in San Francisco. I was an only child. Adopted by this do-good, liberal, professional couple. My dad was an investment banker, my mom ran an international non-profit. I didn't see them that much. They traveled constantly. I was raised by my nanny. They wanted me to understand my heritage, so they hired a Chinese nanny to teach me the language and all the old country customs. My language skills are pretty good"—she laughed —"but the old customs didn't take."

"Are your parents still in California?"

"My mom is. My dad died a few years ago. I don't see her much. We didn't have much use for each other once I became a teenager. She was the kind of woman who needed constant affirmation of her looks from men. She had men friends over all the time when my dad was travelling. Mom was the primary villain in most of my therapy sessions. And yes, I'm aware that my need for male attention has a lot to do with her. What about your folks?"

"My parents both died before I graduated from college, and I haven't been back to West Virginia since." Dean looked at the building and sighed. "Look, we've given it our best shot. Let's go back to the hotel, get something to eat, and relax. I've got an idea for the morning if she still isn't home."

The next morning, over room service breakfast, Dean looked at the online real estate listings for Doris's building address and located a local print shop a block away from the hotel on their way back to Doris's building. They dialed her phone again, got no answer before entering the building and approaching the doorman. "I'm a real estate broker and I'm showing Unit 2216; do you have the key?"

The doorman looked at Dean and then took a much longer look at Melinda, who was wearing a tight short skirt and very high heels. "Sure," he said, still eyeing Melinda. "I'll need your card."

Dean took a card he'd had printed a few minutes before from its leather case and handed it to the doorman, who didn't even look at it. He fished the key from a desk drawer, and asked Dean to sign in. "Make sure you remove your shoes. That unit has white carpeting."

"Sure thing," Dean said as they entered the elevator and took it to the twenty-second floor.

"You could be an excellent conman, you know," Melinda said when they were alone in the elevator.

"Why do you say that?"

"With those honest blue eyes, and that fake Southern-boy accent, you could get anyone to believe anything."

"The accent isn't fake, Melinda."

"Oh, so you're saying the accent isn't fake, but everything else is?"

The exited the elevator, and Dean took out a small black leather bag of tools in front of the Doris's condo which was just down the hall from the unit for sale. Seconds later they were inside the two-bedroom, two-bath unit, with large windows overlooking the strip. "I bet this view looks pretty cool at night. You take the living room, bathrooms and kitchen," Dean said. "I'll take the bedrooms."

The apartment was sparsely furnished, so the search took only about ten minutes before they reconvened in the living room. "She hasn't been here for a while," said Melinda. "There's nothing in the fridge."

Dean held up a pocket-sized book. "I found her address book. And I'm betting someone in this book knows where to find her." He placed it in his pocket and they left the unit.

"Tom, I can't believe that bullshit story you gave to Rigo actually worked," said Charles. "You have always loved being onstage, ever since you starred in *Streetcar Named Desire* at the University of Wyoming." They were watching the network coverage of the event in their hotel suite.

Tom laughed, "I can't believe it either. But I had to try something. He was just having a crisis of confidence. The story may be bullshit, but I do know the feeling. And it looks like it worked out really well. The network coverage has been amazing."

One of their security people walked into the room with Dean and Melinda. "I'm so glad you're in town," Tom said to them. "Sit down and catch me up on the developments."

Dean and Melinda outlined their trip to Chicago, the information they got from Hoffman, and their attempt to track Doris to Florida and Vegas. "It looks like she's purposely disappeared since Mario was killed. I'm guessing that she's afraid because of something she knows, or something she has. Like a certain video. Or maybe a pile of missing cash. We picked up some other leads to follow up from her apartment. We'll stay on her trail until we find her," Dean said.

"You do that. I don't have to tell you how important it is for you to find that damn video before the FBI does. Any luck in finding your laptop, Dean?"

"I think we know who took it—an associate of Boris Birkov. But he's also disappeared. They have an alert out for him in Wyoming, but he hasn't turned up."

"Do you think there's anything on the laptop that can hurt us?"

"I'm not sure. There were some notes that I made on the investigation."

"Anything that wasn't included in your original report?"

"Of course. You omit non-relevant information when you put a report together." Dean knew he wasn't being completely truthful with the Senator. His notes included his speculation about how Rosati was possibly blackmailing the Senator and why it was probably working, which was not in his original report. But he didn't think telling the Senator about it at this point would be useful.

The next day Senator McGraw looked in the makeup mirror as the network makeup artist applied concealer to freckles that dotted the space around his nose. Toby Landers had arranged for an exclusive interview with influential print and broadcast journalist Larry Bloom directly after the convention speech, to be aired on *60 Minutes* on Sunday night; the network had set up the cameras in a suite in the same hotel where the Senator was staying in order to tape it that morning.

"Almost done," the makeup guy said. "You know, you need to stay out of the sun; you've got quite a bit of sun damage on your face. I'm leaving you a tube of the best moisturizer and sunscreen on the market. It'll work wonders for you. We have to make sure you look really good at your inauguration. We're counting on it." By we, Tom thought he must mean the LGBT community, which was now giving him a lot of support. He didn't know exactly why. While it was true that he was the only Republican candidate to offer support to the LGBT community, there were Democrats who had made much more policy than he had.

"Thanks so much. I'll be sure to give it a try," Tom said.

Larry Bloom walked into the room. "Wow, that was quite a reception you got out there, and that was quite a speech too. You must be flying high, Senator."

"I thought it went pretty well."

"I just wanted to say hi before we start taping. I've been following your campaign and I was expecting a typical stump speech, but you gave us a lot more to talk about in our interview."

"Then let's do this. I'm flying to Jackson Hole for the weekend as soon as we're finished."

Larry Bloom stared right into the camera and spoke with a tone as silky as Georgia molasses. "I'm sitting with Senator Thomas McGraw, Republican candidate for president, and he has just delivered a most remarkable speech to the Convention of the Coalition of Job Creators. Senator, if I didn't know who you were, I would never have guessed that you're a Republican. What caused this break from the principles of your party?"

"As I've tried to explain, Larry, I don't think it's a break at all from Republican principles. I think my party has abandoned the principles that governed them for decades."

"OK, let's take these things point by point. Explain this new phrase you used tonight, the Capitalist Oligarchy. I haven't heard you use it before."

"Well, how much money does it take to get elected president today? A billion dollars. Where does a candidate get a billion dollars? Either he is a capitalist with a billion or more of ready cash, or he has to sell his soul to a cabal of capitalist oligarchs who want to buy US economic and tax policy for their benefit."

"But aren't the people who were in the audience tonight... aren't *they* also capitalists contributing to your campaign?"

"There's a big difference between these capitalists and the ones supporting the rest of the candidates from both parties, Larry. For one, these are

American entrepreneurs, running American manufacturing businesses, selling American-made products. And they're paying an American middle-class wage to American employees, and they're paying the full taxes on their corporate profits."

"Are you saying the capitalists that manufacture overseas are un-American?"

"That's exactly what I'm saying. Their manufacturing facilities employ workers making a subsistence living in unsafe conditions, they pollute the environment, not only of that country but contribute to world global warming, and in doing this they stash away trillions. That's right, Larry, trillions of dollars in overseas tax havens and they don't see any obligation to contribute to the financial support of the society that they live in and enjoy. They are not patriots. Patriots pay taxes! The patriots are the men and women in the audience tonight."

"What's this I keep hearing you say that you don't think America is exceptional? I know your fellow candidates are giving you a hard time about it."

"It's not that I don't think that America is exceptional, but we've become enamored with bragging about how exceptional we are instead of just being the example of exceptionalism. We're like the rich guy who drives up to the local blue-collar bar in his Cadillac, walks in with a blonde on his arm, buys everyone in the bar a drink, and brags about his last big deal. Sure, they'll take the free drink, but when he leaves, what do you think they're saying behind his back? 'What a prick.'

"The true American hero knows where he came from, knows his faults, and doesn't think he's morally superior to the rest of the world. We should have the humility to acknowledge that we exterminated an entire race to get from sea to shining sea, killed hundreds of thousands of people fighting a war because half our country couldn't see that owning another human was wrong. We're the richest country in the world, but have children living in squalor with poor nutrition, no health care, and who can't walk to their substandard school without getting shot at. That's how exceptional we are."

"Senator, you have to admit, what you've been talking about the last year or so, it's a big departure from your party, and from your career thus far. Are you having a mid-life crisis?"

"Mid-life crisis...." The Senator gave the laugh that he used to dismiss his critics. "Kind of conjures up sports cars, trophy wives, and hair plugs, doesn't it? I've never really thought about it that way." He paused, then spoke more quietly. "But maybe I am. I looked at myself a while back, and I didn't like what I saw. I didn't stand for anything except furthering my political career. And I made a decision that I was going to stand for something. Maybe America needs a mid-course correction. Maybe America needs to look at itself in the mirror and ask if this is who we want to be to each other and to the world. But if the American people send me back to Wyoming to raise cattle, I'm fine with that."

"So, Senator, you're saying that your re-evaluation of your legacy caused you to make this change. Do you have any more surprises in store for the American people?"

"I certainly hope so."

Chapter 27

Ronald Flag was watching the Fox News coverage of the Job Creators' Convention and knew he was in trouble. "Look at this fucking thing, Luis." Flag was addressing his long-time manservant, Luis Lopez. Flag didn't have a lot of close friends in his life, but Luis had been with him for over twenty years and had become the repository of his most unguarded opinions. "That documentary of those twin Mexicans made them out to be some kind of saints. Then the Senator gave a speech about how he's the only one who cares about American jobs, and how un-American anyone is who uses foreign manufacturing or takes advantage of our God-given tax code to save money. And what really pisses me off is that it's not just the liberal media eating this shit up, it's even our conservative media that's now questioning foreign investment. I've reached out to him multiple times, but he's given me the cold shoulder. Somebody's got to stop this guy, interrupt this fairy tale he's telling. He's no white knight. I know he has as many skeletons as any of us."

Luis smiled. "You're right, boss. When he was

at the fundraiser here, he was really disrespectful to you."

Flag's mobile phone rang, and he waved Luis out of the room. "Hey. Yeah, I saw it. Can you fucking believe what's going on? You're in Vegas, right? It's a shame we couldn't get this all arranged earlier. I know, I know there are a lot of moving parts, but he has all the attention now. If this had happened yesterday, it would have worked out so much better, but all the arrangements have been made now. OK, let me know when it all goes down. Hopefully, this will get the attention off the foreign jobs thing and show the world what these guys really are. Talk later."

Flag hung up the phone and turned back to the TV. "We'll see if you know how to play politics with the big boys, Senator."

Joe Buford never thought he'd be this close to a president, or at least a guy who might become president. When he came home from Viet Nam in '74, he'd been a twenty-one-year-old with no education and no job skills, facing an economy in the shitter, and the only work he could find was as an over-the-road truck driver. Somehow the owner of the company had taken a liking to him, and here, decades later, he was the President and CEO of a transportation company with terminals in seven states. Sometimes he had to pinch himself. The only time he'd met the guy who'd sent him to this convention was two years ago at a meet-and-greet when his company had won the bid for the transportation contract from one of Flag's logistics companies.

Joe was shocked when he got the call from Flag's people asking him to join the McGraw PAC. He wasn't a political guy at all. His way of getting by was to keep his head down and work hard. His mentor had showed him how to sweeten deals with under-the-table incentives for the decision-makers at his customers', or prospective customers', companies, but he'd never even thought of getting involved in local, much less national, politics.

Flag had insisted that he take time out of his schedule to attend the convention, and it was Flag who was bankrolling the after-party tonight for the biggest contributors of the PAC. He'd even rented out an entire floor for the party, hired the bartenders, caterers, and entertainment. Joe was to be the host, but it was Flag's show. He didn't understand why he wasn't to tell anyone about Flag's involvement, and then one of his vice-presidents had sent him the *Wall Street Journal* article about the feud between the Senator and Flag, and Joe had become even more confused. He'd always voted—every election he could cast a ballot, he was there—but like an average, non-ideological Republican who thought his taxes were too high. McGraw's message that night, however, rang true —the part about the real patriots being the entrepreneurs who hire Americans, who pay their taxes, who play fair. Joe felt as if the Senator had been talking about *him*, and about the thousands of Joes all over America whose voices had been drowned about by the international conglomerates. He'd been truly moved by the speech, by the presentation of the Chavez brothers, by this whole experience. Joe jumped up for McGraw's standing ovation and pumped his arm, even wiped away a few patriotic tears. Then he remembered he had to hurry, and headed for the elevators, swollen with pride that he would get to be the host tonight. But there was something gnawing at him. If Flag hated McGraw so much, why was he bankrolling this big shindig in his honor? No doubt some political stratagem that he would never understand.

When Joe arrived at the party floor, the celebration was already underway. A couple dozen attractive young women and another half-dozen just as attractive young men were in the lounge area. A muscular man in his forties with a dark tan, wearing a tight black suit over a tee shirt, approached, looked at Joe's badge, and then held out his hand. "Mr. Buford, I've been expecting you. You're the host of this shindig, right?"

"Yes, Joe Buford." He winced as the giant gold pinkie ring on the other man's finger cut into his.

"My name's Joe, too. Ron hired me to coordinate this. We've got everything taken care of, and we even brought in some hostesses to create a convivial atmosphere for the guests. We have food and beverage in the lounge here, a jazz trio and dancing in another suite on this floor, and several other suites for people who want a little more private setting. Ron made it clear to me that you're in charge of this, so if you need anything at all, just flag me down. I'll be around all evening, and I'm here to serve you anyway I can, sir."

Buford nodded and walked to the bar, avoiding both a blonde and a redhead who tried to make eye contact along the way. Grabbing a scotch, he staked out a spot near the elevator to await the VIP guests. For the next hour, he greeted the biggest contributors to the Coalition of Job Creators as they got off the elevator. Joe would encourage them to have a good time and then hand them off to one of the hostesses who would accompany them to the bar. He was disappointed when he heard that McGraw had already left without attending the party, but another of the hostesses kept his glass filled so he didn't need to leave his station near the elevator, and he was enjoying playing the role of the CEO who had sprung for such a lavish party.

Maybe it was the flattering way the other Joe had called him sir. The manner of address seemed to imply that he knew he had a personal relationship with Ron Flag—or maybe it was the fact that he'd consumed more scotch than he could remember but, for whatever reason, he found himself daydreaming about politics for the first time in his life. In his fantasy world, Senator McGraw would be so delighted with the party that he'd offer Joe a job in his administration. In his scotch-fueled fantasy, he imagined he was some kind of liaison between Flag and President Elect McGraw. As the evening wore on, his eyes grew heavier and his thoughts became more convoluted, and he took a seat in a thick leather chair in the lounge.

The young woman who had served as his personal waitress plopped herself down on his lap.

"Are you off duty now? So am I! Why don't we find someplace quieter and have some fun." She pulled him up from the chair, and he stumbled, willingly following as she led him down the hall, numbed enough by scotch to allow himself to be seduced by the illusion of power, and the just rewards that came with it.

Joe had passed out but was jerked awake by a glass of ice water thrown on his face by a bulldog-faced, crew-cut man wearing a yellow vest labeled *Las Vegas Police* in large block letters. "Are you Joe Buford?" He repeated this twice more before the ice water shocked Joe's brain into limited coherence.

"Yes, I'm Joe Buford. What's going on here?"

"Are you the host of this party?"

"Yes, I'm the host."

The cop nodded. "You're under arrest for pandering and drug trafficking. Several of your guests are undercover Las Vegas vice agents. Put your pants on, you're coming with us."

"Under arrest? This is a huge mistake. Where's the other Joe, the big guy in the black suit?"

"You're drunk, buddy. Put your pants on. You don't want to be booked half-naked."

Chapter 28

DEAN sat at the blackjack table in the casino at the MGM. He was about two grand ahead and, as was his usual practice, he told himself he would walk away when he made another grand. Of course, if he did make another grand, he would make another deal with himself and extend his session. As a result, Dean never walked away from a blackjack table ahead.

Melinda, who had been playing slots, walked over and put her arms around him. "I'm tired. I'm going to the room and take a hot bath. See you up there later, OK?"

Dean kissed her on the cheek and turned back to his table and split his aces.

Two hours later, when he was back to break even, he left the table and headed back to his room, taking a detour to the men's room, but not because he'd allowed himself to indulge in the free drinks while gambling. He hadn't had a drop of alcohol since the trip to Chicago—he'd even lost a few pounds and was feeling clearheaded—but he had consumed a gallon of soda water at the blackjack table and had refused to leave until the table turned cold. He was reading the ad for an escort service printed on a playing card that had been taped above the urinal by an enterprising Las Vegas entrepreneur when he felt something press against his back, and a split second later his nerve endings were sprayed with electricity, as if he was shot with a thousand hypodermic needles all at once. In an instant, he was flat on his back, looking at the ceiling, paralyzed and unable to move but completely aware of his surroundings.

A huge figure stood over him and a voice behind the big man said, "Get his dick back in his pants and pick him up." The big man tucked him back in, fastened his pants, and they each took an arm and carried him like a rag doll out of the men's room. A couple joined the trio in the elevator, and the young man grinned at them. "Our friend couldn't resist the free drinks at the blackjack tables. Doesn't know his limits."

The hotel room Dean was held in was on a floor directly below the one he shared with Melinda. The feeling in his arms and legs had come back to him, but they ached, as if he'd been stung by a nest of hornets. His eyes, hands, and feet were wrapped with duct tape. He had a tiny view of the room from a gap in the tape in the lower right-hand corner of his eye, but the entirety of his vision was dominated by the enormous belly of a man sitting on a stool in front of him. Another man, so close he could feel the heat of his breath in his ear, whispered, "Where is she?"

"Where is who?"

"Doris Bertucci. Where is she?"

"I have no idea."

Evidently at that moment, the whisperer indicated something to the enormous-bellied man and either a fist or a club exploded deep into Dean's side, the pain taking his breath away. The man waited a moment for Dean to be able to speak and repeated, still in a whisper, but now a bit more forceful. "We're prepared to take it easy on you, if you give us the information we want. If you don't, well, then, I don't know if you'll survive, but I know your ribs won't."

Dean could hardly breathe, but he managed to creak out, "I told you. I don't know where she is."

Four more explosions on each side of his chest cavity took not only the rest of his breath away but also his consciousness. A glass of cold water splashed on his face, and he awoke moaning, each breath sheer agony, not knowing how much time had passed.

"One more try. This time your answer is more important than last time we asked. Do you understand what I mean?"

Dean grunted a hoarse, "Yes."

"Where is she?"

"Fuck ... you!"

This time it was a club to the back of his head that brought the enormous pain that gave way to darkness.

Sometime later, she came to him, a blonde out-of-focus angel, and softly touched his forehead.

Dean looked up and grimaced as he tried to force a smile. "Where have you been? I've needed you."

"I'm always around, but I've been trying to let you live your own life. You need to start living in the present, and it looks like you've done that very well from what I've seen. She's hot, I have to give her that. But I'm not sure she's your type."

"Well, she's not you, that's for sure. But ... I needed something...."

"I know, honey, I know you did. And it's fine. I'm not upset with you. Just be careful." She leaned down and kissed him gently on the lips. And then her image began to recede into the distance.

Dean reached for her, tried to climb out of the bed as he shouted, "Wait! Wait! Don't go, not yet ...." Two nurses, one male and one female, appeared. The man held him down while the woman injected a sedative into his arm, and he relaxed and fell into a tormented sleep.

When he awakened, another face was looking directly into his, a pretty Asian woman with dark eyes. "Great, you're awake."

"Yes, where am I?" With the act of speaking, Dean felt a sharp pain in each side.

"In a hospital in downtown Las Vegas. You didn't come back to the room last night. I fell asleep, and when you didn't answer your cell phone this morning, I started calling hospitals. The police found you dumped by the side of the road. Someone doesn't like you very much. What happened after you left the blackjack table?"

Dean thought for a moment, looking past Melinda to the police officer standing behind her. "I left the table to come upstairs. I don't remember anything after that."

"You don't remember anything about being attacked?"

"Nothing at all."

That was when the uniformed officer who'd been standing out of Dean's sightline moved to his bedside. "You two are law enforcement officers from Wyoming? What are you doing in Las Vegas?"

"Oh, we're not here on official business," Melinda answered quickly. "Just a little weekend R&R."

"Do you remember leaving the hotel after playing blackjack, Mr. Wister? You were found on the side of the road near a strip club."

"Like I just said, I don't remember anything."

The policeman paused, and Dean could see that he wasn't sure he believed him. "Well, if you remember anything, please give me a call. And you might want to limit your drinking a little bit."

"Thanks, officer," Melinda offered. "I'll monitor him. I can assure you he won't be drinking again while we're in town."

Melinda waited until the officer had left the room, then scooted up on the edge of Dean's bed. "Is that true, you don't remember anything?"

"Of course not. I remember everything." He told Melinda about being jumped, tied up, interrogated, and beaten.

"Are you able to identify the two men? Do you have any idea who it could be?"

"I know exactly who it is. There were two guys. The huge guy, I've seen before. It's Mario Rosati's bodyguard, Pete Pisano. There was another guy with him. He interrogated me, but I never saw his face. It has to be Mario, Jr. They're looking for the same thing we are, right? So, we need to get moving. Let's get out of here and go through the address book. We're ahead of them and need to stay that way."

"You're not going anywhere for a day or two. You've got several broken ribs and the doc wants to make sure you don't puncture a lung or some-thing. The address book, do you know where it is?"

Dean groaned as the answer hit him. "Try my jacket pocket."

Melinda went to the closet in the corner of the room and searched through his clothes. "Not here."

"Fuck. And I didn't even have a chance to go through it."

Chapter 29

CHARLES Kidwell and Senator McGraw took Charles's private plane to Jackson Hole after the Larry Bloom interview. On the plane, they talked about the taping. "That was different than any interview I've seen you give before," Charles said.

"Well, that's Larry's thing, isn't it? The intimate profile."

Charles looked at Tom and spoke quietly. "So, am I part of your mid-life crisis?"

Tom sipped his drink. "Probably, but that's not a bad thing. Being with you, that's who I am." Charles was quiet for a minute, and Tom asked, "What's wrong?"

Charles looked away. "Well, you know we've never been intimate. You've been intimate with Charlotte, but not with me. Is that because you can't stand yourself being with a man? That, somehow, when I dress like Charlotte, the fantasy makes it easier for you to accept your sexuality?"

Tom took another long sip of his drink. "At first, yes. It took me a long time to admit to myself that I'm gay, to accept myself. The dress up part, it was a novelty." He shook his glass, so the ice cubes clinked, filling in the silence. "Since we've been together, Charles, I've changed. You've changed me. I'm ready now to be with you, Charles. Without Charlotte."

When they arrived in Jackson, Charles and Tom were still in the bedroom at the back of the plane, on a high from Tom's successful speech and the endorphins from the activities in the bedroom, so they made a stop at The Rose, the upscale bar located in the hottest local music venue in downtown Jackson, the Pink Garter Theater. The Rose was packed this weekend night and when the Senator entered the bar, he was recognized by the bar patrons who gave him a spontaneous ovation. His speech had been on the bar TV earlier in the evening and the patrons called out their congratulations and support as he walked through to a table, and many of them sent shots of whiskey to his table into the wee hours of the morning. Back at Charles's house, the Senator undressed and lay on his back, naked on the four-poster, handhewn, king-sized bed, his mind running through the day in Vegas and evening at the bar while Charles was in the bathroom.

When Charles emerged as Charlotte, her transformation meticulously executed with her red wig, eye makeup and lipstick, red bustier and heels, she dimmed the lights and crawled on top of the Senator. "Sorry, I took so long. I promise it will be worth the wait." But the Senator was snoring loudly, his mouth open and, with each raspy breath, a potent puff of Wyoming Whiskey was exhaled into the room. Charlotte smiled, patted his cheek and rolled off him. Slipping off her heels, she snuggled into his arms and they fell into a happy drunken coma-like sleep.

The morning greeted them with the cell phone ringing inside the Senator's trouser pocket. He fell out of bed and, still in an alcohol haze, crawled on hands and knees to locate his pants. "Hey, TL … what's up?"

"Sorry to bother you, I know you got in late last night. But you better turn on CNN right now. There's something you need to see."

He found the remote and clicked on the TV. The voices of the newscasters woke Charlotte and she sat up to look with him at the huge high-def screen on the wall. Scrolling across the bottom of the screen was a summary of the highlights: "High rollers arrested in prostitution/drug sting at Senator McGraw Las Vegas event." The news anchors were laughing and making jokes about the arrests as mug shots flashed across the screen. TL was on the speaker phone now, talking to both of them as one of the anchors continued to fill in the details: "—a hospitality suite of one of the donors was raided last night. Twelve were arrested, including at least two of the people on the Board of the Job Creators."

"How could they be so stupid?" Charlotte groaned.

"This is what guys do at conventions in Vegas," said the Senator. "The cops generally look the other way. You know that. You're from Chicago.

This time they didn't." He grunted. "It has to be a setup."

"A setup? You mean someone arranged this with the cops? Who would do that?"

"A lot of people would do that. Anyone who wants to derail my campaign. Remember what Lee Atwater did to Gary Hart."

"All that goodwill. All that great publicity, down the drain." TL shook his head.

"Well, not all, but it's a setback," said the Senator. "I'll get back to you later in the day. Try to find out more about this and figure out how we can spin it." He hung up and turned to look at Charlotte. "When did you change into that?"

"Last night. When I came out of the bathroom, you were passed out on the bed."

"Well, I'm not passed out now. And I'm nearly sober." He grabbed her and pulled her on top of him. "Let's not let anyone spoil the rest of our weekend. I've decided to have both of you over the next two days. Technically, that's not considered a ménage à trois."

Chapter 30

Two TV pundits were screaming, one demanding Senator McGraw be arrested for treason, the other suggesting that he was clearly having mental health issues. Dean couldn't understand why they were screaming because they seemed to be pretty much agreeing with each other, so he gave up on the TV, flipped off the remote, and picked up his cell phone to call Mark Jeffery in Chicago.

He and Melinda had returned to Jackson for a few days for Dean's ribs to recuperate. It still hurt like hell when he coughed or laughed, and lovemaking required several compromises. The first time they'd attempted sex after his injury, Melinda had told him, "Don't worry, you just lay there and let me do all the work." When she returned to the bedroom, she was wearing a cowboy hat, boots, and nothing else. Cowgirl style had definitely worked for him, but now that he was feeling better, maybe they'd be able to change it up a bit.

He put those thoughts away when Mark answered. "Hey, Mark, I'm about ready to get back on the road. Do you have any leads for me on Doris?"

"I was just getting ready to call you. I located her mother. She lives in Wrigleyville. I'll email you her address. You sure you're up to traveling?"

"I'm feeling much better." He coughed and winced. "And I need to get out of here. It's hard to watch TV—it seems there's nothing on the news except coverage of all the pussy hounds at Mc-Graw's Vegas convention."

"I know. Did you see the *Daily News* headline? 'McGraw's Convention for Full Employment of Sex Workers'."

"Yeah, I did. And it caused me a very painful laughing fit."

Marion Aurelio lived in a modest bungalow about five blocks from Wrigley Field. Dean rang the doorbell and a thin, silver-haired woman in her late seventies opened the door. "May I help you?"

"Ma'am, my name is Dean Wister, and I'm with the Teton County Sheriff's Department in Wyoming." Dean spoke in the slightly exaggerated version of his drawl that he used to charm middle-aged ladies. "I'm trying to locate your daughter, Doris. Can you tell me anything about her whereabouts?"

Marion smiled at Dean and then looked over his shoulder at the short Asian woman behind him, and her grin faded. "Where did you say you were from?" she asked, but she didn't take her eyes off Melinda.

"I'm with the Teton County Sheriff's Department. In Wyoming."

"Wyoming? My daughter doesn't live in Wyoming." She didn't look at Dean. Her eyes remained fixed on Melinda.

Melinda touched Dean's shoulder and said, "Excuse me, Dean, I have some calls to make. I'll just wait for you in the car."

Dean shrugged, not looking at Melinda, staying focused on Doris's mother. "Mrs. Aurelio, may I come in?"

The old woman seemed to relax as Melinda retreated from her doorstep. "Oh, I suppose it would be OK."

The living room was dark, the curtains and furniture covered in red and gold brocade. The overall effect was to remind Dean of a Southern funeral home. "Can we sit here, ma'am, for a bit? I just want to ask you a few questions about your daughter."

The woman nodded, and they sat side-by-side on the fancy sofa. "Ma'am, are you aware that your daughter was involved with a man who was killed last year, Mario Rosati, Sr.?"

"Oh, yes. Mario was a very nice man. It was terrible what that Senator did to him. And he got away with it too."

"Well, there are some people who may want to hurt your daughter, and they've been looking for her. I'd like to help her, but we haven't been able to locate her. It's important that we find her first, so we can offer her some protection. When is the last time you heard from her?"

The woman thought for a moment. "Well, she called last week. She calls me on Sunday morning every week. She doesn't get back to Chicago much."

"Do you know where she was when she called you?"

"She said she was in Las Vegas."

Dean sighed. "Has anyone else been here asking you about her?"

The woman paused for a moment, as if she was wondering if she should share anything else with Dean. Then Dean smiled at her and touched her arm. "I really want to help your daughter."

"Well, last week there were two men here. A young man who was very good looking, and another one who was really fat. The young man was very nice at first, but when I told him I didn't know where she was, he got really nasty."

"Did he threaten you, ma'am?"

Marion shivered. "Yes. He said it wouldn't be very good for my health if I didn't help him find her."

"And what did you do then?"

"I asked him to wait a minute. I said I might have something that would help. And I went to my bedroom and got my shotgun and came out and stood in the hallway and told him to get out of my house right now or I'd blow a hole in his belly the size of a bowling ball."

Dean smiled. "And what did he do then?"

"Well, he didn't do anything. He just turned around and left."

"Did you call the police, Mrs. Aurelio? You should file a report on this. Based on what you told me, they could arrest him for assault."

At the mention of the police, her face completely changed. "I hate the fucking police. They're fucking worthless. I'm sleeping now with the shotgun next to my bed. If he comes back, I won't be so nice to him." She cackled the wet gravelly laugh of a long-time smoker, and Dean thought she probably wasn't kidding.

"Well, I'm sorry that you had to go through this, Mrs. Aurelio. But I'm afraid that man may come back if we don't find your daughter." Dean pulled a card from his pocket and put in on the table in front of them. "If you hear from her, please tell her to call me. It's important that I talk to her." He stood and walked to the door. "Mrs. Aurelio, where did you learn to use a shotgun?"

"I used to go hunting with my husband all the time when he was alive. I was actually a better shot than he was, but I never let him know that."

"And do you think you would actually have been able to shoot him?"

"Oh, I'm sure of it." She said it with such determination that Dean was sure of it too.

In the car, Dean filled Melinda in on the conversation with Mrs. Aurelio. "Why did you go back to the car?"

"I was obviously making her uncomfortable."

"Generally, I find it makes the process easier if there's a female officer present when I question a woman."

"That may be true most of the time, Dean. But some women, especially older women, are extremely prejudiced against Asians. And I could see that in her eyes when we were at the door."

"Really?"

"Really. I can't believe you aren't aware of this. Also, I recognized the sweet Southern boy thing you were doing. Bet that works in the Chicago bars too, doesn't it?"

"To tell the truth, it's been a long time since I've tried it out."

They returned to the hotel and showered before dinner. Dean had his head full of shampoo when Melinda opened the shower door and joined him. "Wash your back?"

"Sure." She took the soap and lathered his back and worked her way down, massaging his muscles that still hadn't fully recovered from the beating that he had taken. He turned to face her when his cell phone, charging on the bathroom counter, rang.

"Let it go to voicemail," said Melinda.

"Can't," said Dean. "Could be about the case." He also knew he wouldn't be able to fully enjoy the encounter with the unheard voicemail distracting him. Dripping and trying to keep his balance on the slippery tile, he picked up the phone. It was an area code he didn't recognize. "Hello."

"Is this Dean Wister, the Wyoming cop?"

"Yes. Who's this?"

"Doris Bertucci. You were at my ma's house looking for me?"

"Yes, Doris. Thanks for calling me back. I was involved in the Mario Rosati case and there are some loose ends that I need to go over with you."

"What kind of loose ends?"

"Well, those bad guys that visited your mother. I'm sure she told you about it, right? They're also looking for you. Maybe I can help get rid of them. Where are you right now?"

She paused for a minute. "I'm in Chicago. But I should come to you. I can be there in an hour. Where are you?"

Dean looked at Melinda, standing naked outside the shower, toweling off, and mouthed "Doris" to her.

"Doris. Are you at your mother's house? If you are, check out the cars up and down the street before you leave to make sure you aren't followed."

"I'm not at her house. Don't worry. I know the drill. Don't forget, I spent many years with Mario Rosati."

The woman that walked into the hotel lobby looked a lot like the picture they had seen in the Florida photo, albeit about twenty years older. She still had a nice figure, and was wearing a tight red dress that showed off a lot of cleavage, and Dean couldn't help visualizing the photo of her in Key West draped in nothing more than tropical paint. He and Melinda took her up to their suite and they all had seats in the sitting area.

"The only reason I'm meeting with you is I don't want my mother to be bothered anymore. That little shit Mario, Jr. threatened her, and I'm afraid he'll come back."

"Do you know why he's looking for you?"

"He probably wants money, but I don't have any to give him. I have the places in Key West and Vegas, but beyond that I don't have much of a nest egg. Mario gave me a monthly allowance but that's gone now."

Dean thought she was probably lying about the money. She didn't want him to think she had five million stashed. "Doris, I don't think he's after just money. He may be after money too, but what I think he's really after is a video that his father may have made of Senator McGraw in a compromising position. Did Mario talk to you about that?"

"Yeah, he mentioned it. I never actually saw it, but he said he had something on him and it was going to help him get connected to the top levels of government."

"Well, Junior is looking for it. And frankly, so are we. It's important that we find it before Mario does but, until we do, your mother isn't safe, and frankly neither are you. He's really looking for you, he thinks you probably have the tape, his father's money, or both. Does your mother have somewhere she can go until this blows over?"

"I tried to get her to go live with her sister, but she's hard-headed. She said she has her gun loaded, and she has a bullet with his name on it." Doris chuckled. "I know it isn't funny, but what can you do?"

"The FBI has been through all of Mario's things, but nothing turned up. Did he give you anything?

A computer or a flash drive or a DVD, anything like that, for safekeeping?"

"No, he didn't. As a matter of fact, I saw very little of him the few months before he died. He didn't say, but I think he traded me in for a younger model."

Dean and Melinda exchanged glances. "Do you have any idea who it might be?"

She laughed. "I suspect it probably was a young blonde with big boobs in Chicago. But that only narrows it down to about a million possibilities. I wasn't in Chicago that much at the end. I was alternating between Key West and Vegas. At first Mario would come see me nearly every weekend. And then the time between visits became longer and longer."

"If you had to guess, where do you think Mario would have hidden this video?"

"Well, if I had to guess, I'd say you were on the right track. He gave me various things to hide for him over the years. And the fact that he didn't give me this, well, I was sure he had another girl. Find her and you just might find the video."

Chapter 31

Toby Landers walked into the Senator's hotel suite in Denver. Surprisingly, the Senator seemed to be in a good mood when he saw his campaign manager. "TL, sit down and have some breakfast."

"Sorry, Senator, I can't eat. And I can't believe you can either after that debacle last night. Have you seen what the media is saying about the debate?"

"TL, do you know how much I care about what the media is saying about me? Not two shits... not even *half* a shit."

"Well, you should give more than two shits." TL pulled out his notebook and started reading "'McGraw trounced on his home court.' 'McGraw not too quick on the draw this time.' 'McGraw traitor to conservatism.' I googled the words McGraw and Liberal together, and you know what I got? Five hundred thousand hits. Senator, I'm sorry, but I have to ask, are you running in the right party?"

McGraw dabbed his mouth with a napkin and took a long swig of water. "TL, do you really believe that the average American voter looks at who the media favors when they walk into the voting booth? As a guy running as an outsider, in some ways it actually helps me when I'm criticized by the media. We had this talk once before, a while back, didn't we? Didn't I say that I was going to be myself, come hell or high water, and let the buffalo chips land wherever they may? Damn it, that's exactly what I'm doing."

TL rubbed his face. "I understand. But have you seen the *Wall Street Journal* this morning? They haven't endorsed anyone for the nomination yet, but they just adopted an 'anyone but McGraw policy.' They say you've declared war on capitalism with your plan to tax profits on foreign manufacturing, and your program to repatriate corporate earnings amounts to blackmail."

"That's exactly what I was hoping for. I'm removing a substantial part of the incentive to manufacture overseas. As for the blackmail part, it's hardly that. I'm actually letting them bring their money home tax-free if they invest in new manufacturing jobs. Look TL, I expected this attack from the captains of industry, but I believe the American voters will have an entirely different opinion about my plan."

"I get that, but did you have to refer to the *Wall Street Journal* as the 'bought-and-paid-for rag of billionaire slave traders'?"

The Senator snorted. "That may have been a little over the top, but still, pretty damned good line, huh?"

"I'm not sure the American people thought it was such a great line. You're down in the overnight polling, and with many of your 'job creators' laying low since the convention, we don't have the money to make it up."

"Well, that's why I hired you, TL. You figure out how to sell the truth to the American people. At least my version of it. Now let me go back to eating this fantastic breakfast of steel cut oats and fruit. It's possible you're right. Maybe my political views have been messed up by this fucking liberal vegan diet you have me on."

Chapter 32

MELINDA and Mark sat around a small table in the Chicago hotel room while Dean paced the room. "We're back to square one. I believe that Doris doesn't have the video. What do you think Melinda?" Dean asked.

"I agree with you. But if she's right about Mario having a replacement girlfriend, how do we find her?"

"Everyone in his organization was interviewed about the women in his life," said Mark. "The only one that came up was Doris. If there's another, she's a mystery."

"OK. So, he didn't take her to his usual places, where his boys would hang out. Where did he go that was more respectable? You guys were tailing him for some time, Mark. What do you think?"

"Well, he would meet with public officials, and he even met Charles Kidwell at the Palmer House, the same hotel that this elusive video was from. We could start there and see if anyone remembers him with a woman."

"It's a start, I guess. Melinda and I will do that. Meanwhile, Mark, can you go back to your contact

at the FBI and have him, or *her*, review the surveillance records and see if any other women turn
up?"

"I'll see what I can do, but I'm already pushing
my contact pretty hard."

"Well, then you may just have to put a ring on
it, Mark, if you want to get closer," said Melinda
with her trademark smirk.

Dean and Melinda were ushered into the General
Manager's office of the Palmer House. The GM
was a short pudgy man who looked as though he
couldn't resist the free buffets and restaurant tast-
ings that a GM at a major hotel would be privy
to. "What can I do for you? What are a couple of
Wyoming cops doing in Chicago?"

"Did you know Mario Rosati? He was a regular
at your hotel before he was killed."

"Oh, I heard all about it, but I never met him. I
came here shortly after that whole mess."

"Well, he was involved not only in money laundering in Chicago, but in sex-worker trafficking
in Wyoming, and we're tying up some loose ends.
We're looking for a woman Mario might have been
seen with at this hotel."

"As I said, I wasn't here then. You'd have to talk
to my predecessor about that."

"How would we do that? Can you give us the
contact information?"

"I can't. I'd love to cooperate, but I can't.
You see, I kind of got transferred here at the
last minute. The former GM, her name is Gina
Cochran, quit without giving notice. When I got

here, I tried to reach out to her to answer a few questions about some of our corporate clients, but her cell phone was disconnected and she never answered any of her emails. She didn't leave HR with any forwarding address."

"And why did she leave?"

"She didn't give a specific reason. She just told corporate she had to go right away, for personal reasons. She left a few pages of notes on her desk for the person who took over for her, but that was it."

Dean exchanged a look with Melinda. "Could we talk to the restaurant manager, or maybe some of the servers? They might be able to help us with anyone he might have been here with."

"Sure. I'll set it up for you."

The restaurant manager was the opposite of the GM, a thin, wiry man with a thick Mexican accent. "Sure, I knew Mario pretty well—he came in here a lot. I know they say he was a mafia guy and stuff, but he was really nice to the staff, and a really good tipper."

"Did he ever come in with a woman?"

"Not that I know of. He was generally here with businessmen. I think this was his business restaurant—he was in here a couple times a week."

"How close were you to your former GM? Did she tell you anything about why she left?"

"I didn't know her well, and she didn't say anything to me about leaving. I just came in one day and she was gone."

"And this was about the time that Mario was killed?"

"I think so. I can't say exactly, but not long after."

Dean stopped and looked down at his notebook, and then back at the manager. "Did you ever think those two things could be related, Mario getting killed and Gina disappearing?"

"Why would you ask that?"

"From what I've been told, her leaving was all so mysterious. I'm just wondering. Did you ever see Mario with Gina?"

The restaurant manager paused. "Look, I don't gossip. I purposely try to not know too much about this kind of thing." He looked around, then gestured for Dean to come a little closer, so he could speak quietly. "Mario's business meetings would often run late into the evening. A couple of times, after the kitchen closed and we were closing up, I saw Mario and Gina sitting at a table alone."

"What do you mean alone?"

"Just the two of them. But they were sitting real close, you know? Like a man and a woman do when it's more than just business."

When they walked out of the hotel, Melinda said to Dean, "So how do we find this Gina Cochran?"

"We'll put Mark on it. I bet he can track her down."

Mario, Jr. flipped open his pocket knife and slipped it between the doorjamb and the deadbolt that was lit by the narrow beam of the penlight held by his much larger partner. He applied pressure and the door lock popped. They quietly opened the back door of the bungalow and entered into the kitchen. As they walked past the counter, Double P grabbed Junior's arm and Mario froze, listening in the darkness for a sound he presumed the big man had just heard. Double P reached into his jacket, pulled out a gallon zip-lock bag and put it on the kitchen counter. He grabbed a fistful from the plate piled high with chocolate chip cookies, slipped them into the bag, and then let go of Mario's arm and nudged him forward.

They waited a moment for their eyes to adjust to the darkness and moved through the hallway to the bedroom in the back of the house. They looked down at the old lady, sleeping on her back, breathing quietly. Mario nodded and Double P put his huge hand over the woman's face, covering her mouth and pinching her nose at the same time. Her eyes popped open, darting back and forth between the two of them.

"Surprise," Mario said and sat down on the edge of the bed next to her. "You were very rude to us the last time we were here, so we decided to pay you another visit."

The woman's face was getting redder now and she began to struggle. "Now, just hold on, we're going to let you breathe, but if you scream... well, then we're going to have to cover up your nose and mouth again. Do you understand?"

The woman nodded and Double P uncovered her nose and mouth. She struggled to get out of the bed, but Double P grabbed her and threw her back down. Once again, he covered her face, not saying anything to her as her skin became redder and redder and her eyes began to roll back in her head. Mario nodded, and Double P let go of her again and she gasped for breath.

"You don't seem to be taking us seriously. All we want is for you to tell us how to get hold of your daughter. Give us that, and we will be on our way. Don't make us tear up your pretty little house."

The old lady was trembling now, coughing and gagging before catching her breath. "There's an address and phone number in the kitchen, on the counter next to the phone."

Double P turned and walked to the kitchen, returning in a moment with a piece of paper in his hand and nodding to Mario.

"Thank you, ma'am. Thank you very, very much," said Mario, as he got up from the bed and took the paper from Double P's hand. "Oh, and, Double P, thank the nice lady for the cookies."

Double P put his ham-sized knee on the woman's chest and, before she could resist, covered her mouth and nose once more with his sweaty paw. As she struggled, he reached into his pocket and pulled out a cookie. Crumbs dribbled from his mouth to the woman's face, and as he munched nonchalantly, she kicked furiously at the covers. After a minute or so, her kicks became slower and slower, like the battery in a children's toy running out of juice. Finally, she lay still, her eyes fixed and vacant.

Dean pushed a sleeping Melinda off his shoulder, rolled over and picked up the ringing phone from the nightstand. "What's up, Mark?"

"Doris's mother is dead. A neighbor found her in her bed this morning. Could be natural causes. There was no sign of a struggle, and nothing in the house seems to be disturbed, but when the cops came, they found pry marks on the back door."

"Fuck. Mario, Jr. came back."

"Could be," Mark agreed.

"You guys going to pick him up, turn him over to the Chicago PD?"

"Well, we've got a little problem with that, Dean. She never filed a police report about the threat. The only reason we know about it is that you interviewed her. And I can't tell the people here that I know about it. Maybe Chicago PD will turn over some forensic evidence, or maybe we'll find out she died of natural causes in her sleep."

"Maybe. But I know that fucking Mario, Jr. His dad was just a run-of-the mill Chicago mobster, but his son? His son is truly evil." Dean was getting worked up now. "I hope I get another shot at him. I'll wipe the smirk off that little motherfucker's face."

"Well, I think he's getting a little panicked. He knows that getting his charges dismissed is going to hinge on finding some useful info. So far he hasn't come up with shit."

"This isn't panic. This is the little sociopath just having fun. There was no reason to kill her. She humiliated him, and this was payback. I'll try to contact Doris and tell her what happened, and that Mario may have gotten some info from her mother about her whereabouts."

When Dean hung up the phone, Melinda touched his shoulder. "What was that about?"

"I think Mario, Jr. killed Doris's mother last night."

They met Mark for lunch, and he joined them with a smile on his face.

"What are you so fucking happy about? One of your informants killed an old lady. You work for an organization that was complicit in a murder last night," Dean said.

"I know, I know. Don't give me shit, Dean. I've already committed several crimes since I've been working with you. I was smiling because I have a lead on our hotel GM. I was able to access some Illinois payroll tax records and she's working at the Ramada Inn in Alton, near St. Louis."

"Shit, that's a pretty big come down from being the GM at the Palmer House in Chicago," Melinda said.

"It looks like she wanted to get out of town," Mark offered.

"OK, let's check it out and see what she has to say."

Chapter 33

THE sign outside the Ramada Inn in Alton, Illinois read "Welcome Miss Madison County Pageant", but the threadbare carpet in the lobby and chipped laminate on the front desk counter revealed what a low-rent pageant that really was. Dean flipped his badge and asked to speak with the General Manager.

When the young woman appeared, Dean could see why Mario went for Gina Cochran. She was blonde, voluptuous, just a little too made up, but she had a broad, friendly smile—a younger version of Doris Bertucci. "What can I help you with?" she asked.

Dean flashed his badge. "Miss Cochran, is there some place private we could talk?"

Her smile disappeared as she led them into her cluttered office. "We're tying up some loose ends on the Wyoming side of the Mario Rosati case." Dean paused. "And we understand that you were in a relationship with him."

She looked stunned and didn't speak for a moment. "How did you find me?"

"It wasn't that hard to find you, Gina. And if we can, then other people can too. People who won't be as friendly as we are."

"How did you find out we were in a relationship? It wasn't that long. And I was so careful at work."

"Why is it that people who are sneaking around always think no one knows," Melinda asked. "People who are around you all day, your co-workers, they always know if something is going on at work."

"Look, we don't want to cause you any trouble, Gina," Dean interjected. "We know that Mario gave you something for safekeeping. We figure that you knew some people might come looking for it, and that's why you took off. We need what he gave you. Just give it to us and we'll walk out of here, and you can go back to your life. No one ever has to know where it came from. No one cares about you, just about what you have."

She looked at the picture of the Chicago skyline on the wall of her office. "I loved Chicago. I was doing so well there. And then I fucked it all up by getting involved with him." She thought for a moment. "You're promising that you won't say where you got it?"

"That's right. No one needs to know. You give it to us, and we were never here, never met you. As I understand it, it's a video of someone in a compromising sexual situation. And there's nothing illegal about that. Do you know how it was taken? It was taken in a room at your hotel?"

"Yes, but I didn't even know it existed until Mario showed it to me. Apparently one of his men knew a maid who worked at the hotel and she placed the camera in the room."

"Where is it?"

"It's at home."

"Is there more than one copy?"

"No. It's on a memory card. I didn't make a copy."

"Here's what we are going to do. We're going to drive you to your house. You get it for us, and then we leave, and you can come back to work. And that's it."

Gina sighed. "I just want this whole part of my life over. I came here to start all over. It's not glamorous, but after what I've been through, I don't want glamorous. I just want to be left alone."

Gina lived in a small house in a blue-collar residential area about five minutes from the hotel. The house was modestly furnished but very dark inside, with heavy curtains and dark-wood, seventies-style paneling in the living room. Dean and Melinda waited in the small living room while Gina went to the back of the house and then returned with a small plastic case containing a memory card. Melinda took the card out of the case, placed it into the tablet she was carrying, and a video began running.

The camera had been positioned in a wall over the foot of a bed for a clear shot of two people having sex. A thin, redheaded woman was riding a man, and the man was moaning—"That's right, fuck me, baby, fuck me harder." The voice sounded very much like Senator McGraw, but there was no clue at all to the identity of the woman. Her face wasn't visible, only her back.

The three of them watched more of the thrusting and moaning for a couple more minutes, until the man's body jerked upwards and he groaned, "I'm coming, I'm coming, sweet Jesus, sweet Jesus—" As he cried out, he sat up and put his arms around the woman to kiss her and, as he did, he moved his head to the side of hers and looked up, straight into the camera. It was without a doubt, Senator Thomas McGraw *in flagrante delicto.*

"Holy shit!" said Dean.

"Yep," Gina agreed.

Melinda just giggled.

When Dean opened the door to leave the house, he was staring directly at a very large gun attached to a very large arm. "So good to see you again, Dean," said Mario, Jr. over the shoulder of Double P. We had such a good time in Vegas."

Inside, the three of them were forced to sit side by side on the living room sofa. "I have to say, Dean, I'm surprised that you're still playing detective—I gave you a pretty strong warning the last time we met. How're the ribs?"

"Fuck you!" Dean glared at him.

Mario chuckled. "I have to say, I'm very glad you're so persistent. You're a much better detective than me and Double P here. I have to thank you for that. Now I don't want any more violence, Dean, but that's up to you, really. We're leaving here with the video one way or another. You can give it to me, or Double P and me can have a little fun with these two very attractive sluts here and leave behind your dead bodies. Now there's pluses and minuses to both alternatives, but on balance it's kind of win-win for me and Double P here either way. Which one would you like Double P? Daddy's fuck toy... or little Yellow Fever here?"

"Whatever you want, boss."

"How is this Chinese chick in bed, Dean? I'm sure you know. It's such a tough choice. It would be sort of incestuous to fuck my daddy's mistress, but then again, that might make it more fun."

"Just shut the fuck up, Mario. I don't care if you are working for the FBI. You know you can't get away with killing law enforcement officers. Even you aren't stupid enough for that. Melinda, give him the video so they can get the fuck out of here."

"Dean, you are such an angry man, and still always so chivalrous. Trying to protect the virtue of women." Then Mario's demeanor became all business, "But you're right about one thing. The lay wouldn't be worth the hassle." He turned to Melinda, "OK, sweetie, turn it over."

She took the memory card out of her pocket and dropped into his hand.

Double P tied them up with electrical cords from the lamps in the living room.

"That should keep you long enough for us to get a good head start. Dean, I hope we're done with each other. I'm giving this to the people I work for. It's just business. Don't take it personally."

"Junior, it's always personal with me. Always."

It took about ten minutes to untangle themselves from the cords after Mario and Double P had gone. When they went outside, the tires on their rental car were punctured. Dean turned to Melinda. "The Senator is going to kick my ass. I really fucked up here."

Mark sat, openmouthed, in the lounge of the Four Seasons in Chicago as Dean debriefed him on the events in Alton. "I'm really fucked here, Dean. Do you realize that? I checked with my source before I came over here, and Mario has not checked in today with his handler. You say he has the video, and now I know how he came about getting it, and I can't say a word. You realize if all this comes out that I could go to jail?"

"There's no trail that leads anywhere near you, Mark. Melinda and I sure as hell aren't going to ever bring you into this."

Melinda patted Mark on the back. "You've committed far fewer crimes than your boss. As far as I'm concerned, the Director is an accomplice in Marion Aurelio's murder—if it was a murder."

"Oh, it was a murder all right," Mark snapped back at her. "She was suffocated. She had broken ribs and bruises on her face where her mouth and nose were covered, and there's evidence someone pried open the back door. No fingerprints, but get this—there were cookie crumbs all over her face. The cops are running the DNA on it. I'm betting it comes back positive on one morbidly obese convict."

"Look Mark," said Dean, "it's going to be kind of hard to justify having a guy working for the FBI that commits a murder. I don't think you have much to worry about. The Director has other tracks to cover."

Mark seemed unconvinced. "So, where do we go from here?"

"Well, Melinda and I are flying back to Jackson right now. The Senator is going to be there, and I have to break the bad news to him."

"Let me get this straight. You're saying that my face is definitely recognizable in the video?" The Senator was amazingly calm, Dean thought. He was much calmer that Dean would be in the same circumstance.

"Yes, sir," Dean admitted.

"And what about the other person?"

"The other person you can only see from the back—thin and redheaded. I looked pretty closely at the video, and I don't think you would be able to draw any other conclusion from it about her."

"OK, that's good."

"That's good? That's *good*?" TL was the red-faced one. "After the hits we've been taking, with the job creators' sex scandal, and your comments about the twin pillars of decadence our country was founded on, and now this... How can you be so calm?"

"Well, I am still way ahead in the delegate count."

"You are now, but the biggest states are coming up. Believe me, you're going to give up the lead. It's unlikely you're going to walk into the convention the presumptive nominee. This could very well be an open convention now," TL said

"TL, you always anticipate the worst-case scenario. I guess that's what I pay you for, but we need to be calm. It just looks like I had a little diversion with a woman other than my wife. This is not the end of the world."

TL didn't respond but got up and walked out of the room.

"There's one other problem, though," Dean warned.

"What's that?"

"My computer that was stolen. My notes on the computer indicate pretty specifically who the other person is in the video. The file was hidden and encrypted, but if a computer expert wanted to analyze the hard drive, it probably would be uncovered. If that happened, the video plus my notes would probably confirm the identity."

"And if the public knew who the other person in the video actually was," added the Senator, "they may not be quite so open-minded about it. Yes, that might change everything. So yes, I guess now you should refocus your investigation to finding your computer."

"I'm so sorry, Senator. I totally fucked up. I should have realized that we could have been followed and taken better precautions."

"What's done is done. You shouldn't apologize for being less devious than a sociopath." His words were understanding, but he didn't look happy. "Just put this behind you and find your computer."

TL walked back into the room and clicked on the TV on the wall. CNN filled the screen along with a blurred-out version of the hotel room video. The announcer was saying, "The website TMZ has acquired a video purporting to show Senator Thomas McGraw in a sexual encounter with a woman who does not appear to be his wife. We have reached out to the Senator's campaign for comment but have not heard back."

The Senator turned to TL. "Turn it off and draft a statement. Dean, I obviously have some work to do. Let me know when you've recovered your laptop."

Chapter 34

A few weeks later, when TL met with Senator Mc-Graw for his morning briefing, he seemed more downcast than usual. "Our campaign is in deep trouble. Your poll numbers are terrible since the sex video came out. Now it's not a matter of being able to win the nomination on the first ballot, it's about doing well enough in the final states to stay in this and be a player in what we hope will be an open convention. We need to do something to change the conversation."

"I agree," said the Senator. "We need to do something different. I've decided to go on the trade commission trip to China next week."

TL did a double take, which made the senator laugh. "I think that's a terrible idea. You're going to suspend a week of campaigning to go to China? You'll leave the entire campaign trail to your opponents if you're overseas."

"Not if I make news while I'm there. I'll say my opponents are engaging in politics as usual, while I'm out looking for our lost jobs and working on getting them back. Maybe we can do live video posts from China every day. Also, I'd like to visit a couple of orphanages if I can. My assistance program for parents with disabled children isn't getting much publicity, and this might be a chance to attach some little faces to it. "

TL thought for a moment. "I still don't think it's a good idea, but"—he threw up his hands—"I don't have a better one. I'll put together a briefing that we can release to the press."

"Put Melinda and Dean on the security detail. I'd like them to go with me. I think the whole search for Dean's computer has stalled, and it doesn't seem as if they have any hot leads. Melinda could be a big help; she could serve as my unofficial translator, and I know this adoption issue is important to her."

"What about your wife? Will she be OK with that?"

"Well, she's not speaking to me anyway after the video. She may suspect who the woman is in the video, and it's clearly not Melinda."

Senator McGraw, Dean, Melinda and TL sat in the lounge of the Four Seasons in Shenzhen, China. The Senator had motioned them away from the main group after the formal luncheon, and they'd adjourned for an impromptu meeting and afternoon cocktails.

"This trip has been a fucking waste of time," Senator McGraw said. "It's been nothing but a propaganda trip for the president. They've controlled everything we see. So far there's nothing I can use in the campaign."

"We can't even do the live broadcasts we were planning for, and they've blocked us from visiting any orphanages." agreed TL. The idea of the Senator sending back live video broadcasts from China never materialized because the government prevented them from having Internet access except through the American trade offices within the country.

The server brought their drinks, and when TL laid down a credit card, Melinda added a generous cash tip on top. The server seemed startled, and said, "Thank you very much," in heavily accented English.

Dean looked at his drink, a red, orange and yellow concoction described on the menu as a "Shenzhen Sunset." "Do sunsets in Shenzhen really look like this?"

"They do," said Melinda. "Do you know why? It's the pollution. The reflected light off the millions of particles of pollutants create a prism effect in the atmosphere. It's kind of ironic, but the worse the pollution, the more beautiful the sunset."

They were quiet for a moment, and then TL said, "Really? I wish we could see one."

Dean looked up. "Why not? Melinda, the server seems enamored with you. Call him over and ask if he can get us a car to take us on a little unofficial tour."

Melinda waved at the server as TL said, "You've got to be kidding. We can't just slip away. We'll be followed."

"Maybe, maybe not. What are they going to do to us?" asked McGraw, looking around the lounge.

"I don't see anyone in here keeping an eye on us. I think they forgot about us."

Melinda talked to the server in his language. He nodded as he walked away but returned a few minutes later with a wink in Melinda's direction.

"Let's go," she said. "His cousin has a car waiting for us at the workers' entrance."

The server led them back through the kitchen, down a set of stairs and through a long hallway. They came out a door into an alley in the back of the hotel and hopped into an old Chrysler minivan.

Melinda spoke to the driver, who nodded and accelerated so quickly that the team was pushed backwards in their seats as the van bounced through the alley and onto the main thoroughfare.

"I'm surprised the server would risk his job for this," TL said.

"You shouldn't be surprised what people will do for money," said Melinda. "He's getting a month's pay for arranging our little tour."

As the driver drove through the city, TL pulled out his cell phone and took video of the tall buildings in the financial district that were shrouded in haze. "Look at that," he said. "It's a clear day, and you can hardly see the buildings."

"You're all too young to remember," said the Senator, "but every major US city looked like that in the sixties. Cars parked on the street overnight would be covered in soot. On most hot summer days, you were warned not to leave you house if you had a respiratory ailment. Even in Cheyenne.

My party wants to gut the EPA, and if it does, our cities will look like this again."

They drove out of the city, where they could see the Maozhou River from the highway. The driver had the windows open in his unairconditioned van, and as they got closer to the river, the odor of rotten eggs, human waste, and pungent chemicals created a stench that burned their lungs with each breath. Dean coughed, Melinda gagged and covered her mouth with a tissue, and TL turned his camera phone on the Senator.

"We're approaching the Maozhou River now, one of the most polluted rivers in the world," the Senator said, picking up the narration of TL's little home movie without missing a beat. He pulled a handkerchief from his pocket, partially covering his face, for effect. "The stench is unbearable. It's the odor of human waste, open sewage, and toxic chemicals from manufacturing. But it's more than just a foul smell. It's the stench of a government that doesn't care about its people. American rivers used to have this stench, and some still do. We decided decades ago that we didn't want to live this way. Some of our leaders want to take us back a century or more. They want to undo the progress we made in cleaning up our environment."

The driver pulled onto a road that led from a factory parking lot down to the river. The party got out and walked along the river bed. All manner of garbage could be seen floating in the sludge-gray water.

"Look at that," Dean pointed to the horizon. Above the river, a beautiful mosaic orb floated, red, orange and yellow streamers shimmering on its surface, like an exhibit of living nuclear art. "The goddamned Shenzhen Sunset. Son-of-a-bitch."

As the Senator made an impromptu speech—TL's camera phone trained on him, and the sunset and the polluted river behind him—Dean wondered if anyone would ever see it. Or even if they did, would anyone care? Was the American dream really just to get the cheapest price on whatever was needed to maintain our culture of materialism? Then he remembered. The smartphones that every American used for hours each day to link themselves to each other and the world, the same ones they were using to take the videos of Senator McGraw, they were all made in this country. He shook his head as they piled back into the van and headed back to the hotel.

Chapter 35

Yao Chen quietly opened the door to the children's dormitory and crept to the back of the room to Jia's bunk. He looked at her sleeping face and felt a pang. The little girl had been through so much, and through all of it her spirit had not dampened. Her friend was sleeping next to her with her back the wall, so Yao brushed her hair back and whispered into her ear. "Jia, it's time to get up... We are going to visit your brothers today."

Instantly, her eyes opened and, without saying a word, she jumped out of the bunk and started getting dressed. "Don't you have any other clothes?" asked Yao.

She shook her head and continued to put on the gray smock and pants that she wore to work in the factory. As they walked the quarter mile to the train together, Yao fretted about leaving the factory for the morning. Although the line had been running smoothly the last few weeks, he didn't trust Wei Jinping. He was bright enough, but he seemed to lack common sense. There were weekly accidents, and although there had been no serious injuries, Yao knew Wei wouldn't be able to handle a crisis. Li Ming was aware of his absence, and was capable, but his indifference to safety issues on the factory floor provided Yao a different set of worries.

The cardiologist appointment, his excuse to get away from the factory and take Jia to see her brothers, was on time and brief—his EKG was fine, and the orphanage was just a short bus ride from the doctor's office. They stopped at a department store around the corner from the orphanage, and Yao picked up some food and necessities, for the boys. He noticed Jia browsing the racks. "Go ahead, pick out some clothing and toys. Something they'll like."

"Oh, thank you," said Jia. She bought them some items of clothing, including identical onesies, some puzzles, and each of them a hacky sack identical to her own.

Wei Jinping was jumpy. Although he had been apprenticing under Yao Chen for some time, he'd never been left alone before. During Yao's leave of absence, Li Ming had micro-managed everything he did, checking the machinery and monitoring the production floor both from his office and in person throughout the day. Both of his superiors were missing this morning and weren't expected back until the afternoon.

The main problem, Wei thought, was the heat. They were in the tenth day of a record heat wave, and the large fans that would remove the heat of the machines and the fumes from the chemical adhesives were groaning. Something was going on with the power, and the fans would slow down and then speed up again. As a result, there was more coughing and choking than usual on the floor today, more from the elderly supervisors than from the young workers. They would leave the floor for a minute or two to get a drink and splash their faces with water, but Wei was there to remind them to keep their absence brief. He was determined not to leave the floor today. This was his chance to prove himself with Li Ming. The old man couldn't keep it up forever, and he was in line to replace him. *Sooner rather than later*, he thought.

Wei Jinping's experience on the factory floor was sporadic. Since he wasn't fully trusted by Yao Chen, most of his work was at his desk, and he hadn't spent a whole day on the production floor since his first month on the job, when he was learning the assembly process. It was hotter than he remembered, and the fumes much more overwhelming. Just this week Li Ming had replaced the adhesives they had used for several years for a less expensive substitute. It would add a point to the factory margin, but its odor was much worse than the previous one. Wei suddenly felt his breakfast rice surging from his stomach into his throat, and he walked as fast as he could to the private washroom in the hallway. There was no way he could let anyone see him throw up.

Mao Shu was watching the television in his office when Yao and Jia walked in. He looked up but didn't speak, his attention absorbed by the news program on the flat screen mounted on the wall above his desk. The program was describing the visit of American politicians to Shenzhen. Then it showed a picture of US Presidential candidate Senator McGraw. The newscaster was describing him as an enemy of the Chinese people, a man who wanted to shut down American companies manufacturing in China, and they depicted his views as so extreme that he'd been censored by his own political party. Yao watched too. He'd been following the coverage of the American presidential election as reported by the Chinese government-controlled media. He could read between the lines. This McGraw, he was a champion of worker rights, not trying to shut down American manufacturing. He had spoken with American businessmen, and he knew the protections afforded workers in America far exceeded those in China. The news program said that the Americans were in Shenzhen today, but would be traveling to the US Consulate Office in Guangzhou before leaving for the United States.

The program ended, and Mao turned to the two of them. "Yao, I know we had discussed a visit, but you should have made an appointment. I'm much too busy today to spend any time with you at all." He glared at Jia, and Jia returned his stare without blinking.

"I apologize for not calling," said Yao, "but this opportunity came up at the last minute. I promise we will stay out of your way. We've brought a few things for the boys, and Jia would like to spend a few hours with her brothers."

"I'm afraid that this is out of the question. I have to leave for a meeting in an hour, and I refuse to have outsiders in the building while I am gone."

Yao could see that Jia's face was starting to turn red, and he was afraid she would have an outburst. He patted her on the head. "Then we will make the most of the hour, and I will make an appointment for us to come back soon and spend some more time."

"You must be out of here in one hour," demanded Mao, and he turned his attention back to the pile of papers on his desk.

Jia's brothers were sitting in a "playpen" in the back of a large communal room which contained primarily infants, but there was no playing in what was most definitely a pen. The boys were filthy. Feces and dried food covered them and the thin, plastic-covered mattress they were sitting on. Instead of playing with the boys, as Yao had envisioned, they spent the next hour bathing them and scrubbing their plastic bedding. But the boys were thrilled to see Jia, and they laughed and giggled as she bathed and dressed them. Yao could see that it was going to be difficult for Jia to leave the boys, and he made a promise to himself to bring her back soon.

"Yao Chen, can't you tell time!" the snaggle-toothed man screamed as he walked into the room. "You were supposed to be out of here twenty minutes ago. You need to leave immediately."

Yao looked up from the boys and walked directly to Mao, until he stood only inches from his face.

"I know that you pay off the inspector to look the other way, or possibly not even to come by and, so, I am going to come back here soon. I will most definitely not make an appointment. If I find these boys in this condition again, then I will personally pay the inspector to shut you down."

Mao started to speak, and Yao pushed him in the chest. "Don't mess with me. I have connections too, and I will pay whatever it takes to shut you down if I have to." Without turning to look at her, he said, "Jia, let's go."

The little girl had never seen the kindly older man angry before, and it scared her. So even though she was reluctant to leave, she hugged and kissed the boys and let Yao pull her away. They walked to the train together, neither of them speaking for a long time. When Yao finally looked down at her, she stared directly into his eyes. "Are you really going to have the orphanage shut down? Then my brothers will have nowhere to go."

"Don't worry, Jia. I was just trying to scare him. You and I will pay a visit every week to clean up your brothers and make sure he is taking better care of them." He patted her on the head as the train rumbled north.

Wei knelt in front of the toilet and heaved, the nausea coming in waves. He'd thrown up his meager breakfast minutes ago, and now just drops of yellow bile dripped from his mouth with each retch. Finally, as the gagging stopped, Wei wiped his dripping eyes and splashed water on his face.

He waited a few minutes to make sure the heaving had subsided. He couldn't risk anyone seeing how it had affected him. He'd been in and out of the production area throughout the day. There was something in the air that wasn't right, and finally on his last trip, nausea had overtaken him. Carefully, he walked back to the factory floor and opened the door that separated manufacturing from the offices.

What he didn't hear disturbed him. He noticed right away the silence of the fans. The huge rooftop fans usually hummed continuously, and, like the concussion section of a strange factory symphony, they provided the continuous bass notes to the higher registers of the machinery. He looked to the ceiling. None of the fans were running.

Seeking out the main production supervisor, a heavy-set woman in her fifties, he could see she wasn't at her usual post, an elevated podium from which she could observe the entire floor at once. He jumped up the steps to the podium and saw her black rubber-soled shoes jutting out from beneath the table next to the podium. Kneeling down, he lifted her head, slapped her face sharply and shook her. "Wake up," he repeated several times, but he could see that she was unconscious and white foam was leaking from her tightly closed lips. He stood up to look for the other supervisors who were assigned posts in a geometric pattern on the floor. None of them were standing; no doubt they had also collapsed at their stations.

His brain was trying to process what he was seeing, but suddenly he felt foggy, and each inhalation brought a terrible burn, as if he were being stabbed in the chest each time he took a breath. His thoughts were coming in confusing images without words, and he was no longer sure of exactly where he was. Looking toward the far corner of the factory now, he thought he was in a game of dominoes. The biggest damned domino board he'd ever seen. Small children were standing on the huge domino board, and something knocked down the child at the far corner and, in turn, more children fell, one by one, row by row, until the huge domino board was filled with toppled dominos—the domino children now laying stiffly at all angles on the factory floor. *How do you even score that?* was the last thought his poisoned brain processed before he, too, collapsed into a writhing, foaming lump on the concrete floor of Hua Jiaju Manufacturing Company.

The factory was quiet when Yao and Jia walked up to the entrance. The familiar buzz of the fans and the clamor of high-pitched machinery was missing. Yao knew instinctively that something was wrong, so he took Jia to his office.

"Jia, stay here. I have to meet with Li Ming. I will be back in a little while—until then, do not leave my office. Do you understand?"

Jia could see the concern in his face. "Yes, I understand, but what's wrong?"

"I don't know."

Jia nodded, and Yao headed down the hall to Li Meng's office. He knocked twice on Li Meng's closed door and then entered. "Li, what's happening with the production? Do we have a power outage?"

Li didn't answer. He was sitting behind his desk, staring at his computer screen, his face frozen.

"Li, what is it?" When Li still did not answer or even look up from his computer, Yao walked behind him and looked at the screen. A frozen video showing the manufacturing floor at the beginning of the production day filled the screen. Yao leaned over to click on the video, and Li grabbed his hand.

"No, do not look at this." Li spoke as if in a trance. "The production floor... it's poisoned. It was the new adhesive. They're all dead... all of them. Everyone one of them... all dead. It must be erased. It must be erased now."

Yao forced the mouse from Li's hand and knocked it off the desk. Emerging from his trance now, Li raised himself from his chair and moved fast, grabbing Yao by the throat, forcing him to his knees. Yao could feel himself choking, weakening as his windpipe closed. Closing his hand into a fist, he thrust as hard as he could into Li's crotch. Li grunted in pain and let go of Yao's throat, falling to the floor, moaning as his hands grasped his abdomen. Yao, gasping for air, looked to the desk and spied the heavy acrylic paperweight commemorating the twenty-fifth anniversary of Pretty Flower Manufacturing. He lifted it from the desk and, with all his force, brought it down on the top of Li's head. Li crumpled to the floor, a red gash on the crown of his head pumping blood with each breath. He would not be getting up again.

Yao sat in Li's chair and caught his breath be-fore clicking on the video. The video clip showed a normal start to the work day. He could see that Wei was on the floor, monitoring production. He fast-forwarded until he saw some of the supervi-sors throwing up and leaving the floor, Wei exhort-ing them to get back on the job. Then he saw Wei also leave the floor for several minutes. While Wei was gone, Yao noticed the lead supervisor collapse at the elevated podium moments before Wei re-turned. Then he watched as Wei found her body, and as the young workers toppled one by one, with Wei finally following suit.

Shocked by the images, Yao decided he had to know for sure what had happened. He got up and walked down the hall, covering his mouth with a handkerchief, and opened the production door. He made several trips in and out, hold-ing his breath for the time he was on the floor. Each trip left him breathless and wheezing, and he would pause to take a few deep breaths before he returned. He didn't stop until he confirmed there were no survivors to this horrific event. On his last trip, he found the body of Jia's friend, Juan Fu. Although the telltale white foam coated her mouth, her eyes were open and her face re-laxed; she didn't look as if her last moments were painful. In her arms was her precious China doll. He touched her face and gently closed her eyelids, took the doll from her arms, and walked off the production floor. Yao had seen all that he needed to see. There was nothing more that could be done here.

As he stood in the hallway, breathing heavily, he knew what he needed to do. It wouldn't be easy. It probably wouldn't work, but he had to try. He made a mental list of the steps required, and then remembered Jia. Opening the door to his office, he saw that Jia was still sitting at his desk drawing pictures on copy paper. "Jia, I'm almost done. Then we are going on another trip together. Just another few minutes. Stay here, and I will be back to get you." Jia nodded but did not look up from her work.

Back in Li's office, he saw that Li was still on the floor, breathing but not conscious. Yao opened the desk drawer and found the stack of blank memory cards Li used to store the production videos, He put one in the computer, copied the video of the day, and then clicked on the webcam and pressed record.

"My name is Yao Chen, I am the production manager at Hua Jiaju Manufacturing Company. This is my confession..."

Yao opened the door to his office and looked at the little girl drawing pictures behind his desk. "Jia, we are going to take another little trip today. I will explain to you on the way, but we must hurry."

Yao walked so quickly that Jia nearly ran the quarter mile to the station. He bought tickets and they boarded the train that would take them to the station close to the US Consulate Office in Guangzhou. Yao didn't know if they would be able to find Senator McGraw there, but, somehow, he'd convinced himself that the burly American who was so hated by his government would help them. If not, maybe someone at the consulate would grant them asylum. He didn't care about himself, but how could they turn down a little girl?

Suddenly Yao remembered the doll. He pulled it from his bag and handed it to Jia. "This is Juan Fu's doll," she said and wrinkled her forehead. "Where did you get it?"

Yao looked out the window. He seemed to be in another place and said softly, "I saw her right before we left. I told her we were going on a trip, and she said to give this to you for good luck."

"She told me it was lost. I'm glad she found it, but it was her good luck charm. Why would she give it to me?"

"I told her you were going on a *long* trip. And she said that you needed it more, and that you should have it."

"I wish I could have seen her before we left. Where are we going? Will we be gone long?"

"We are going to see an American. I'm going to ask him if he will take you and your brothers to America."

"America?" She remembered the videos she saw in the children's barracks. "Can I see Big Bird?"

Chapter 36

It was the last day of their trip. The Americans toured two factories in Shenzhen, and then traveled to the US Trade Consulate in Guangzhou. As they exited their cars just inside the gate at the consulate, Dean noticed an old man and a little girl standing just outside the wrought-iron fence. The old man seemed to recognize Senator McGraw, shouted his name and then other words in Chinese. Dean and the Senator walked to the gate, and the man put his hand through the railing and continued to shout in Chinese. At the same time, two policemen jumped out of a car in front of the entrance. One grabbed the little girl and the other put his arms around the old man, who had a tight grip on the metal railing. The policeman pulled at the old man, but he held on tenaciously and extended his other fist toward the Senator. Dean stepped forward to grab hold of the man's hand just as the policeman pried his fingers lose from the railing. They dragged him away, put him and the little girl into the car, and sped away.

"What was that about? What was he saying?" The Senator looked for Melinda, but she hadn't seen the ruckus. She and TL were talking as they walked toward the main entrance to the consulate building, out of earshot.

After a short meeting inside, a joint press conference was held where the American Ambassador and his Chinese counterpart spouted platitudes about improving trade relations. The Senator, meanwhile, stewed in the back of the room. Then the entourage was driven to the airport and boarded a plane back to the states. The dignitaries sat in front, and Melinda and Dean continued to the back of the plane.

"The Senator said there was some kind of commotion at the front gate?" Melinda asked when they were settled in their seats.

"Yeah, there was an elderly man and a little girl at the gate. The old man was calling for the Senator, and then some policeman grabbed them and took them away." Dean opened his palm. "The man slipped me this. I didn't want to draw attention at the consulate. I thought I'd wait to look at it when we were out of the country. Let's see what we have here…"

He took his laptop out of his bag and put the memory card in it. There were two files on the card, and he clicked twice on the first one. The elderly gentleman was sitting at a desk in an office. He was speaking in Chinese, so Melinda quietly translated to Dean as they watched the video. "My name is Yao Chen and I am the Production Manager for Hua JiaJu Manufacturing. This is my confession and acceptance of responsibility for the tragedy that happened in our factory."

He explained that the financial pressures to be cost-competitive with factories in other countries had required his company to cut costs, and that meant he had to comply with the demands from his superiors to eliminate safety controls on the factory floor. He then outlined the day on which he'd returned from his medical leave and discovered that the factory was now employing dozens of children from the local orphanage as laborers. Finally, he explained that the malfunction of the ventilation system had resulted in the death of those children from the poisonous fumes from the adhesives used in the process, ending with: "I am ashamed and humiliated about what you are going to see. I have stolen this video from the cameras used to monitor the production floor, and I hope to be able to get this video to Senator Mc-Graw, who could take it to America so that others can see what is happening here."

Dean wondered how he even knew who the Senator was, but Yao's tale continued. He told the story of Jia and her twin brothers, and that he was going to try to deliver her to the American Consulate in Guangzhou. "I don't care what happens to me, but her bravery needs to be recognized by the world."

When he was finished, Dean and Melinda looked at each other. "Let's play the other file," he urged.

The video file began with the camera scanning the production floor and, except for the fact that children were the production workers, it seemed routine. Dean fast-forwarded to the part where the workers started collapsing like dominoes and lay lifeless on the floor. The file was hi-def, so Dean was able to zoom in to see that some of the children were writhing in convulsions and foaming at the mouth. When the video ended, neither Dean nor Melinda could speak. Dean pulled Melinda close, putting his cheek on hers, and they could feel the moisture of their mutual tears. "Let's show this to the Senator," Dean whispered.

At the front of the plane, Dean explained how they had come into possession of the file, and Melinda and Dean watched the Senator's face as he viewed the videos, Melinda again translating. His expression registered curiosity, then concentration, and finally horror.

After the second video played, the Senator said nothing but looked out the window of the plane for a minute, composing himself. When he turned back to them, Dean saw a somber side he'd never seen before in the jovial man. "As soon as we land, I'll call the President. I'll tell him we've got something so explosive that I won't put it in anyone's hands but his."

Chapter 37

SENATOR McGraw stood in the Rose Garden, just off the Oval Office, and waited for the President. It was a beautiful late spring day in DC, and the Senator imagined what it would be like to live in this place, with all of its history, and wondered if he would be worthy of the responsibility. The President's Chief of Staff opened the door. "Senator McGraw, the President is ready for you now."

The President was standing and was attended by his Chief of Staff, the Secretary of State, and a person the Senator didn't recognize. He shook the Senator's hand and said, "Senator McGraw, I've known you for a long time, so when you called and said you had an urgent matter to discuss with me about your trip to China, I took you at your word. I requested that Secretary Stephens join us, and, as you requested, a state department translator."

"I know you're very busy, Mr. President, so I'll get right to the point. I obtained a disturbing video while I was in China. It was passed to one of my security detail by a local Chinese man on our last day in Guangzhou, and it's something you need to see. Can you get us a computer so that we can view it together?"

The President's Chief of Staff brought in a laptop and McGraw produced the memory card. The translator narrated as Melinda had on the plane. When the video was finished, the President got up and walked to the window of the Oval Office. No one said anything for a long time, and then the President returned and sat down. "Thank you, Senator McGraw, for bringing this to my attention. I concur that this is very disturbing. It also is a very sensitive matter. Who else knows about the video?"

"Just my Chief of Staff, and the two members of my security detail who brought it to me. No one else."

"Good. We need to keep it that way. I'm so glad that Secretary Stevens is with us. I'm directing that the process of negotiating the release of the man in the video and the little girl and her brothers begin right now. This may take some time, but I'm making it a high priority. Can you take this on, Mr. Secretary?"

"Of course, Mr. President."

"And we will need to keep the memory card."

"I understand," said the Senator.

The President stood. "Thank you again, Senator. I'll be in touch when we have something to report. And once again, I want to emphasize that nothing about this is to be distributed to anyone outside of this room. It would impede negotiations, or maybe even result in the termination of *any* negotiations."

"Yes, I understand, Mr. President," said the Senator. "You have my word."

The President nodded to his Chief of Staff, who ushered McGraw to the door.

"Senator Stevens," urged the President, "please stay. There are couple other items we need to discuss."

A week later the Senator walked into TL's office. "I just got off the phone with the President's Chief of Staff. He's made a deal to bring Yao and the little girl Jia and her brothers to the United States."

"Well," TL answered, "that was faster than I expected."

"However, there's a major condition. The video must never be disclosed or distributed, and there's a gag order on anyone who has seen or heard of it."

TL nodded. "How can they fucking enforce something like that?"

"The President has classified the video for national security reasons. Any disclosure of its contents violates federal law. Any of us could be subject to arrest and imprisonment if we talk so, as much as I share your reaction, right now there isn't much we can do about it."

"But this was going to be the major PR coup that our campaign so badly needs. Now we just have you spouting off about lost American jobs. It would mean a lot more with this video on the news every day. And it would guarantee support for your plan to provide assistance to families of children with disabilities."

"I know. But the President's not going to give me anything that will help our campaign—we knew that going in. This is a larger issue than just the little girl and her brothers, but we're not going to be able to exploit it until after the election. What's doable now is that we're going to be able to get them out of the country. Jia and her brothers will have a better life. Let's focus on that." The Senator paused. "How are we coming with the campaign ad from the video showing the pollution we saw in Shenzhen? I think that could be an amazing spot. I still believe hammering on foreign jobs is what separates us from the rest of the candidates."

TL nodded. "I'll check and see how they're doing ..."

"And call Dean and Melinda and make sure they're aware of the gag order," McGraw said as TL walked out the door.

Chapter 38

Tatiana Petrov was waiting impatiently in the long morning coffee line at the mini-mart on Highway 89 in Jackson Hole, her arms cramped from holding two large boxes. Amber was out of diapers again for the twins, and Daryl wasn't going to make his monthly trip to the Costco in Idaho Falls for supplies for another week. She watched as an agitated young woman ran from the back of the store, pushed open the door, and chased after a black SUV as it pulled onto the highway, yelling and waving and then finally walking slowly back to the storefront, her head down in defeat. She was wearing a cocktail dress and spiked heels at eight in the morning. Carrying her sack of diapers, Tatiana walked over to the bench on which the young woman was sitting, staring off into space as a tear dripped down her face, smearing her heavy eye makeup.

Tatiana spoke to her in Russian. "Are you one of Boris's girls?"

The girl looked up in shock. "What?"

"I was one of his girls too. I can help you if you want."

Dean, Melinda and Mark were in Jackson on the last ski weekend before the resort closed for the season. Dean had taken a bad spill on the last run, and now they were sitting in the lobby of the Four Seasons nursing lattes.

"Spring skiing sucks here," Dean complained. "Nothing but ice. Colorado is much better."

"Oh, is poor Dean souring on his beloved Jackson Hole?" said Melinda. "I thought this was your paradise."

"It's not that." Mark laughed. "He's just pissed off because he sucks as a snow boarder."

Dean didn't say anything, just swallowed the last few drops of his latte and pushed the cup to the bartender. He thought how much he'd love to have a double shot of Wild Turkey, but instead said, "Another, please."

"Now that I think about it, it probably isn't that he sucks as a snow boarder," Mark said. "He's always sucked at it, but he still likes doing it." He shook his head. "No, it's because this whole case has stalled. The Russian guy who took his computer has disappeared, and there's not a trace of where he went. Not a word. And the laptop hasn't turned up either."

Dean looked up. "It doesn't make any fucking sense. Boris must have it—and if he has it, he didn't locate the memo."

"Possibly... but not likely," said Mark. "You did attempt to hide it, but I would assume the whole purpose in stealing it was for your data. He would have had someone do a data search who knows something about hidden files and encryption. Any expert would have found it. He's probably waiting for the right time to use it. Or maybe he already is using it and we just don't know." He took another sip of his latte. "Maybe this will cheer you up, Dean. Director Fanning was so pissed at Mario leaking the video of the Senator that he's recommending Mario, Jr.'s charges not be reduced. Mario is supposed to report next week, and then he'll be arraigned, and the charges will be formalized."

"And what about Double P?"

"Double P has disappeared. They didn't charge him with Mrs. Aurelio's murder because they thought he would report back for sentencing, and they didn't want it to come out that he was working for the FBI. But he skipped anyway."

"Of course he did," Dean said. "As a repeat violent offender, he's looking at a life sentence. Hard to believe they didn't realize he would skip if he didn't get a reduction. The whole system is fucked up." His pocket buzzed, and he pulled his phone out and looked at the screen. "It's Daryl—says I should call him... it's urgent."

After dropping Mark at the airport for his return flight to Chicago, Melinda and Dean drove to Daryl's home. Daryl ushered them into the living room, where Amber sat breastfeeding one of the twins while the other slept in a crib set up in the corner. "Hey, Dean. I'd get up and hug you, but as you can see, I'm sort of occupied right now."

"Quite all right." Dean walked over and kissed her on the cheek. "How are the babies doing?"

"Oh, they're doing great, but I'll be a lot happier when they can do more than eat, sleep, and crap."

Dean turned to the small young woman sitting on the couch beside Amber and gave her a hug. "Tatiana, it's great to see you again. You look fantastic."

She smiled. "So do you." She looked past Dean. "Hello, Melinda, we met at the meeting here a few months ago, right?"

"Yes, we did."

Daryl turned to Dean and nodded to a young woman sitting next to Tatiana. "This is Tatiana's friend Lana—Svetlana, actually, but she goes by Lana. They met at the gas station out on highway 89. The Russian guys who were taking her and some other girls to the airport for their flight back to L.A. stopped for gas and then left without her when she was in the restroom. Tatiana saw her, realized she didn't speak English, and asked if she could help, and well—she brought her home. But she has quite a story to tell, and Tatiana and I thought you should hear it."

"She doesn't speak much English, Dean. I will translate for you." Tatiana spoke a few words to the girl and the girl began to tell her story, slowly at first and then faster.

As Lana spoke, Dean observed that she was a bit taller than Tatiana, but Tatiana was unusually petite. She was thin with a pale, flawless complexion, jet-black hair and big, round, dark eyes. The story of how she came to America was eerily similar to the one Tatiana had told the year before. There were many young Russian girls like her in California, recruited to come to America for modeling jobs, and housed at a couple of locations around Los Angeles. They were flown by private jet weekly to "modeling jobs" all over the country. There was very little actual modeling being done, unless you consider modeling to be rich, middle-aged men taking pictures of the girls, getting high and performing at the orgies that were held at their multi-million-dollar mansions.

When she paused, Dean asked, "So where was the party located in Jackson?"

Daryl responded, "At Ronald Flag's home."

"No, shit?"

"Yes," said Daryl. "According to Lana, he has parties every month, sometimes more often. Whenever he's in town, there's a party."

Dean thought for a moment. "OK, so here's what we're going to do. Tatiana, could you have her write down her whole story, in her own handwriting. It's not a problem that it's in Russian. Make sure she includes everything she can remember about how she came to America, the names of everyone involved, and make sure she includes all the details about the parties at Flag's house. Then, after she writes it all down, you can put together a separate English translation. I'll take all this to Senator McGraw, and he can arrange about handling this with the FBI. Meanwhile, don't let her go outside of this house. Ask her if she ever met Boris Birkov, or Ivan Chersky."

"I already asked her that. Ivan was the driver for one of the parties. She's never seen Boris—I showed her a picture of him—but she heard some of the men talk to him. Some, but not all the people that took care of the girls in California were Russian. And the men who picked her up at the Jackson airport were Russian, and they spoke to Boris on the phone when they picked up the girls."

"Make sure she puts all those details in her report too." Dean turned to Lana. "I want to apologize about how you have been treated in our country. We were able to help Tatiana, and I give you my word, we'll help you too."

Two days later Dean sat at Charles's home in Jackson while Senator McGraw read Tatiana's translation of Svetlana's account. When he was done reading it, he tapped his fingers on the table and didn't speak for a moment. "This is very disturbing, Dean. Frankly it's a little hard to believe. Flag is an asshole, but to be involved in this? Do you think there's any chance she's making this up?"

"Respectfully, Senator, I'm not sure how you can ask that question. There are so many similarities between her story and Tatiana's experience."

"Yes, that's my point. Isn't it a little too similar? Could she and Tatiana have cooked this story up?"

Dean was astounded at what he was hearing, and even *he* was surprised at how his voice boomed when he spoke: "Cooked what up? Why would they cook something like this up?"

"Well, revenge for one thing. After all, Boris is out of jail. I'm considering what this means, Dean, and I don't appreciate you raising your voice."

Dean tried to calm down. "Are you going to take this to the FBI?"

"I need to process it before I can decide how to proceed."

"Process what?" Dean was shouting again. "We have one of the richest men in the world molesting children. What the fuck are you processing?"

The Senator spoke evenly but forcefully. "I appreciate your passion, Dean. As I said, this information is disturbing, and I'll take it under advisement. Now, I've been keeping former Director Vorhies waiting for a meeting."

Dean walked to the door and grabbed the handle so hard his knuckles turned white. "I thought you were one of the good guys," he said as he walked out.

Melinda was waiting for him when he returned to his home south of Jackson. "How'd it go?"

"The Senator is 'taking it under advisement.' He said maybe Tatiana cooked it up... whatever that fucking means."

"He's probably just being cautious. It doesn't mean he's going to bury it."

"He'd better not." Dean was pacing, and Melinda had never seen him like this. He stopped and stood by the window for a long while. "I've got to get out of here. Let's go back to Chicago and see if we can track down that little fuck Mario before they take him back to jail. I wouldn't be surprised if he knows something about this."

Chapter 39

WHEN they arrived at Dean's apartment in Chicago, Dean was exhausted but still fuming about his meeting with Senator McGraw. Melinda led him into the bedroom. "Dean, you need to calm down. You're going to have a stroke or something. Let me give you a massage."

Reluctantly he agreed and removed his clothes and lay face down on the bed. "You just think you can take my mind off all of this with sex."

"Don't challenge me... I'm sure I could distract you with sex if I really wanted to, but I really just want to give you give you a massage. To help you to relax." She took her elbow and dug it into a place in Dean's shoulder blade that made him yelp in pain.

"So yes... this is going to hurt, but you will feel a lot better when I'm done." She was right. For the next hour she used her elbows, fists and fingers to release the anger that was paralyzing the muscles in his shoulders, back and legs, and then he fell into a deep sleep. When he awoke, he turned over and found Melinda asleep beside him. He looked at her voluptuous body, the curve of her breasts, her smooth and creamy white skin, and he did feel the sexual desire that he always felt when he looked at her naked. But there was more, something that he hadn't felt for a long time.

She opened her eyes and saw him staring at her. "What." Dean didn't say anything.

"What's wrong?'

Dean hesitated. "I'm falling in love with you."

"It's just the massage. It's the endorphins talking."

"I haven't felt this way since—"

She sat up and kissed him softly. "You are so sweet." She got up and put on a robe. "I'm going to get something to eat. Can I get you something?"

When Dean awoke, he wasn't sure where he was. He looked at the clock on the nightstand—the one that he and Sara had bought on their honeymoon in Barbados—and he remembered he was back in his Chicago apartment, with Melinda. It was 3:15 AM. He got up and walked barefoot through the darkened hallway, into the living room. There were no lights on, but he could see by the light of the computer screen that Melinda was seated with her back to him at the dining room table at the end of the room, typing. The rhythmic clicking of Melinda's fingers on the keyboard punctuated the low bass register of the furnace hum, and Dean stood for a moment listening to this after-midnight duet. Remembering their conversation earlier in the evening, he walked softly up behind her, his barefoot steps as quiet as a lynx on the plush carpeting, intending to put his arms around her, but he suddenly felt a strange force pulling at him, and he abruptly stopped. She was typing an email fast, concentrating as her fingers tapped rapidly on the keyboard, and she didn't sense that he was behind her. Dean could read the text on the illuminated screen, but he didn't recognize the email address.

> *Hi, Ron, I don't know where Lana is. McGraw has moved her to a safe house. Will try to find out where. Dean says he is in love with me. Can you believe that? Can't wait till this is over. Maybe we can spend a week in Jamaica. Remember last year? Don't worry, he doesn't suspect anything—*

Dean froze. Then he turned around and walked quietly back to the bedroom. He lay awake, shocked and numb. An hour later, when Melinda returned to bed, he took her roughly from behind, and deposited all of his frustration, hurt, and betrayal deep within her.

"Melinda, wake up." Dean shook her. "I've been on the phone with Doris."

Melinda wiped the sleep out of her eyes. "Doris? What does she want?"

"She found a box with some of Mario's stuff. The box contained a flash drive of another sex video of the Senator and Charles, and she says this one is very clear and even more explicit than the other one."

She was wide awake now. "Are we going to go pick it up?"

"No. She's really spooked after what happened to her mother, and she knows that Double P is still out there. She wouldn't tell me where she is. She's going to text me a location in an hour or so where she'll drop off the flash drive and we'll go pick it up. Get dressed."

Melinda and Dean were sitting in the coffee shop, throwing back their third espressos, when the text came in. The location where Doris had dropped the flash drive was about thirty minutes from where they sat.

"We've got the address, let's go," Dean said.

On the way, they drove by a McDonald's, and Melinda grabbed his arm. "I'm sorry, I need to use to the restroom. Can you stop?"

"Of course," said Dean.

When she returned, she had a strained look on her face. "Everything OK? Dean asked.

"This is embarrassing. But can we make a side trip back to your apartment? My period just started."

"Sure, no problem. You don't need to be embarrassed."

"And would you mind making a stop at a pharmacy? I also need some feminine supplies."

"Sure."

So far, so good, Dean thought. He figured he was playing his role perfectly, and so was she. He waited patiently in the car while she went up to his apartment, and again at the Walgreens on the way to the drop-off point. When she got in the car from the Walgreens, he said. "Got everything?"

"Yes, thank you."

"Need anything else?"

"No, I'm good."

"You don't look so good. Are you feeling OK?"

"I'm feeling fine, why are you acting like an asshole?"

"I'm sorry, Melinda, you're right. You've been so great throughout this whole investigation. I can't imagine it would have gone this well without you," he said, giving her the sincerest look he could muster.

Dean pulled in slowly to the drop-off point, a convenience store on the south side of Chicago, and parked across the street.

"Are you sure this is the place? I'm surprised she would want to drop something off in this neighborhood if she was concerned about her safety," Melinda said.

"I'm not that surprised. Do you see what I see?" Dean asked.

"What?"

"Those drab cars. FBI drone cars. They got here before us."

At that moment, Mark Jeffrey and another agent came out the front of the convenience store with Mario Rosati, Jr. in handcuffs.

"What—" Melinda affected confusion.

Dean stared at her, looking straight into her indigo eyes. "Oh, I think you know, Melinda. Didn't you tip Mario off in the restroom at the coffee shop, and then use the tampon trick to give him enough time to get here first?"

"What are you saying, Dean? That I'm somehow working with Mario, Jr.?"

"Not Mario, Jr. But Flag. It's over, Melinda. I'm a little slow on the uptake… but I finally figured it out."

"I can't believe you would think I'm working with the other side." She raised her voice. "Last night you said you loved me. And now you think I'm working with Flag?"

"Wow"—Dean had to laugh—"you're really good. I probably would believe you if I hadn't caught you red-handed." He turned away, unable to look at her. "Last night I saw the email you were typing to him."

Melinda stared at him. "There's no second video?"

"No."

"You just made it up… thinking I would flush out Mario, Jr. for you?" She slumped low in the car seat. "Well played."

"I can't believe I fell for you. The oldest ruse in the book, right? I really thought we had something together."

"We did, Dean. I wasn't fucking you just to get the info. I'm sure you would have given it to me anyway. I'm genuinely attracted to you, and you're great in the sack. But you are so fucking serious. You need to lighten up."

Dean looked at her in disgust. "You know your whole career is over now."

She laughed. "No, Dean. My career is just starting. I think I'm going to do very well in the Flag organization. Much better than trying to succeed with the Wyoming State Police. At least Flag actually respects me as more than a piece of ass. There's nothing the Senator or state police can do to me. Our whole investigation is borderline illegal, and it would create a ruckus the Senator can't afford."

Dean contemplated the casual way she took the news of being caught. Twenty-four hours earlier, he'd thought he was falling in love with her. And now all he saw was a selfish, amoral young woman who would do anything for money.

"Get out of my car."

"Just take me back to your apartment so I can get my things, and I'll be out of your hair."

"I said, get out of my car."

"You can't put me out in this neighborhood. What happens if I'm attacked?"

"Then I would feel sorry for the guys who tried to take you on. You're armed. And with a lot more than the Glock you're carrying. I'm sure you can take care of yourself. If you feel it's not safe, call Flag or the Chicago PD. I'm not spending another second of my life with you. Now get the fuck out of my car."

Chapter 40

Dean met Mark that evening at Kingston Mines on Chicago's northside. Mark was accompanied by a thin, auburn-haired young woman with a face full of freckles. "Dean, this is Colleen O'Hara. I hope you don't mind that I brought her along. You can speak freely—she's the person who has been helping us out with information."

"It's great to finally meet you, Colleen."

"So, this is the great Dean Wister I've heard so much about. I have to say, I was expecting someone much tougher looking. You don't look nearly as dangerous as your reputation." She touched his arm. "I'm really sorry about Melinda. Mark filled me in. Betrayal is tough."

"I'm glad I found out before she could do any more damage to the investigation."

"Or to you," said Mark.

Despite Mark's reassurance, Dean didn't feel comfortable discussing the case in front of Colleen. Mark and Colleen drank beer, while Dean stuck to club soda. As they listened to retro Chicago blues, Colleen told stories about growing up in the tough "Back of the Yards" neighborhood in

Chicago. Mark was the child of Lincoln Park academics, and Dean found it amusing that he was involved with a tough, south side Irish girl. At the end of the evening, they went back to Dean's apartment and finished off a large deep-dish pizza they picked up along the way.

"Well, I've got to call it a night," said Colleen. "I have to shop for wedding dresses tomorrow morning."

"Damn, Mark. This is how you tell me? Congratulations, guys."

Colleen laughed. "No, no. Not for me. It's for my sister. I'm in her wedding."

"Oh, sorry," Dean mumbled.

Colleen chuckled while Mark and Dean squirmed. Mark started to get up to follow Colleen out the door, but she stopped him. "No, you stay here. I know you guys need to discuss the case, and I know Dean wasn't comfortable talking about it in front of me. I don't blame him after what he's just been through with his partner." She smiled at them, said goodnight, and let herself out.

"Mark, she's great... Is this serious or are you just playing her for info?"

"I'm not just playing her for info, and I can't tell you how serious it is. But I do know one thing; you look really down. I know the Melinda thing is a shock, but you didn't know her that long, and to tell you the truth, I never thought she was that nice. I think you were just under the spell of her sex appeal."

Dean offered a half smile. "I *was* under her spell, wasn't I?" He shrugged. "I know she was a rebound thing." The truth was, since he'd discovered Melinda's betrayal, he wasn't feeling broken-hearted, more like guilty. He hadn't thought of Sara since he'd become intimate with Melinda. He wondered if that as how it was going to be—when he was in a relationship, would Sara disappear? Maybe forever? He wasn't sure any relationship would be worth that amount of pain.

"But she was good for one thing," Mark said. "She got you off the booze. Are you going to be able to keep your drinking under control after this? You know it was out of control there for a while."

"Yeah, I know it was. Don't worry, I've got it—it wasn't so much Melinda that got me off the booze, it was being back on the job. I need to work." Dean grabbed a couple of bottles of water from the fridge and handed one to Mark. "We have another issue. I called TL this afternoon and briefed him on the Melinda problem. That wasn't a pleasant conversation, as you can imagine, but he told me something that is fucking unbelievable. The Chinese have reneged on the deal. They're sending the girl, Jia Lin, and her brothers to the US, but they aren't sending Yao Chen. They've closed the factory and arrested the officers of the company, including Yao. There's a rumor that he's going to be executed along with the other corporate officers."

"But he was the whistleblower. The good guy!"

Dean nodded. "The Senator still isn't doing anything about Flag and his underage sex parties. The deal he made with the president? It resulted in this. I know that video is classified, but if I had a copy, I'd find a way to get it released."

They both were quiet for a moment, then Mark asked, "When you played it for McGraw on the plane, you played it from your computer?"

"Yes, and then I took the memory card out and gave it to McGraw. I didn't make a copy."

"Let me see your computer."

"Help yourself... it's on the desk. But I know I didn't make a copy."

"Maybe you didn't. Maybe you did." Mark went to the laptop and started surfing through Dean's file manager. A half minute and three key strokes later, Yao Chen was on the screen, confessing to his crimes.

"What the fuck—"

"I noticed when you played a video for me a couple of weeks ago, you clicked twice, on download first and then on play. So, as a matter of habit, you downloaded it first before you played it. It was still in your download folder along with... oh, about a thousand porn videos, so you might want to do something about that."

"I haven't been dating, what can I say? Save Yao Chen's confession to a memory card, I'll set up a fake email address and send it to Larry Bloom."

"You've come a long way in tech sabotage, Dean, but we need to plan for the investigation of the leak. I expect they'll be questioning everyone in the campaign, and will be looking at your laptop too. So I'll take your computer and wipe any traces of the downloaded video. You're on the right track with the email, too, but we'll need to send it from an anonymous, untraceable email address. There are sources on the web that will let us do this, but if I tried to tell you, you'd screw it up and we'd both get arrested. I'll take care of it. It'll be in his inbox late tonight."

"Can you make it look like it originated from Russia? That will send them down a whole different and interesting rabbit hole."

"I'll see what I can do."

When Larry Bloom opened his computer the next morning, there was a curious email from an unknown address, but the subject line—Video from McGraw China trip—intrigued him enough to open it. He was afraid to download the attached file, so he called in his IT manager to check for viruses before he viewed it. Once he got the clear from IT, however, he sat, perched on the top of his desk, a hand covering his gaping mouth. He immediately recognized the political bombshell, and his first instinct was to call McGraw for confirmation, but he assumed the video had been leaked to him specifically from the McGraw campaign. He'd hit it off with the Senator in their one-on-one interview, and Bloom knew he needed to be cautious.

There was a reason McGraw hadn't released the video when he got back from China, or even made it an issue in his campaign. Bloom had been jailed for six months, decades earlier, when he'd refused to divulge his sources in a story that had revealed a top secret but potentially illegal government surveillance program. He knew the record of all his

calls from this point forward could likely to be sub-
poenaed by the government if he chose to do anything at all with the tape that had just fallen into
his hands. A call to McGraw could be construed as
a confirmation of the leak from the McGraw campaign. If the government had suppressed the release of the video, it might be better for both him
and the Senator to keep some distance.

TL rushed into the Senator's office, his face was
flushed, his breathing heavy. "Larry Bloom just
released the China video. It's all over the Internet
and we're getting calls for a statement. Please tell
me you don't know anything about this."

Senator McGraw looked up from the briefing
sheet he'd been studying. "I don't know anything
about it. Believe me, I wanted that tape released
as much as anyone, but I'm not going to violate
federal law. Who do you think did it?"

"We first viewed the tape on Wister's computer.
That's the first place I'd look."

McGraw paused for a moment, thinking. "I
know Dean is really pissed at me," he said, "but
this could be good for the campaign. I hope Dean
covered his tracks."

"We're going to need to release a statement."

"How about this? We have viewed the video, and
we are unable to comment on its contents. This
is a State Department matter, and all questions
should be addressed to the Secretary of State and
the President of the United States."

TL smiled, marveling at his boss's brilliance.
The press would read a statement like that as

meaning the McGraw campaign was prohibited from commenting. It would put the onus on the President to explain what happened.

And that could not be bad for the senator's chances of taking over his seat.

Chapter 41

Senator Thomas McGraw stood in his suite at the Chicago Four Seasons, looking out a window at the sailboats navigating the white caps on this beautiful but windy June day. He thought about the challenge before him. There hadn't been an open Republican Presidential Convention since party-insider Gerald Ford beat Ronald Reagan in 1976. That had been a chaotic and riotous affair, featuring hours of drunken deliberations, fist fights on the convention floor, and a desperate move by the father of the modern conservative wing of the party to win over the liberal wing by naming a surprisingly progressive running mate. The Senator smiled at the thought. There actually were Republicans in 1976 who didn't hide from the L word. Of course, none of it had worked, and the party insider won the right to lose to Jimmy Carter, another outsider, in the bicentennial election. Now another party insider, Senator Howard Grimes from California, led in the committed delegate count.

There were, however, important differences between this year and 1976. This year there were four candidates, not two, who held a significant percentage of the committed delegates, and since there were no uncommitted delegates, the nomination was open to the candidate who could make a deal with the competition. Herein lay the challenge that confronted McGraw. After a fast start at the beginning of the primary season, the Senator's controversial statements deriding American exceptionalism—accusing the big money financing of campaigns as creating a "capitalist oligarchy", and espousing the necessity of harnessing the unbridled avarice of capitalism—had lost him the goodwill of party regulars. After the sex scandal at the Job Creators' Convention, and the release of his very own sex tape, the religious wing of the party had pretty much abandoned him. The only reason he had remained competitive through the end of the primary season was the crossover of a substantial number of Democratic voters.

The trump card he had counted on—the industrial tragedy in Shenzhen—had promised to raise his prospects before the California primary, but the president had quashed that by quarantining as classified the explicit video that could put a human face on the foreign jobs issue. The mysterious leak of the video, however, might still prove to be a game changer. The press had hounded the President until McGraw's role in the rescue of the little Chinese girl and her brothers had been revealed, and this had helped him gain some momentum. But he was still a limping, wounded animal coming into the convention and was being written off by the political media. Senator Grimes

from California now had 35% of committed delegates, Senator McGraw had 30%, Senator Greenburg from New York had 19%, and Congressman
Smith from Ohio trailed with 16%. Grimes could
acquire enough delegates by making a deal with
either of the two lesser candidates, but for Mc-
Graw to obtain enough delegates for the nomination, he would need to make a deal with both of
them. He was limping and wounded, but he was
also familiar with stories of hunters being taken
out by a wounded grizzly in the Wyoming wilder-
ness.

The Senator walked away from the window to
join TL at the large conference table in the war
room they had set up in the hotel. "I've arranged
to meet with Greenburg and Smith after they meet
with Grimes. They've agreed to hold off on making
a decision until after our meeting," said TL.

"And do you believe they actually will wait? You
don't think Grimes can close them at his meeting?" asked McGraw.

"With Grimes's social skills? Not a chance. I
hinted that you have something pretty special in
mind, so I think they'll want to see what you're
offering. Was I lying? Have you figured out what
incredible thing you're willing to put on the table?
I expect Grimes will offer them each the chance at
being his running mate, and he only needs one of
them to bite."

"I don't plan on offering the VP spot to either of
them. Greenburg is way too close to Flag, as is
Grimes. And Smith is incompatible with pretty
much everything I stand for. Besides, I've already

promised the VP slot to Governor Robbins from Pennsylvania. She was responsible more than anyone for pushing me over the top in the primary there. I'm not very popular with women right now, and after what's happened the last few months, I'm really going to need a woman on the ticket."

TL didn't say anything for a moment. "Well, then, I don't know how you think you're going to get the nomination."

"TL, you're assuming that both of them want to be VP. Maybe both of them do. Or maybe neither of them do. Or maybe there's something each of them want more than being VP."

"And what might that be?"

"I'm still working on it. I have a couple of ideas, but I'm waiting for some information that will help me put together offers specially designed for each one of them, offers that will be irresistible for different reasons."

TL was curious about the nature of the offers, but the Senator was being deliberately secretive, and TL had been around politics—not to mention the Senator—long enough to know it might be safer for him to remain in the dark.

The next afternoon, Senator McGraw met first with Preston Smith, Republican Whip in the House of Representatives, who was, in McGraw's opinion, a sanctimonious little prick. It wasn't just his attitude. He had a small narrow face that reminded McGraw of a wolverine, and his attempt at a smile would more often not not morph into a snarl due to his underbite and pointy lower incisors. TL would make fun of his "snile" whenever he and the Senator watched Smith on television.

"Good afternoon, Senator." Smith greeted them with his signature predatory grin.

The Senator shook his hand and offered him a seat on the couch. "Thanks for taking the time to meet with me, Congressman."

"You're welcome, Senator. But I want to be frank with you. This is a courtesy meeting. I've already decided to be Grimes's running mate. And you and I, well, you know we don't see eye to eye on most things—almost anything really. It just wouldn't work out."

The Senator smiled. "That's a little strange, Preston. I wasn't aware that I had offered you the vice-presidency."

"Well, isn't that the purpose of this meeting? You can't get the nomination without me, and I don't know what else you would have to offer."

"Actually, I did want to talk to you about your candidacy for vice-president. I'd already heard that you've agreed to be Grimes's running mate. Congratulations on that. You've come quite a way from your time as the high-school wrestling coach of the year in Massillon, Ohio. Did you enjoy teaching?"

"Oh, I loved it. It was very satisfying. I look back on that part of my life with a lot of fondness."

"I think I read something about that in your bio. You had a dozen state champions there, and also coached an Olympic Gold Medalist. Is that right?"

"Yes, we had quite a run at Taft High. Were you a high-school wrestler, Senator?"

"Actually, I wasn't much of an athlete. State champion in high-school debate, though." The Senator smiled, as if he was still basking in the glow of that long-ago victory. "Preston, as you know, your whole life becomes an issue when you run for national office. I just want to make sure you're ready for your coaching career to be reviewed." He paused, then looked Smith straight in the eye. "I'll get to the point. The young man that you coached, the Olympic gold medalist? I just came into some information about him." He reached to the coffee table in front of them, picked up a manila envelope and handed it to the Congressman.

"Whatever this is, I'm not interested in it." Smith placed the envelope back on the table without opening at it.

"I guess I can understand that, given its contents. Let me summarize it for you. It's your medalist's sworn statement describing his relationship with you when he was in high school. It's a long and tawdry story, and he gives a lot of explicit details. Details that make pretty compelling reading—lots of times, dates, locations. I'll give you the condensed version. You had a sexual relationship with him from the time he was fifteen until he was eighteen. When he graduated high school, you cut him off. Seems you like them a little younger."

Smith's face was flushed a red so bright even McGraw was alarmed. "That's a total fucking lie.

It's fabricated bullshit. Is that what you're doing now? Paying for fake stories?"

"I considered that possibility. But the younger model you traded him in for? Well, there's also a statement from him in that envelope. The investigator who turned up this information, well, let's just say he is very experienced in such matters. He did a lot of investigative work on the Catholic priest sex scandals. I wouldn't bring this to your attention unless I had complete confidence in this evidence."

Smith didn't say anything for a moment. Then he put on his reading glasses, picked up the envelope and read through its contents. When he was done, he threw the envelope back on the coffee table, took off his glasses and put them in his pocket. "You are an underhanded, fucking asshole."

"I'm not in the name-calling business, Preston, but if I were there are much worse labels that could be used to describe the person in that folder. I could have given this to the press, or to Grimes, or maybe even the FBI—I don't know what the statute of limitations would be on these matters in Ohio—but I decided you have the right to know that I know about it before you make a decision on the vice-presidency."

McGraw stood and walked back to the window with the glorious view of the lake. "There's another reason I'm reluctant to go to the press or law enforcement. These two young men? Unbelievably, they told my investigator that they still have feelings for you. They don't want to ruin your career, but they would appreciate very much if you would reach out to them. They want to give you a chance to make amends. I quite frankly don't understand their attitude, but I haven't been in their shoes, thank God."

"So, what you are saying is that if I run for vice-president, you will see this gets out… But if I withdraw and endorse your candidacy, you'll bury this?"

"I'm not saying that at all. I'm just saying there is a much greater chance that this gets in the press if you're running for VP. There is just so much digging, so much scrutiny, at the top of a national ticket, and if I don't become our party's candidate, well, I'll have a lot of time on my hands … I just couldn't abide seeing a pedophile a heartbeat away from the presidency. On the other hand, if I am our party's candidate, well, you know… I'll be pretty busy with the campaign and you yourself can focus on making amends to these men. That's something I'd like to see from you—you make amends, and also make sure they get the counseling they're going to need for the rest of their lives."

"This is fucking blackmail, Tom."

The Senator nodded, thinking. "I'd call it more like giving you an opportunity to make reparations, but you go ahead and do what you think is right. If these are all lies, then you should go ahead and run. I haven't let rumors and innuendo affect my candidacy, and neither should you." The Senator stood, indicating the meeting was over.

Two hours later TL brought a plump, ginger-haired man into the Senator's suite. Senator Greenburg, the junior Senator from New York, wasn't at all charismatic, but he was an intellectual—one who cultivated a disheveled look, more college professor than a politician. Greenburg's popularity with his constituents was almost exclusively due to his prosecution of several corrupt politicians, including the former governor of his home state. This not only endeared him to the voters of New York but removed the suspicion that voters in the heartland often have about eastern politicians. Greenburg greeted McGraw with a smile and a hug. "Hi, Tom. Great to see you again. This promises to be an exciting convention, doesn't it?"

"Well, it should be a very interesting one. How great it turns out... well, that will depend on the outcome, as far as I'm concerned."

Senator Greenburg nodded. "I know. I'm not too optimistic about how this is going to work out for you *or* me, though. I think Grimes is cutting a deal with Smith for VP, and that should pretty much cut off any chance that you or I may have."

"You might be right. But I'm working on getting Smith's support. Assuming that I can get his, your support would put me over the top. I'd like to see what we can do about that."

"You're interested in running with Smith?"

"Of course not. That could never work. Let's just say that I may have hit on something he wants more than being VP."

Greenburg's smile faded. "I have to tell you, Tom, I'm not interested at all in running for VP, if that's why I'm here. I like the job I have right now a hell of a lot better than that. If the convention doesn't work out for me then I'm going to be in a very strong position to run for governor next year."

"I'm not surprised. I figured you wouldn't be interested in the VP slot. Consequently, I wasn't going to offer it to you. We've known each other for a long time. We came into the Senate together. I don't know if you remember, but I recall a party we went to the first week we were in DC. We both got pretty hammered and ended up at a blues bar in Georgetown. Do you remember that?"

Greenburg looked surprised. "Yes, I do. Fondly."

"We talked about how we got where we were. I told you that the Senate was pretty much my dream job, and you said it wasn't yours."

"I don't really remember the conversation, Tom. The end of that evening is awfully blurry. I'm not even sure how I got home that night." He laughed nervously.

"Well, I remember it well. It made an impression on me. You told me that you ran for the Senate only to make your father happy. You said your dream job was to be a Supreme Court Justice."

"Tom, that was just a combination of youthful exuberance, and maybe bourbon acting as a truth serum. I can get like that when I've had too much to drink. I gave up that dream when I left the law for politics."

"What if I could give it back to you?"

"Tom, that's kind of far-fetched. I have zero judicial experience and, besides, there's no opening on the court."

"You're a historian. There've been dozens of justices without judicial experience. With your legal background and straight-shooter reputation, it'd be a slam dunk to get you confirmed. You're right, there isn't an opening now, but there may be soon after the next president takes office. I think Justice Moran is holding on, waiting to retire when a Republican can appoint his successor."

"If this is a quid pro quo, that would be illegal, Tom."

"It's not a quid pro quo, but let's be honest. Your chances of getting the nomination are slim. You already said you're not interested in being VP. I'm just telling you that if I'm elected, and a spot opens up, I can't think of anyone else who would be a better judge than you. Would you rather be governor or on the Supreme Court?"

Greenburg joined the Senator to look out the window at the sailboats on the lake. "What about Smith?"

"Grimes is getting the nomination unless I get the both of you. Would you rather see me as president, or Grimes? Isn't that what all of this boils down to? Let me worry about Smith. If I can't handle him, then none of this matters anyway."

Chapter 42

Dean was surprised to receive a call from Senator McGraw. Their last meeting hadn't gone well and, after that blowup—and discovering Melinda's betrayal the following day—Dean had decided to skip the coverage of the Republican Convention. He and his beloved dog Cheney went on an extended backpacking trip in the Wind River Range in Wyoming. When he got back on the grid, he was shocked to learn that two of the candidates had withdrawn and endorsed Senator McGraw, who was about to become the Republican nominee. After checking in with Mark, he'd returned to Chicago to follow up on any leads he might be able to dig up on the whereabouts of Double P but, as soon as his plane had landed, he'd received a call from TL summoning him to Senator McGraw's hotel.

Dean had cooled off since his camping trip and was in a good mood when TL led him in to the Senator's suite—though he still wasn't quite sure what to expect. He offered McGraw his hand when he entered the room. "Congratulations, Senator.

You did it, and I'm not sure I want you to tell me how."

The Senator laughed. "No, you don't. Have a seat, Dean. I'm glad you're here. You can be a tough man to get hold of. The last time we talked it didn't go all that well, and I feel badly about that. And about saddling you with Melinda. It never occurred to me that she could be a mole. As I think about it, I'm sure she sabotaged much of your investigation. The whole investigation would have had a better result if I hadn't made you take her on. I apologize for that."

"Thank you, Senator. But you couldn't have known. She fooled me too."

McGraw nodded. "She's something else, isn't she? We're going to agree not to discuss her again, and we're going to agree not to discuss the video leak either. The President was so happy to share credit with me for getting Jia and her brothers to the US, the whole investigation of the leak has been dropped. I was relieved to hear that your computer turned out to be clean, but again, let's agree to be thankful for the favors we've received and not bring this up again."

"What about Yao Chen? Is he still in danger of execution?"

The Senator shook his head. "I'm not sure. There isn't much I can do about it right now, but if he's still alive when I'm elected, it will be a priority to work on his release. I promise you that, Dean."

"Thank you, Senator."

The Senator shrugged off the gratitude. "I do want to update you on the Flag investigation, as I know that means a lot to you. But first, I'd like to ask you a favor."

"Sure, Senator, how can I help?"

"Well, I hope you know that I've come to respect your law enforcement skills, and even more your instincts. So, I'd like you to help with security tomorrow night at the convention. I think it would be good to have another set of eyes on the crowd."

"Why me? I'm sure the Secret Service has it all under control. Those guys are always on top of everything."

"Ah yes, the Secret Service. They're efficient all right, but you and I are different. I've seen that you have a nose for trouble. You're not afraid to break the rules if need be, and I don't mean that in a bad way. I'd just feel more comfortable if you were there."

"Of course, Senator. I'd be happy to do what I can to help."

"Good, I'll have TL put you in touch with Secret Service and they can walk you through the process and give you an assignment. Now, let me update you on the Flag investigation. I haven't forgotten about it. I brought in ex-FBI Director Vorhies to take a look at what you found. I want to be frank with you, Dean... he advised me that there isn't enough to warrant bringing the FBI in at the present time. I am asking you to trust me on this. I'm not going to let it go. But this isn't the right time to pursue it."

Dean didn't say anything. He just let his disapproval be known by his silence.

"I can see that this bothers you. I assure you it bothers me as well. The important thing right now is that the young girl you brought to me is in a safe place."

"What about the other girls, the ones who continue to be abused until it becomes the 'right time'? What about them?" Dean spoke in a flat, deliberate voice, keeping his temper in check.

"I think about that every day, Dean. I am asking you to trust me. I'm not letting this go."

Dean nodded, but otherwise didn't respond to the Senator's request. Instead, he stood. "Have your security detail call me. And good luck tomorrow night, Senator. I know you've gone through a lot to get the nomination. I hope it's worth it."

"So do I, Dean, so do I."

That night Dean tried to sleep but his conversation with the Senator still bothered him. Despite everything he knew about McGraw, Dean had him figured as a good guy at heart, and it bothered him that maybe he'd been fooled. Dean understood political expediency, but it was hard for him to accept that McGraw may have backed off the investigation of the sexual abuse of children because it was inconvenient to his campaign. He turned over and closed his eyes, but sleep wouldn't come.

A body moved close against his back, and Dean mumbled groggily, "Melinda?"

"Geez, you forgot about me that quickly?"

Dean jumped up with a start. "Sara? Where the fuck did you come from, and where have you been? I've been calling for you for months."

"I needed to give you some space. Just now, you were dreaming about her, weren't you?"

"No, I wasn't."

"You were. I know. I don't blame you. She was sexy as hell, that's for sure. But you were falling for her, baby, and she was just a sex toy. I know you're a guy, but you've never been one to go around thinking with your dick."

"I know. I know. I was in a bad place."

"It's good you got your heart broken. She was good for a rebound girl. Now that you've got that out of the way, you can move on."

"I don't want to move on, and, really, I wasn't thinking about her. The Senator wants me on his security detail at the convention, and I'm not sure I should do it. I just don't trust him anymore, not since it looks as if he's ignoring the evidence of the child abuse I brought to him."

Sara reached up and stroked his face. "I know you're a black-and-white guy, darling. There aren't too many shades of gray with you. Didn't he ask you to trust him? You know from what Mark has said that the FBI is really sketchy right now. Maybe he thinks it will be better to wait until after the election to follow up."

"Maybe. But meanwhile more and more young women are being abused. And what if he doesn't get elected? I'm just having a hard time with this."

"I can see that. But I'd advise you to calm down and give it some more time. Once you burn your bridges with him, you're not going to be able to re-build them." Sara pulled him close. Dean buried his face in her hair, wrapping his arms around her, inhaling her unique fragrance that he knew so well. Her body was so familiar that it was al-most an extension of his own, and he didn't see how it could ever be the same with anyone else.

Chapter 43

FLAG paced back and forth in his Jackson Hole home, waiting for Colonel Ned Wood to arrive. He still had a hard time figuring how and where he'd gone wrong. He'd spent a fortune promoting Grimes, and Grimes was the delegate leader coming into the convention. He'd squeezed McGraw's funding, and McGraw's staff was running on fumes through the whole campaign. He'd sabotaged the Wister investigation by paying Melinda and Mario, Jr. to obtain the McGraw sex tape, and the release of the tape *had* derailed the McGraw campaign. He'd sabotaged the Job Creators' Convention in Las Vegas, and the McGraw campaign had come to a near standstill. He'd convinced the President to bury the video from Shenzhen, removing a potential blockbuster PR coup for the Senator.

Despite all of his efforts, McGraw had gotten to the convention with the second-highest number of delegates, and still Flag saw no path for him to get nominated. He'd pulled every possible string to get Grimes nominated, and when Grimes had made the deal with Smith to put it over the top, it was a done deal. Flag was on his private jet, ready to take off for Chicago, when the news alert had come on his phone. At the last minute, Smith had withdrawn his candidacy for personal reasons, then endorsed McGraw's candidacy and gone underground. And now, he wouldn't even return Flag's calls. Flag was shaken, but he had one more tool in his bag. It was time to break the glass. Luis knocked lightly. "Mr. Flag, Colonel Wood is here."

"Well, bring him in, bring him in."

The Colonel, wearing his usual paramilitary uniform, entered the room and didn't wait for Flag to speak. "What the fuck happened? I thought you said it was a done deal."

"I'm not sure. I think maybe McGraw had something on Smith. That's the only thing I can figure."

"So that motherfucker McGraw is going to get nominated now."

"Unless we can figure something else out. Not all of Smith's delegates will go to McGraw, but certainly enough to give him the nomination. What about the Stauffenberg solution? Are you still up for that?"

"Oh, so you finally figured out what that was? Well, it's a little late for that now. You can't put an operation like that together at the last minute. You should have listened to me months ago. That cowboy? He bested you, Flag."

Flag made an unholy effort to control his temper. "Not yet he hasn't. I was listening when you were talking Stauffenberg, but I only wanted to consider it as a last resort. I have the assets ready to go. I have a guy in place in Chicago—on the ground, ready, willing and able to carry this out. I need you to handle it, manage the operational details. My plane is already gassed up and ready to fly you to Chicago."

Dean had been sitting for two hours in a small room deep in the bowels of the Convention Center. He'd been told someone would pick him up at eleven AM at Gate D, but he'd been there for thirty minutes and, finally, he'd called TL's number and left a message. TL had called him back and told him to keep waiting. Forty-five minutes later a Secret Service agent walked up to him at the gate. "You Wister?"

"Yes," Dean affirmed.

"You have ID?"

Dean produced his Illinois driver's license and showed it to the agent.

The agent looked at it, and then at Dean, confirming the picture matched the man before him. "You're on the Midwest Organized Crime Task Force, right? Don't you have a badge?"

"I thought it was explained to you. I'm actually not working there anymore. Senator McGraw asked me to help out today."

The agent sighed. "Nothing was explained to me. I got a call from Toby Landers saying the Senator wanted to put you on security tonight, but I have to tell you, we're not looking for any more help. I don't need another untrained guy to worry about." He looked at Dean as if he were a homeless person trying to crash a party. "Look, I'll give you a walkie talkie, and you can wander around observing the crowd. If you see anything, alert us on the unit. But I can't have you carrying a weapon inside." He waited until Dean took out his Glock and handed it to him. "We'll get it back to you tonight. Follow me and I'll get you set up with a lanyard and a jacket, so we can identify you."

The agent walked Dean into the basement of the convention center and handed him off to a young man, wearing a blue blazer and khakis, who looked to be about fifteen. The young man had him stand against a gray wall and took his picture with a digital camera, then instructed him to sit in a small room that contained only a plastic folding table, four metal chairs, a coffee machine and a small refrigerator with bottled water. "Wait here while I process your ID."

Dean looked around the room. It reminded him of a dozen other rooms in the bowels of auditoriums when he'd moonlighted at times as security for concerts. He'd once nabbed a pickpocket ring at a Billy Joel concert, and he thought a pickpocket could do pretty well at this convention. It was stifling hot and he was starting to sweat through his shirt. Thirty more minutes of cooling his heels and the young man came back and gave him a lanyard with a picture ID, a walkie-talkie, and a thin, red, windbreaker-style jacket.

"What's with the red jacket?" Dean asked.

"It's so we can easily identify the security people that aren't part of the Secret Service," advised the young man.

"OK. So now where do I go?"

The young man shrugged. "I have no idea. I was just told to get you an ID, a walkie-talkie and the jacket."

He left, and Dean sat and stewed. Was this the Senator punishing him for being insolent? Telling him he wants him on the security detail, then parking his ass in a dungeon? After two hours of waiting, Dean stood up. "Fuck this," he cursed aloud, and walked out of the room and took the elevator to the main hall.

Chapter 44

DOUBLE P sat in his car outside the 18th Precinct station of the Chicago Police Department, two empty McDonald's sacks keeping him company in the passenger seat. It was near dinner time, and although he'd already finished off three Big Macs, two large orders of fries, and a couple of apple pies for lunch, he was getting hungry again. He sure hoped Sergeant Esterhaus was off duty soon —he couldn't leave his outpost until Esterthaus came through that door.

Double P had felt lost since Mario Rosati, Sr. had been murdered the previous year. Then Mario, Jr. had come along, giving him some hope of getting his sentence reduced. But then they'd both been screwed by the FBI. He wasn't surprised. He hadn't wanted to work for the FBI, but he didn't have much of a choice. He'd been facing an effective life sentence as a repeat offender, and helping them out in the hunt for a video of the cowboy politician was his only chance at getting it reduced. But then they'd fucked him, all because the old lady mother of Mario's mistress got in their way.

Damn that little twit, Mario, Jr. It was all his fault. He wouldn't have killed her, but Mario, Jr. told him he had to. The old man's kid was a mean little fucker. And he knew he'd blame the old lady on him. So, he'd skipped. He'd thought about heading to Key West or Vegas, maybe hide out at one of Mario's homes. If Doris was there, he'd have to take care of her, but he liked Doris and didn't really want to kill her.

His head hurt trying to figure all this out. He'd never had to plan any of his crimes. Even as a young hood, he'd always just followed the instructions of someone else. Then, just as he'd been stuffing his face at his favorite south side pizza joint, sitting at the back table with a sixteen-inch meat lover's with double cheese, a guy had dropped into the seat next to him wearing a baseball cap, sunglasses, and what Double P presumed was a fake beard. Double P figured this was the guy that Mario, Jr. had told him about. They'd had an FBI handler, but Mario, Jr. was also in contact with someone else who'd wanted the same video and had been willing to pay big bucks for it. Junior hadn't actually met the guy —it was all spy shit. Voice mails left on burner phones and cash-in-envelope drops. Mr. Spyman had arranged for Double P's bail, and Mario, Jr. had given him a burner phone that he'd periodically use to update him on their progress. After they'd obtained the video, Junior had said they needed to split up. He'd given Double P his cut of the money he got for the video—ten grand—

wished him good luck, and that was the last he'd seen of him.

So, he wasn't totally shocked when the guy in the ball cap now sat down beside him. What did shock him was what the guy wanted him to do, but Double P was thrilled the guy had a plan for him. If everything worked out, he'd have a slick new life, with plenty of cash, a new passport and ID papers that would enable him to hide in a foreign country, or even in plain sight in any US city that was big enough. Double P didn't really want to go to a foreign country. He'd never been outside of the US. He was thinking either Miami or Phoenix, someplace warm. The man had all the details worked out. He seemed like a real pro. He'd even promised an explosion that would help the getaway.

There'd been one issue with the plan, though. He needed a Chicago Police uniform, and Double P had the solution for that. But he needed Esterhaus to make it work, or, at least, he needed his uniform. Mario's guys had always teased Double P that Esterhaus was his twin on the Chicago PD. It's true that they looked a little alike and were approximately the same size, which is to say Esterhaus was the only cop Double P ever saw that was even close to matching his girth. Additionally, Esterhaus had always been willing to take a few bucks to help them out when he was a beat cop. Double P put down his candy bar and started his car when he saw Esterhaus emerge from the front door of the station house. Following him through a Burger King drive thru just down the street, he had the urge to pick something up himself, but he couldn't afford to lose him.

Five minutes later, Esterhaus turned into the driveway of a neat brick bungalow and got out of his black Crown Vic with an empty bag in his hand. Double P watched and waited on the street for five minutes, and then knocked on the front door. A morbidly obese man wearing a wife-beater and boxer shorts opened the door with a can of beer in his hand. "Hey, Double P, what are you doing—" was all he got out of his mouth before he was pushed into his living room, and Double P brought the gun up to his head.

Double P was relieved to find a new uniform hanging in the bedroom closet, still in its plastic dry-cleaning bag. He hadn't been looking forward to putting on the one that Esterhaus had worn all day. It fit him pretty well, he thought, as he looked in the mirror. Actually, it was a little big on him.

"You've got a real eating disorder, you know that?" he said to the fat man duct-taped and on his back on the bedroom carpet, struggling to breathe through his nose. "You need to try Weight Watchers or something."

Double P fastened his holster, put the Sergeant's badge and wallet in his pocket, placed his cap just so on his head, and walked out the door. He looked good, he thought, in his freshly pressed blue uniform. Tonight, he would avenge Mario Rosati, Sr., make a big enough score to set him up for life, and change history. Just like that soldier who tried to kill Hitler, what had that man said his name was, Stupenberg?

Dean wandered around the main hall looking for a spot with a good view of the crowd. There were speeches going on, but the hall was nearly empty. The important event, the acceptance speech of Senator McGraw, was going to happen later that evening. Dean didn't see the Secret Service agent who had met him outside the hall, so he stationed himself on the first-floor mezzanine, about twenty feet directly above the convention floor, and very close to the stage. The only weapon he carried was a walkie-talkie on his hip. His sole job was to scan the crowd and use his radio to summon the cavalry if he noticed anyone suspicious. As the afternoon wore on, so did the speeches, as the up-and-coming politicians and party officials who'd been promised a chance to address the convention got their shot, even if not in prime time, and the crowd slowly filed in.

It wasn't until an hour before the Senator's speech to accept the nomination that the hall became standing room only. Someone had come up with the stupid idea of creating a rock concert-like pit in front of the stage, and several hundred people were now herded into it. As more and more people attempted to occupy this prime real estate, the herd was pushed closer and closer to the stage. The room was hot. Dean had been in this Convention Center many times over the years, but he'd never seen this many people in it. Perhaps the air-conditioning was overloaded, which was understandable. The weather had turned the last couple of days and now was typical Chicago late summer weather—in the nineties and humid.

The Senator had been nominated the previous night, and his nomination had been made official by acclimation after Grimes had given it his blessing. And he'd done it well, like a good party man, without any outward sign of reluctance. This evening was the Senator's chance to address a national audience, and take the fight to the Democrats instead of the Republican establishment, or any Republican rival. Now there was only one person to beat, the Democratic candidate who would be nominated the following week in New York.

Double P followed the plan just as the mystery man had laid it out to him. He double-parked Esterhaus's black Crown Vic that could pass for an unmarked police car, if you didn't look too close, in the loading area of the convention hall and got out carrying a bouquet of yellow roses up the ramp of the loading dock. A man in a red jacket stood at the entrance with his arms folded. He looked at the fat cop, and held his hand up, stopping him. "I'm bringing this bouquet to Mrs. McGraw. They're from the mayor."

"I wasn't told anything about any delivery," objected the man in the red jacket.

"Look, I'm part of the mayor's security detail. And he told me to bring this over." Double P looked at the badge on the red jacket. "Hey, Steve. You work for the city, right? What department?"

"Streets and sanitation."

"This convention, pretty good overtime gig, huh? Well, Steve, you know the mayor. He'll be really upset if this doesn't get delivered." Double P didn't say anything, just let the statement sink in. In Chicago, what the mayor wants, the mayor gets.

The man in the red jacket looked at Double P's badge for a moment, and then said, "All right. Go on through. I hope she likes them."

Chapter 45

CHARLES Kidwell sat on a chair in the green room off the convention floor with Senator McGraw, TL, and Mrs. McGraw. He remembered sitting in a similar convention center in Cheyenne nearly two years before when the Senator had announced his candidacy for the presidency, and he remembered how proud he'd felt then, but this was entirely different. It had been only a dream then; now it was real. After all the crazy peaks and valleys of the campaign, and living with the constant fear of their relationship being uncovered and the Senator's chances ruined, they had made it. At his announcement speech, Charles had, in his own mind, taken the credit for the Senator's success. Now he realized that he actually had very little to do with it. He'd recognized Tom's potential, had encouraged him, had raised money for him, but Tom had more inside of him than Charles had ever realized. Tom had the ability to charm anyone, the ability to coalesce a wildly diverse group of followers, and he had the killer instinct necessary to be the leader of the free world.

Charles smiled—*killer instinct, in spades.* Tom

had said their relationship wouldn't change once he was elected and, while Charles didn't see how he could keep that promise, he'd kept every single one he'd made so far, so who knew? A Secret Service agent opened the door, and advised, "Senator, it's time."

They left the room with TL in front, followed by Mrs. McGraw, then Charles directly in front of the Senator. As they walked out the door, the Senator whispered in his ear, "Thank you, Charles, for everything."

There were multiple speeches leading up to Mc-Graw's. The chairman of the party was speaking first, charged with introducing the person who was there to introduce McGraw. Dean thought, *There's too much unnecessary liturgy involved in the process; just get on with it already.* Now they were rolling some kind of stairs onto the stage. *What the heck?* Dean was trying to avoid looking at the stage, keeping his eyes on the crowd in the pit at the foot of the stage, constantly scanning. He heard the crowd begin to buzz, starting with a murmur at the front of the hall and working its way to the back in waves, the crowd coming alive in a tsunami of sound. Now everyone was standing and cheering, and Dean wondered who could be creating this level of excitement. He took his eyes off the crowd for a moment and turned to the stage.

A small Chinese girl was climbing the stairs that had been placed in front of the podium. She calmly looked out at the crowd and waited until the audience delirium quieted. Dean figured she must have been coached well, because the ovation was the loudest he'd ever heard—a good five minutes—and she waited for the sound to die down before she spoke. Everyone in the hall was familiar with the story of this little girl. The tale of how the Senator had obtained the video and taken it to the president, and how his actions had resulted in her and her brothers coming to the United States, had been detailed in story after story online and in the newspapers. It had become another chapter of McGraw lore, and had been an integral part of the propaganda video about the Senator shown to the convention and to the television audience earlier in the evening. The issue of China had become more than about jobs. The faces of exploited workers and the shock of child labor had added a human element to which Americans were responding.

The little girl spoke no English, save for the one sentence she had been practicing over and over again for last two weeks. Finally, when the hall was quiet, she paused, looked out at the crowd with her round black eyes, smiled broadly and pronounced loudly, slowly and clearly: "My name is Jia Ling, and I am here to introduce Senator Thomas McGraw, the Republican candidate for President of the United States of America."

Hysteria infected the building. The crowd was screaming and the hall literally shaking as the audience pounded the floor after the introduction by the little China doll. Dean thought the chant of

"USA, USA!" by the crowd was ironic after the introduction of McGraw by a Chinese citizen, but the sheer drama of the moment gave him chills. Say what you want about McGraw, he had a knack for theater.

Dean forced himself to refocus his attention to the task at hand. Senator McGraw was now making his way through the hall from the side and would be passing through a narrow aisle in the middle of the pit. He was accompanied by several Secret Service agents, his wife, Charles Kidwell, and TL. The crowd in the pit surged forward and Dean focused his eyes, scanning the crowd in the pit, when something caught his eye. A Chicago police officer was pushing his way to the front of the pit, toward the aisle. He was a large man, and he took his hat off to wipe his head. His uniform was soaking wet, and beads of perspiration were dripping down his face. Something about him—this was a really big cop, bigger than any Dean had ever seen. The cop's hands were hidden by the crowd, and he kept pushing through, seemingly in a hurry to get to the front. Where had he seen the guy before?

Dean could see him bring his hand up, a black piece of metal in his right hand. And at that moment, recognition clicked in Dean's brain. Pulling his radio, he shouted as loudly as he could, trying to be heard above the crowd noise, "The cop at the front of the pit has a gun, and he's not a cop!" Dean shouted into the radio. Then he dropped the radio to the ground and pulled himself up on the railing. His heart was drumming in his chest, but he was calm and focused. Crouching on the railing, he was unconsciously taken back to his training as a defensive back on the University of Illinois football team. Spearing was illegal, but it was a play Dean had a hard time resisting. He was slower than the wide receivers, so his biggest weapon was intimidation. Even the toughest and most talented wide receivers feared crossing the middle of the field, because Dean would use his helmet as a weapon, and his body as the energy to deliver the weapon to whatever body part was most exposed by the opponent—preferably the head or shoulders. This muscle memory took over his body as he crouched, and waited, waited, waited, for just the right moment, trying to get the timing just right to hit his target. He could see the man raising his gun and he couldn't wait a second longer. He launched his body through the air, a human missile flying directly at the head of the fake Chicago cop.

The crown of Dean's head collided above the man's nose, but the man's hand, cramped and jostled by the crowd, still managed to get off three shots, each one slightly more off target than the one before.

Dean didn't actually see what happened. What he did see was Double P's head coming up fast at him, then there was a jolt of pain as his own head cracked with the contact, and then blackness. When he awoke, he felt the weight of dozens of bodies on top of him, crushing his chest, squeezing the breath out of him and, although conscious for a moment, he went black again as all the air was pinched from his lungs.

The Secret Service agents heard Dean's radio message and turned to look for the suspect in the crowd, identifying him just as Dean leaped from his perch. They pushed the Senator and his wife to the ground, covering them with their bodies. The crowd in the pit panicked as Dean came flying into the mob, and when the cop pulled the trigger, it turned into a stampeding herd of animals, trying to escape the pit.

Senator McGraw heard the shots, felt himself pushed to the ground and held there by the Secret Service, his breath pushed out of his lungs. He tried to find the hand of his wife in the crush. Finally, the arms of several agents surrounded him like tentacles and helped him to his feet.

"Let's get you out of here, Senator." The agent turned, and McGraw could see his wife next to him; the designer dress made especially for this occasion was torn and she held it to her bosom.

"Are you all right?" he mouthed.

She nodded grimly.

Then he looked to the other side and saw a man on the ground, laying face up. His eyes were open and there was a bullet hole just above one of his eyes. At first, he didn't recognize the man, his brain not connecting the lifeless eyes and expressionless face to anyone he knew. It was a moment later that the realization registered. He pushed the Secret Service agent aside and dived for the man on the floor. "Charles, Charles, oh my God!" McGraw cried out, scrambling to reach him.

He was grabbed by several agents. "Senator, no. We have to get you out of here." The agents struggled to pull him down the aisle and through the back door in the back of the hall. It took a seeming eternity to clear the pit, and on the ground lay dozens of spectators, layered on top of one another, writhing and squirming in pain like a school of beached fish. Police and Secret Service surrounded the pit, searching the pile for the assassin. At the bottom, they found Double P and Dean, spooning in an unconscious embrace.

Dean was groggy, seated on a cold metal chair in a room in the bowels of the convention hall. A doctor was monitoring his blood pressure, and at the same time the Secret Service was interrogating him. His head hurt, and he was having trouble understanding their questions. He asked them to repeat each one and then waited for his brain to process like an outdated computer with a dial-up Internet connection. Gradually and deliberately, he was able to get out the story of Double P, how he recognized him, and his desperate dive from his perch on the railing.

"Is the Senator OK?" Dean asked.

"Yes, the Senator is safe."

"Was anyone else hurt?"

"Quite a few people in the crowd were trampled and taken to the hospital. There are a lot of injuries. And Charles Kidwell was shot."

"Charles Kidwell was shot? How is he?"

The agent paused. "He didn't make it."

Chapter 46

DEAN Wister was a sweaty mess as he tried to glide up the last half mile to his house south of Jackson. He'd been practicing cross-country skiing all afternoon, following a morning instructional session, and he thought he had mastered the basic moves. But as exhaustion set in, he'd lost all form. Now he was not only exhausted but frustrated, and drooling like a St. Bernard rescue dog on a warm spring day. He thought about taking off the skis and hiking the last few hundred yards to the house, but the snow was too deep. He slogged on, and by the time he reached the front porch of the house, his lungs were burning and his legs were cramping badly. His faithful Border Collie had beaten him home and was waiting for him, and as Dean kneeled to remove his skis, Cheney walked over and licked his face in sympathy. Dean sat up and laughed. "Are you pitying me, boy? Or just trying to butter me up before dinner?"

Dean was bored. It had been clear coasting for Senator McGraw after the assassination attempt at the Republican convention. The Democratic convention the next week had been completely overshadowed by the media coverage of the event and the subsequent investigation. The Democratic candidate never had a chance. The Senator rode the wave of public goodwill, from his near martyrdom and the death of his chief advisor all the way to the November election, taking with him most of both houses of Congress on his coattails. *Bloody coattails*, Dean thought. Not that he hadn't benefited himself from the entire affair. The FBI had quietly dropped the investigation of the Senator for the Rosati shooting, and Dean had received a commendation and reinstatement to his old job on the Organized Crime Task Force.

That hadn't lasted long. Late one night, a few weeks after going back to work, he'd gotten so frustrated by the interagency infighting that he put his badge on his supervisor's desk and headed back to Jackson. He didn't really need to work— the trust fund he inherited when his wife Sara died was more than enough to live on—but he knew he had to find something more than hiking, camping, and fishing. He needed to be busy. He knew from past experience what happened to him when he wasn't. First would come the brooding, then the ruminating over all the things that he should have done differently over the last decade. Then the spiders would begin to crawl into his brain, at first at night when he would awaken with a panic attack, but later on during the day, too, when he wasn't expecting it, the foreboding feeling would overtake him, and he would be tempted to self-medicate with a bottle of bourbon. He could keep the spiders at bay when he was preoccupied with work. So far, his attempts at hobbies had been futile, and sleep was something he avoided, falling asleep every night on the couch and awakening in the morning to the same twenty-four-hour sports channel he'd left on the night before.

His phone buzzed. He pulled off his glove and looked at the screen—a number he didn't recognize. "Wister, here."

"Dean, how are you? TL here. I haven't talked to you since you left the Task Force. How are you doing?"

"I'm doing great. Keeping busy." He looked down, and saw Cheney looking at him accusingly.

"Glad to hear you're doing well. Listen, the President would like to see you. He's dedicating a memorial for Charles Kidwell in Chicago on Thursday and wondered if you could come. And he'd like to meet with you briefly afterward."

"Well, I'm in Jackson right now."

"Do you think you could make it to Chicago by Thursday? It would mean a lot to the President."

Dean still couldn't wrap his head around the fact that Senator McGraw was now President McGraw. He had kept his distance after the convention. As far as he knew, Flag was still molesting little girls, and as far as Dean was concerned, McGraw had abdicated his responsibility in order to expedite his campaign. But now the President, his president, was asking for him. And it wasn't within him to say no.

"Tell President McGraw I'll be there. Just email me the details."

The address was above the front façade of the new glass and steel building in Chicago's loop, but the building's name was obscured by a large black tarp. Dean checked in with the Secret Service agents in the front entrance and, after going through the metal detectors, was spied by TL, who was talking to a tall thin woman in the corner. "Dean, over here," he called.

TL made the introductions. "Dean, I want you to meet the provost of the new Charles Kidwell School of Business, Dr. Hanna Jenkins." He turned to the woman. "This is Dean Wister, the federal agent who saved the President's life at the convention."

"Of course, I recognize you Agent Wister. And thank you so much for your heroic service."

Dean blushed and murmured, "Just doing my job."

"Please excuse us," TL said to Dr. Jenkins, "he President is waiting for us."

TL led Dean through a corridor to a room guarded by two Secret Service agents. He nodded to the agents, and they let them pass through the door. President Thomas McGraw stood and looked at Dean with a huge smile. "Dean, it's been way too long. It's so good to see you."

"Thank you, Mr. President."

"Please sit down. We have a lot to talk about."

Dean took a seat and the President looked at him a long moment, seemingly thinking before he spoke. "Everything we talk about today is confidential. I don't think I need to say that to you, but TL would have my head if I didn't. OK?"

"Of course, Mr. President."

"First, an update on the investigation of the assassination attempt. None of us think that Double P acted alone, but we never had an opportunity to question him. He never regained consciousness after the stroke he had shortly after they took him to the hospital from the convention. Most likely he was put up to the hit by the same people who bankrolled his and Mario's search for the video, but the main characters—Flag, Melinda, and Boris—have lawyered up and won't say anything."

"You haven't been able to follow the money? Whoever bailed Double P out of jail?"

"Well Mario, Jr. is talking like a little girl gossiping at a sweet sixteen party. He wants desperately to cooperate. But the person pulling his strings communicated with him by burner phone. The bail money was dropped off in cash at his door. He never met anyone. Everyone figured it's probably Flag, Boris, or both."

"Melinda's emails?"

"They implicate her in being a mole for Flag in our search for the video, but that's all. We have nothing to prove a conspiracy for the assassination attempt, and the uncertainty surrounding the investigation can't be allowed to go on. There are all kinds of conspiracy theories out there. It's unhealthy for the country. Our country needs closure. Soon the Attorney General will release a statement saying our investigation has concluded that Double P was acting alone. He was facing a life sentence, he never got over the fact that I shot his boss, and he just went over the edge."

Dean nodded. "I'm sorry, Mr. President, that the other people involved in this aren't going to be punished."

"Well, I'm working on that. That's the second thing I want to talk to you about. Look, Dean, I know you are still pissed off at me. And I want to apologize, and explain—"

"Mr. President, you don't have to—"

"Please don't interrupt me, Dean. Didn't TL fill you in on the protocol in addressing the President?" He laughed. "No, I do need to explain. I left you in the dark about what I was doing about the info you brought to me when you found Svetlana. I asked you to trust me because I had to keep you in the dark, but I can explain it all to you now.

"When you brought me the info on Flag, I wasn't quite sure how to proceed. I knew I couldn't trust the FBI, the Director at the time was very close to Flag and I was afraid he'd bury the information. So I brought in Vorhies to advise me. He agreed that the Director would suppress the evidence and probably warn Flag. We thought we needed more evidence to nail him and decided to wait until we got it. I know that you may still think that was the wrong decision, but it's the call I made, right or wrong. I felt it would give us the best chance to put him away. As you know, one of my first appointments when I took office was to nominate Vorhies as the new Attorney General, and his first act was to replace the FBI Director. With a new FBI director, we reactivated the investigation. I don't know if you remember a man by the name of

Luis? You would have met him at the fundraiser that you and I attended at Flag's house?"

"Yes, I remember him."

"Well, Luis has been a very, very loyal assistant to Flag for the last twenty-five years or so, which also means that Flag had very few secrets from him. And a nice bit of serendipity that fell into our laps was that Luis's son was recently arrested for drug trafficking in L.A. A drug conviction like this would destroy the young man's life, so we were able to use that to get Luis to cooperate in the investigation and corroborate the young Russian girl's story. He also agreed to tip us off when the next party was going to occur at Flag's home in Jackson."

Dean was trying to process all this information. "So, you're saying the investigation is back on?"

"Yes, and its coming to a head. Flag is hosting one of his parties tomorrow night in Jackson, and we're going to bust it. Would you like to be a part of the operation?"

"Really?"

"Sure. Sheriff Cody is working with the FBI on the logistics. She's waiting for you to arrive back in Jackson to fill you in and deputize you. She's pretty pissed off that this sex trafficking is going on in her territory. I want you to keep an eye out so she doesn't go too overboard at the bust. Not that I would blame her. So how would you like to crash the party?"

"I think you know the answer to that, Mr. President. Damned right I would." Dean paused, and said softly, "I owe you an apology. I'm sorry I didn't trust you."

"Oh, don't worry about that, Dean. I don't trust myself most of the time." He put his hand on Dean's arm. "After what you did at the convention, I will always be in your debt."

"Now, Dean, there's another matter. I heard about you quitting the Task Force. We have to get you a job. I've gotten to know you a little bit, and I can see you don't play well with others." He chuckled and pointed his finger at Dean.

"Mr. President, I think I am an excellent team player, it's just that—"

President McGraw interrupted. "No no, that's not a criticism, it's just a fact. I have some of that same weakness myself, so I understand it. Now, in my new job I have a pretty broad view of all the opportunities in federal law enforcement, and I have an idea."

"Mr. President, you don't have to—"

"Dean, hear me out. I think it's a damned good idea. Four things I know about you. You're independent, you like to work alone or with a few select people you trust, you're discreet, and you're a damned good investigator. How would you like to be a US Marshal?"

"US Marshal? But wouldn't that just be working for another agency like the FBI?"

"Not if I make you an independent investigator for the US Marshal's office. Of course, on paper you'll be assigned to DC, but you can work from wherever you want—Chicago, Jackson, or Maui, for all I care. Of course, you'll have a boss, but, ultimately, you'll be working for the Attorney General, who is totally on board with this. I have a feeling we're going to be able to keep you busy with special projects that require more than the usual amount of discretion." He looked at Dean and smiled. "Now isn't that a grand idea?"

For the first time since he entered the room, Dean returned the smile. "It sure is, Mr. President. But can I think about it for a few days?"

"Take whatever time you need, Dean. Just let TL know what your answer is. But I'll be very disappointed if you turn me down."

"I understand, Mr. President. Thank you very much for the opportunity."

"Thank you, Dean. Thank you for everything."

Dean turned to leave, and then he stopped. "Mr. President, one more thing. We looked everywhere for my computer, and the only thing that makes sense is that Boris Birkov had it all along. But I can't figure out why he hasn't used it against you. My memos would make it clear that the person on the tape was not some random woman but was Charles."

The President beamed. "Well, as a matter of fact, he does have it, and he's been trying to use it. He was waiting until after the election to see if he could wrangle a pardon from me. We've been stringing him along, but he's about to lose all his leverage and the info on your computer will be rendered irrelevant. You'll find out why soon enough."

President McGraw sat on the dais next to TL while the Provost gave a speech describing the new school. But he wasn't listening at all. After today the entire country would see him differently; some would hate him for what he was about to say, and some would find him honorable, but he knew no one would be on the fence. The First Lady was back at the White House today and heavy on his mind. They hadn't been intimate for several years, and when McGraw sat her down after the election for "the talk," she'd said, "Of course I knew. I've known forever. Even before you met Charles, I knew. I saw how you looked at each other, but I did appreciate that you kept it discreet."

But two weeks ago, when he'd told her what he planned, she'd said nothing. They'd existed in silence for days. Then last night she'd come to him. "If you are set on doing this, I will stick by you. Our bond has always been stronger than romance, and the truth is, I don't think your Presidency will weather this if I leave. I've worked as hard to get here as you have, and it's unfair that I'd have to be the one to give up my office."

It was true, their bond was more than just romance, which had left him in turmoil over his decision. She'd been the first person in his life who believed in him. He'd been a lost, hard-drinking cowboy when he met her, and she gave him direction. She called him her diamond in the rough, and he was pretty sure that's what he'd still be if they hadn't met. He did love her, just not in the way that he loved Charles. Still, he felt bad about what he was about to do, but this was the last step in his journey toward... What was it called?

An "authentic life." He knew there would be consequences, but being himself had made him President. Charles used to call it the Grand Prize.

Dean sat in the front row mulling over the president's offer and was having a difficult time paying attention to the speeches. It checked all the boxes in what Dean would want in a law enforcement job, but would he truly be independent? The President was speaking now and had paused, and the pause caused Dean to return his attention to the podium.

"Charles Kidwell was in inspiration to me," the President said. "He's the reason I ran for president. He believed that I could do something no other candidate could do, and he convinced me of it. But he was more than that to me. I have never talked about this before, and I know some people are not going to agree or even understand what I'm about to say, but I owe it to Charles—I owe it to myself, and I owe it to the American people—to be the transparent president they deserve. Charles Kidwell was my friend and my trusted advisor. But he was much more than that."

The President paused again, and Dean could see he was struggling to keep his composure. There were tears in his eyes, and he said softly, "He was the love of my life." The room was quiet, but Dean could hear soft murmuring, and the President looked now directly at the crowd, and his voice was strong. "He was the love of my life. And I am so proud to dedicate this school in the memory of this great man, this great and courageous American."

Chapter 47

THE next night, at ten minutes to midnight, eight FBI agents, Sheriff Cody, and Dean Wister stood in front of the palatial estate of Ronald Flag. They'd been stationed at the base of the butte watching the house with field glasses for the past two hours, awaiting the text from Luis that would put the bust in motion. Now the lead FBI agent returned Luis's text, and thirty seconds later Luis opened the door about six inches.

"Follow me, the party is upstairs," Luis whispered.

Two of the agents moved to the back door of the house, two remained stationed at the front door, the rest of the team followed Luis through the front door and up the stairs. Music was playing somewhere upstairs, and it got louder and louder as they climbed the long stairway. Just as they reached the landing, a thin naked girl staggered out of the bathroom at the top of the stairs. One of the agents grabbed her, put his finger to his lips, and sat her down in the hallway, while the rest of the team proceeded down the hall.

The room they entered was huge, with a gigantic moose antler chandelier dominating the ceiling of the room, panties and bras dangling like Christmas ornaments from the points. Bass was pounding, and a rapper was shouting something about the size of his equipment and the number of whores he could do in one night from some unseen speakers. A large, round glass table served as a stage in front of a red-leather half-moon sectional. Three girls, naked except for their six-inch rhinestone heels, danced on the table and, with each gyration came perilously close to a half-dozen silver bowls filled with a white powdery substance. The dancers seemed to be in their own world, their eyes focused on some scene above and outside of the room, ignoring the armed men dressed in black tactical uniforms entering the room. Seated on the sectional were three naked men, and in front of each of them, a kneeling girl serviced them while the dancers writhed to the music.

The team leader nodded, and three of the team members stepped forward, each placing the muzzle of a gun directly on the back of the head of each of the men. Sheriff Cody shouted in the loudest voice Dean had ever heard—loud enough to be heard above the rapper, who was now touting the finer points of sex in an Escalade—"Don't move a muscle, motherfuckers. You are under arrest, and if you move an inch we will blow your fucking heads off!"

The men appeared to be in a state of shock when they turned around and saw the uninvited SWAT team guests. And Dean was surprised they said nothing when Sheriff Cody read them their rights, although they did protest strongly when she would not let them dress before they were cuffed and marched to the vans waiting in the driveway. It was below zero, and Dean was afraid they might suffer frostbite as they waited in the subzero air, first outside the house, and then as they got out of the van at the jail, but the Sheriff insisted on the humiliation. The three men were photographed, fingerprinted, and booked butt-naked in the Teton County Jail.

The arrests had been leaked to the local press and a newspaper and television crew were waiting at the station when the van arrived. The seven girls at the party were permitted to dress and were taken to a local hotel, where a team of female agents and psychologists debriefed them. Later, it would be confirmed that all were illegal underage imports provided by Boris Birkov.

In addition to Ron Flag, Dean recognized one of the other two men as they were being cuffed. "Director Fanning," he said, "fancy meeting you here." Sheriff Cody identified the third man for the FBI agents as local citizen Colonel Ned Wood. The men were arraigned the next morning and released on bail by noon, but the picture of the three men naked and exiting the van at the station house appeared in the *Jackson Hole Daily* and the news footage was distributed worldwide over the Internet by the time they were released.

Dean and Dani sat in Cody's office late into the night, where Dean was overserved Wyoming Whiskey for the first time since the investigation began.

Epilogue

"Jia Ling, for the last time, breakfast is ready. Hurry, you're going to be late!" Elle Landers shouted up the staircase, but Jia was already bounding down the stairs two at a time.

"Mommy, I couldn't find my special dress," Jia said as she scurried past Elle into the kitchen.

"It's no wonder," replied Elle. "Your closet is jam-packed. No more clothes for a while, do you understand?"

"Yes, Mommy." Jia smiled her gap-toothed grin and joined her family already at the big round table just off the kitchen of their Georgetown townhome. Jia took her seat between her brothers and Grandpa Yao. The scars on Yao Chen's face and body, souvenirs of the hospitality of a Chinese prison, were starting to fade, and even his memories of the last year were becoming a little fainter each day as he settled into his American home with his new family.

Jia's smile disappeared, and her face turned cloudy.

"What's the matter, Jia?" asked Toby.

"Where's my congee?" Congee, a watery traditional rice soup was Jia's favorite breakfast, and she would devour a bowl after stirring in a large amount of maple syrup every morning.

"It's time you tried some new foods. You can't eat congee at every meal." Toby pointed at the table in front of them. "We have cinnamon French toast, sausage, and fruit today. Look, your brothers are really liking it."

Jia's twin brothers had flourished since arriving in the US. Proper medical care, nutrition and a tutor had nearly erased the developmental deficits that had stunted them in the orphanage. After the convention, a crowdfunding campaign had raised nearly a million dollars for the children's' medical care and education, and President McGraw had arranged for their adoption by Toby and Elle Landers. Moreover, one of the first legislative triumphs of the McGraw administration was the bill to provide for financial assistance to families of children with disabilities.

Yao Chen said something in Chinese to Jia, and she looked up at him and then picked up a fork, taking a cautious bite of sausage. Jia had made great progress learning English, but Yao still only knew a few English phrases.

"We need to hurry," said Toby. "You remember what today is, right?"

A woman in a headset with a clipboard tapped on the doorjamb. "We're all set up, Mr. Landers. We'll be right outside the front door."

"Sure," said Toby. "Just give us five minutes."

The front door of the luxury Georgetown town-house opened, and Toby walked out with Jia, beginning a carefully staged day that would result in the most popular episode of the highest-rated US television program of the season. *Jia Ling, American Girl* was can't-miss TV for every family in America. Today Jia would tail her adopted father, TL, the President's Chief of Staff, as he sat in on meetings with legislators and cabinet members. It was "Take Your Daughter to Work Day" on steroids, and America ate it up. The dress that Jia was wearing would be featured in the Target commercial for the Jia Ling clothing line, and the Jia Ling American Doll. And its accompanying autobiography would be a holiday gift in such high demand and short supply that toney parents would pay outrageous premiums to make sure their daughters in the young tween market segment would not be disappointed.

The cameras followed the duo as they walked to the limousine at the curb, and cameras mounted inside the limo waited to eavesdrop on their conversation on the way to the White House. Jia looked up at Toby and motioned for him to lean down. She said quietly to him, "I wasn't late this morning because of my dress. I was memorizing my lines. Just like the convention." And then right before she entered the limo, she turned around, looked at the folks that had gathered in front of their house, smiled her gap-toothed smile, and waved.

Dean Wister sat in the hot tub on his back porch

on a moonless night, the only light provided by the emerald glow of the aurora borealis, steam rising in wisps as the 104-degree water met the 10-below-zero air. He closed his eyes and thought of Melinda. He could see clearly now, like Sara had told him, it was more lust than love, though he did miss her body. He thought of how her breasts would bounce against his chest when she was riding him, and he began to feel himself swell in the warm water. He closed his eyes and was drifting away, lost in his thoughts of the warm silkiness of his former partner, when something jerked him awake, and he turned his head.

A familiar blonde woman was sliding into the water next to him. "You were thinking about Melinda again, weren't you?"

"No, I wasn't."

"It's OK if you were, but you need to move on. It's time for you to date again."

"I don't want to move on." Dean put his arms around her, pulling her to him. "Can't you just stay with me?"

"I can tonight." She eased into his arms. "What about that yoga girl?"

"She's just my instructor."

"Dean, you didn't even know what hot yoga was. I'm sure you saw the sign and thought it was something sexual. You had no idea that it was going to be doing all those difficult poses in a studio hotter than hell." She giggled at her own joke.

Dean was quiet.

"What are you thinking?" she asked.

"About the President. About the First Lady."

"It is pretty amazing she didn't leave him after he pronounced Charles was the love of his life. But she's getting kudos for the way she's handled the whole thing." Sara laughed. "Who knew her cause would be supporting women with gay spouses."

"Yeah, there's been a wave of men coming out to their wives since the President did."

"I'm not sure I would be able to handle it that well," said Sara.

They were silent together for a moment. "And I've been thinking about the job offer," Dean said.

"What about it? You're taking it, of course."

"I was thinking that maybe I should stay here and become one of Cody's deputies. Dani is always asking me about it."

Sara was incredulous. "And become the Teton County equivalent of a mall cop? You'd be spending your summers investigating moose versus tourist traffic accidents and your winters trying to recover stolen skis out at the Village. You just got lucky when McGraw got you involved in this huge case. There probably won't be another one this big out here in your lifetime. You killed three bad guys with your bare hands, all because of McGraw."

"That's not true."

"Well, let's see. You shot the guy in the Snake River Canyon. You killed the guy outside the Silver Dollar Bar with your tricky ju-jitsu thing. And old Double P, you speared him with your bare head, not your bare hands."

"You just love to make fun of me, but I hate all the bureaucratic bullshit."

"No offense, honey, but you need to grow up. It comes with the territory. Look, I know you. You're like that Ed Norton character in the movie *Primal Fear*. He's this sweet Southern boy who can turn on a dime into a stone-cold killer. That's you. It scared me when I first met you, but to tell the truth, I liked being near that flame. It's scary and sexy at the same time. You're an adrenalin junkie, and you have this well of anger deep inside of you. I'm guessing it's from your messed-up childhood. Chasing down really, really bad guys, that's your semi-healthy outlet for that anger. It keeps you sane."

Dean considered her lecture. "I know you're right. But I could use a little more gentle persuasion."

All right, I think I can do that." She lifted herself out of the water and climbed over him, sitting down on his lap and wrapping her arms and legs around him. "How about this?"

"You can be a very persuasive woman, Sara." He pulled her into him, holding her so tightly he would have broken her ribs if she were real. And he said a prayer that this moment would never end.

THE GRAND SEXTET, a collection of Dean Wister short stories coming soon from Dennis D. Wilson. Sign up for our newsletter and be the first to know when it is released.

mailchi.mp/waterstreetpressbooks.com/ waterstreetcrimemailinglist

Get the Water Street Crime Starter Library
FOR FREE

Get four, full-length ebooks—***BLOODY PARADISE***, ***FROM ICE TO ASHES***, ***TROPICAL ICE***, and ***SING FOR THE DEAD***—plus two introductory short stories by the author of ***THE GRAND PRIZE*** and lots more exclusive content, all for free!

Building a relationship with our readers is the very best thing about publishing.
We occasionally send newsletters with details on new releases, special offers and other bits of news relating to Water Street Press.

And if you sign up to the mailing list we'll send you all this free stuff:

1.   A free ebook edition of the exotic thriller ***BLOODY PARADISE***—"...a spicy thriller..."

2. A free ebook edition of the crime thriller ***FROM ICE TO ASHES***—"designed to shoot the ice down your spine..."

3. A free ebook edition of the eco-thriller ***TROPICAL ICE***—"...well-spun, tautly written..."

4.   A free ebook edition of the delightfully noirish mystery ***SING FOR THE DEAD***—Foreword Reviews' Gold Medal winner

5. A free copy of two introductory short stores from the author of **THE GRAND PRIZE**—stories that do a deep dive into the histories of two of his most intriguing characters, Sheriff Dani Cody and Mrs. McGraw...

6. Advance notice about the release of the next Dean Wister novel, #3 coming in 2021.

You can get all this and more,
for free, just by signing up at

**mailchi.mp/waterstreetpressbooks.com/
waterstreetcrimemailinglist**

Did you enjoy this book? You can make a big difference for our amazing Water Street Crime authors.

Reviews are the most powerful tools in our arsenal when it comes getting attention for our books. Much as we'd like to, we don't have the financial muscle of a New York publisher. We can't take out full-page ads in the newspaper or put posters on the subway.

(Not yet, anyway).

But we do have something much more powerful and effective than that, and it's something that those publishers would kill to get their hands on.

A committed and loyal bunch of readers.

Honest reviews of our books help bring them to the attention of other readers.

If you've enjoyed this book we would be very grateful if you could spend just five minutes on Amazon or the online vendor of your choice leaving a review (it can be as short as you like).

Thank you very much.

About the Author

After a career working in an international consulting firm and as a financial executive with two public companies, Dennis D. Wilson returns to the roots he established as a high school literature and writing teacher. He draws upon his experiences from his hometown of Chicago; his years of living, working, hiking, and climbing in Jackson Hole; and secrets gleaned from time spent in corporate boardrooms, to craft political crime thrillers straight from today's headlines. Dennis lives in suburban Chicago with his wife, Paula, and Black Lab, Jenny, but spends as much time as he can looking for adventure in the mountains and on his motorcycle. Keep up with him at dennisdwilson.com.

ALSO FROM WATER STREET PRESS

Ready for more thrills?

We suggest **Stained Fortune**, by Joe Calderwood, the first in his Clint Kennedy Crime Series.

Have you read all the books in the Water Street Crime collection? Check out Water Street Press at this link and see all the amazing books we have to offer:

www.waterstreetpressbooks.com

Stained Fortune

Enjoy this excerpt from STAINED FORTUNE, the first book in the Clint Kennedy Crime Series by Joe Calderwood.

Chapter 1

I had not planned on ending up back in jail. But when the rewards are great, the risks are often greater.

I remembered how it felt the first time I'd entered jail, the edge of fear that seemed to jab at my nerve endings like the tip of a knife—a sensation I did not find completely unpleasant. Ambition had landed me here, certainly, but I couldn't discount that the nearly carnal satisfaction of an adrenaline rush didn't have something to do with how high I was willing to aim, or how far I'd go to meet my goals.

The other inmates—six in the cell of the Mexican jail I was led to—were hard-pressed to contain their desire to pounce on me as I took my seat among them on the cold, damp concrete floor. Child molesters, rapists, robbers, murderers, assorted minor scam artists—my new compatriots, their hair gelled to porcupine points at the top of their heads, dusty feet in battered flip-flops, dark and shining eyes assessing me.

The prison housed hundreds in cramped cells like this, dungeons with a toilet as the feature at the center of the room, a dank, brown liquid coagulated at its base and a metal seat for seven or more prisoners to use—no privacy and no toilet paper. Weeds sprouted from the cracks in the concrete floor, and the small, damp room smelled of body odor and spent bodily fluids. It was clear the toilet didn't get a lot of use; the inmates pissed wherever they stood.

Pedro, Luis, Gustavo, Manuel, Jose, Carlos—I was the only one with white skin among the mix of Spanish, Mayan, and Mexican prisoners. Most spoke Spanish, or Mayan, with only a spattering of English among them, but I spoke enough Spanish to make myself understood, and to understand that their conversation was about me, and irreverent.

Fortunately for me, Mexico—unlike America in these early years of the new century—was still an aspirational country. My new prison friends appreciated American men like me: they didn't resent my fresh, new, costly clothes or my expensive haircut; they enjoyed the appearance of money, and their proximity to someone who looked like he had a lot of it.

Chapter 2

The intent to make my fortune was what had landed me in jail the first time, but make my fortune I had, in spite of the temporary obstacle of incarceration. At just thirty-four, and with a fat bank account, I'd moved to Mérida, in the Yucatan, "The White City" named for the common color of its old buildings, and for its cleanliness. I'd bought and restored an eight-bedroom colonial mansion for my home. I spent my days drinking beer by my pool, reading a book or watching an old movie on TV, and feasting on the local dishes my houseboy, Pedro, prepared for me—*Poc Chuc* and *Papadzules*. My nights were spent drinking Scotch and making the rounds of restaurants, art galleries and the symphony that made up the vibrant cultural life of the city. The Mérida population includes the largest percentile of indigenous persons in Mexico—Mayans, most of whom were still struggling to reach even the lowest rung of the ladder their Mexican neighbors sat upon—and so I took it into my head that I would help them in their rise, though perhaps in an even more practical way than I'd been helped in mine: I'd bought three additional old colonials, each smaller than my residence, though just a few streets away, and was in the process of combining them into one building and restoring it as a school for Mayan kids. It was a deeply and not surprisingly satisfying way to spend my time, and my money.

Taavi, for one, wouldn't have been surprised. Maybe he was the one who put the idea in my head in the first place—roused himself from eternal sleep and whispered it to me in my dreams. That would have been something he would have done, if at all possible, and who was to say it wasn't?

In any case, my life was paradise, and it wasn't enough.

Who's to say what's "enough"? What is plenty for one man is paltry to another. I had wads of dollars in my pocket and stacks in my safe and rows and rows of numbers on my balance sheets, but when it came to thrills, I was poverty-stricken.

About three months after my move to Mexico, in the early spring of 2008, I volunteered as a worker for the Yucatan elections—the one hundred and six "municipal presidents", or mayors as we call them in the U.S., that were to be elected that May. Those few weeks of volunteer work consisted mostly of answering phones in various campaign headquarters, posting yard signs where they were permitted—and sometimes where they were not permitted, approaching area business people with a fundraising pitch on behalf of the resident power brokers and decision makers. You could call me a "people person". From the time I was a kid, I could always pick out the ones who would be most beneficial to know. I worked my ass off for the local pols and, by the time the elections were over, I had a whole new group of friends. Politics is an inherently dirty business and the pollution among the Mexican political class is deservedly legendary; I figured someone in that crowd could get me into a little bit of much-needed trouble.

My trouble came with a name: Alvaro.

I met Alvaro—met him *formally*—at the victory party for the candidate in Mérida's Third District. He—Alvaro, not the candidate; the candidate was a forgettable little puke who would later be indicted for removing his opponent's advertising materials and exchanging cash for voting cards—was a solid six feet tall, with a body of lean muscle and a head of wavy, thick black hair. Even at first glance he seemed too lithe and graceful—too *physical*—to be a politician. Periodically he'd throw an arm around the smaller but exceptionally beautiful man at his side; the way he looked down at his companion, the smile he gave him, made me wonder if they were a couple. Both of them were surrounded by the circle of spectators who'd gathered around Alvaro, a crowd of men and women who looked up at Alvaro less as just another guest at the victory party but as if they were his fans. There were a few people among that crowd who looked too alert and wary to be simply guests; they looked like Secret Service guys if Secret Service guys routinely dressed in Irish linen guayaberas.

"Do you know who that is?"

"What?" I turned to the Mayan who'd been on the candidate's PR team. I didn't catch his name, but he looked enough like Taavi to draw me to him when I'd first arrived at the party and he'd taken it upon herself to give me the lay of the land—point out the important people I might like to know.

He gestured now toward Alvaro with the hand that held his frothy cocktail. "You think you recognize him, don't you? He's Alvaro Moreno, the bullfighter—not as well-known as his brother, Oscar, but Alvaro's the one who stabbed and killed the Intimidator."

I nodded. "I've never been to a bullfight in my life."

Chapter 3

"Politicians and bullfighters, there is no difference between them," Alvaro told the crowd. "If you are a bullfighter, the bull is your opponent. He is the one you are trying to beat in the race, the one you do not want to lose the election to, hmmm?" he continued, and the people around him chuckled. "And everything a bullfighter does, every move he makes, is to do one of three things—distract his opponent, so the opponent is confused and can't fight back as well; anger his opponent, so the opponent makes a stupid mistake; cause injury to his opponent, so the spectators will see the bullfighter is strong and his opponent, this massive animal, is weak." By the time he finished, the people around him were laughing in earnest. He didn't need to twist to one side as if to dodge attack, his hands holding an imaginary cape, to keep his audience captive; that flourish at the end was all showmanship.

But when he'd twisted he'd ended up directly in front of me.

I stretched my hand out to him. "I'm Clint Kennedy. New to the area—"

Alvaro put up a hand and let his black eyes wander over my white skin, blonde hair, blue eyes. "New to the area? Who would have guessed such a thing?" he asked, sending the people who were still gathered around him into another gale of laughter.

I might have been put off—distracted—by his greeting, but that was just what he wanted.

"I've never been to a bullfight. I'd love to see you in the ring."

"You would?" he laughed, and he grabbed the beautiful man who'd been standing near to him and kissed him on the neck. "Then what do you say, Javier? I fight again in, what is it? Two weeks? Should we invite this Mister Clint Kennedy to be our guest?"

Javier shrugged, but he smiled as well. "I think Mister Clint Kennedy would like that, Alvaro."

"Then that's what we will do!" Alvaro boomed. He reached out at last to take the hand I had offered him. "Pleased to meet you, Clint. Call me Alvaro—and this is Javier, my brother-in-law."

Brother-in-law, I thought as I began to loosen my hand from Alvaro's grip in order to shake hands with Javier. *This relationship might be more complicated than I assumed...*

But I didn't get to either finish the thought or offer Javier my hand. Alvaro kept his fist tight over mine and yanked me toward him to whisper in my ear, "I know who you are, Mister Clint Kennedy."